The Pitfalls of Being a Goddess

Between the Lines Publishing
1769 Lexington Ave N., Ste 286
Roseville, MN 55113
btwnthelines.com

Published: March 2023

Original ISBN (Paperback) 978-1-958901-17-5

Original ISBN (eBook) 978-1-958901-18-2

The Pitfalls of Being a Goddess

Eva Leppard

To my boys, Jasper, Archer, Billy and Micah.

To my parents, Lynden and Chris.

And to my oldest friend Arielle, because she always assumed I'd become an author

One

It wasn't a particularly good pub, but it was her local, and Brigid had developed a fierce, dogged attachment to it over the past twenty years. She liked the way it did "Irish pub" in that peculiar, completely inaccurate way that Australian pubs try to imitate Irishness. She liked the way the bar staff occasionally remembered her name and pretended they knew her usual order. She also liked the way that the chicken parmigiana was always almost, but not quite, completely overcooked. Consistency was, after all, one of her main drivers and (although she had not yet come to terms with this), deepest resentments.

This particular evening was damp and squally, as was often the case in April, and Brigid quickly made the short walk from her house to the pub. The clouds hung low over Fitzroy, in both a meteorological, and, more specifically, karmic sense. For in the above reaches of the atmosphere, several extremely focussed and determined lesser weather deities battled for possession of the storm pattern over this patch of town. Rain fell in bursts, interspersed by moments of bright moonlight as the clouds were pushed away and vaporised, only to be replaced by new ones.

Brigid was oblivious to all of this. Her focus was on her homicidally suicidal umbrella; an umbrella that seemed to be trying to simultaneously stab her in the eye and throw itself into the street. If she had looked up, she would have seen commiserating black clouds, but sadly, the worship and adulation that she was receiving entirely passed her by. Which is a pity, because having a weather system in love with you is quite special if you can wangle it.

Finally, the umbrella was yanked out of her grasp by a last, amorous gust, flew through the air for twenty metres, and lay in the middle of the street, twitching like a terminally damp dragonfly scooped from a puddle by an enthusiastic toddler.

Deciding that said umbrella was now no longer her problem, Brigid left the rainy street and walked through the door of Irish Bridies. She headed past the amusingly tipsy wooden leprechaun; edged past a cluster of worried looking tourists who were trying to decide if dinner here was a commitment that they were ready to make; raised an eyebrow of solidarity at a group of already catastrophically drunk first-year teachers, one of whom she recognised as her student teacher from two years before; stopped to glare pointedly at the group of glossy young girls who had taken her favourite booth; and finally, decided on a solid, roomy table closer to the fire.

She pulled off her heavy winter coat, and unwound her scarf, irritated in the process to notice that it had caught on one of her earrings. She had known wearing jewellery today had been a foolishly optimistic move. Frowning, she tried to pull the thread back into the cashmere material while at the same time spreading her coat and handbag over the table and chairs in an "I have friends and they will be arriving any minute" manner. Realising that she was making things much, much worse, she gave up, shoved her scarf in her bag, and pushed herself in behind the bench.

The pub had decided on an industrial method of seating that harkened back to the early 1800's policy of "jam as many people into the factory/ tenement/ school as possible and we will take care of details such as functionality later", which meant that unless you had the hips of a snake, getting in behind the sturdy table was going to be a struggle. She weighed the pros and cons, concluding that the effort of shoehorning herself in meant she wouldn't be called on to go to the bar for a round. She was here to sit, and drink, and by God it was a commitment that she took seriously.

Laying her head back against the chipped timber laminate of the wall, Brigid closed her eyes and took a moment to breathe. It was Friday, it had been a hectic week, there were sixty exams to mark by Monday, and she had to finalise a performance review this weekend. But this was her moment. Her bright spot. Her Zen. Although Zen wasn't, as she understood it, a state of drinking too much then eating a dodgy souvlaki on the way home. Maybe bliss then. This moment was her bliss. She breathed deeply into her belly, her round face softening and the lines around her eyes smoothing out for a moment.

"Jesus," said Lauren, hauling the table out and plopping herself next to Brigid. "Were you involved in that shit show at school today?"

Brigid turned her head and narrowed her eyes at her friend. "You're going to need to be more specific. Which shit show exactly?"

"The kid who was caught vaping in the grade 7 history class this afternoon."

Give me strength, intoned Brigid internally. "How do you know about that?"

"Some other kid snapchatted it and sent it to his mum, who put it on the school's Facebook page. Everyone knows about it now.

"Well, to be fair, that's when we found out about it too," said Brigid. "We still wouldn't know if someone hadn't recorded it. It was that bloody relief teacher."

"That's why you should tell your assistant principal to get me to do relief again," said Lauren. "That kind of thing wouldn't happen on my watch.'

"Really? Would you come in and do relief again if I need it?"

"God no. Those kids are monsters."

"I'm on record as saying that the school's Facebook page should be read only. If Barry from IT wants to "curate a rich and complex diversity of human experience by using social media" that's all well and good, but he's going to have to deal with it when the rich and diverse community post their opinions about our classroom management."

"Or lack thereof."

A burst of laughter rose from the bar area, as a short and stocky man made his way through the thickening crowd towards them. Tony, a local-government official who high fived everyone who made eye contact with him, and who could share an in-joke with every bar keeper in the greater Melbourne area did not, on paper, sound like the kind of person who Brigid would have chosen to spend her free time with. But given he always brought them a tray of drinks and a triple serving of hot chips, and also considering that he knew the kind of gossip about politicians that was always useful to have up your sleeve, he had seamlessly become a natural part of their Friday night drinks.

"How are you feeling?" he asked Brigid. "How's the breakdown coming along?"

"How does he know about my breakdown?" Brigid pointedly asked Lauren. "I wasn't sharing that until I've firmed up the details."

"Isn't it obvious?" Tony glanced nervously towards Lauren. "I mean, I thought it was obvious. The whole 'woe is me; my life is shit, and everyone is incompetent' thing. I mean, I thought you were doing that on purpose."

Brigid's mouth thinned. "I am here," she hissed, "for a relaxing ale. Not a life critique. What do you think?" She swung around on the unsuspecting Lauren. "Do you think I'm on the verge of a breakdown?"

"I thought you didn't want a life critique?"

"Why don't you just go for it, since we're here" said Brigid, waving her glass around recklessly. "The evening couldn't get any worse, apparently."

Above her, the clouds, sensing a slight tremor in the energies emitting from the building below them, really hit their stride with the hailing and the blustering. They could sense, in the curiously sentient way of really dark and rain-filled clouds, that their mistress was on the precipice of something incredible, something truly life changing, and they wanted an appropriate amount of spectacle to go along with the event.

One of these mighty gusts blew the door open and, along with spatters of rain and swirls of dejected leaves, a dark figure slipped in. Ignored by everyone, he passed by the tourists, who had made the decision to risk a meal and were staring perplexed at a plate of what had been described on the menu as *Fermented Farfalle sliders with Beer Braised Acorn and Cider Nublets*. The smell of wet dog steamed from people's coats, a fug of stale beer and body odour circulated in the vapour above their heads, and the figure decided he was already heartily sick of the place.

A group of earthbound spirits who had carved out a space for themselves high in the fug raised their glasses cheerfully at him, and he thought grimly that it was a testament to the inebriated state of the inhabitants of the bar that no one noticed disembodied beer steins bobbing around above their heads. The spirits should consider themselves lucky he had far more important things to worry about tonight than the Rules of Engagement.

The figure caught sight of the reason for his visit through the bodies and tables that filled the room, and found himself a seat nearby, to watch, and wait for his moment.

Two

From A Concise History of Shadow Lands, Volume 181, page 916.

The workplace stress that comes along with being a goddess can be, to put it mildly, immense.

Most people think that deities are born with the innate ability to rule omnisciently, to intuitively understand the ebbs and flows of the Earth's seasonal fluctuations, to carefully monitor the machinations of the human mind and how to, when required, deal with them. It's almost universally assumed that all those born into the higher vibrational pantheons just know all this stuff and can jump right into it, guns blazing.

In reality though, much of this needs to be learned. Cultivated. Perfected. It's a long, involved process, and it is a rare thing indeed that a deity is let out on their own for at least a few hundred years, at least in any area where they could have any real impact or, more accurately, do any real damage.

As you can imagine, the difficulties here are magnified infinitely if the goddess doesn't know that they are, in fact, a deity. If say, for argument's sake, she is a forty-something woman living a common-or-garden life in Melbourne, Australia, wondering how she is going to salvage any excitement from her rapidly stagnating life, it can be quite a trick indeed.

Enter Brigid Humboldt.

She was, of course, a goddess. But she had no more knowledge of this than of the fact she was presently being stalked by a reaper, who needed her to recalibrate the disturbing and potentially disastrous lack of balance that was currently being experienced in the liminal worlds that exist above the consciousness of most inhabitants of the planet.

She didn't know this, of course. How could she? All she knew was that her life was bland, her options were diminishing, and she was intent on getting quite drunk.

"Okay." Lauren took a gulp of her beer and ticked off a list on her fingers. "You're miserable and grumpy, over opinionated and critical, and you seem to hate your life and everything in it so, yes, I'd say you need something."

Brigid was slightly affronted by how quickly Lauren had come up with this checklist.

"We're a bit worried," continued Tony, "and we thought you might want to have a brainstorm around what you could do. You know, an action plan. You like action plans. You like them for other people anyway." His voice trailed off.

Brigid sighed heavily and dropped her head on her hands. Her dusty red hair fell forward into her beer, and Lauren quietly lifted it out, flicking off the coating of foam.

"It's just," Tony said in a voice usually reserved for the inhabitants of aged care homes and kindergartens, "you're really good at sorting out other people, but we just feel like you're—"

"Really shit at sorting out yourself," finished Lauren.

"I don't *like* sorting out other people," Brigid said through her hands. "I don't *like* telling people what they are supposed to be doing."

"You do it pretty bloody boisterously for someone who doesn't like doing it, you have to admit."

Lauren shot Tony a warning look.

"I think I should have a baby."

The look Lauren and Tony were exchanging turned to one of nervous bemusement.

"A human baby?"

"It would give my life meaning and purpose and a new peer group of people to hang out with," said Brigid raising her head.

"A group? How many kids are you planning on having?"

"Mums. Other mums. I would make new friends and playdates, and the government would give me money so I wouldn't have to work, and the only thing I'd have to worry about is keeping it alive for a few years until it can look after itself."

"What the fuck are you talking about? You hate other people, and the government would give you shit all money, and you'd hate it. And I feel like the mechanics of keeping something alive is harder than it looks. Look at your pot plants."

"I don't hate other people. Do I come off as if I hate other people?"

"Just a touch," said Lauren.

"At the moment," confirmed Tony.

Lauren put her arm around her friend, looking at her with a gentle concern. "I'm not sure you're ok. Do you feel okay?"

"Clearly she's not ok," said Tony, "otherwise she wouldn't be considering having a random baby. That's not clear thinking. There is nothing about that that indicates clear thinking or good life choices. And who would be the father anyway? You don't even have a boyfriend."

"How about you? Do you want to have a baby with me?"

Tony pushed himself back from the table and stood up.

"Nope," he said, shaking his head. "Nope. I'm out. Lauren, she's all yours. This is above my pay grade, and I'm out." He headed over to the group of drunken young teachers.

"I wouldn't make you change its nappy," Brigid called after him as he disappeared amongst them. "I just need some sperm."

Lauren quickly distracting her with the bowl of chips, and for a few moments they ate in silence.

"All right. Here it is. Hating your job is fine. It's perfectly normal, and it would be slightly strange if you didn't. Being grumpy is, well, not that unusual for you. Wanting to get pregnant using Tony's sperm however is, I'm going to be honest here, totally out of left field and just . . . " her voice trailed off.

"It makes sense though, doesn't it?" said Brigid hopefully. "I've been thinking about it, and it really makes sense. It's—"

"Horrific and gross, and inappropriate," finished Lauren. "I'm almost completely sure it's sexual harassment. You can't just go around propositioning men for their sperm."

Brigid opened her mouth to protest.

"You absolutely and literally can't do that."

There was a long pause. The sounds of the bar were muffled around her as Brigid clasped her beer despondently. She couldn't think of any other options. She hadn't always hated things in her life, she was sure of it. And it wasn't as if she could isolate exactly what it was that she didn't like. She just had this dull nagging feeling that she had forgotten something extremely important, and nothing in her life would make sense until she remembered what it was.

"Do you want to have a baby?" asked Lauren softly.

Brigid shrugged noncommittally.

"Do you have a deep need to be a mother, then?"

"Not specifically."

Lauren's face set into the expression of someone who knew that it was going to be a long night, there was going to be the need to call on the skills of sympathy and empathy, there would be tears and hugs and possibly some emotional breakthroughs, and not a single bit of it would be fun or entertaining or in any way what she looked for in a Friday night out after work.

Over at the bar, Tony had begun downing shots of tequila in what looked like blind panic. Lauren and Brigid gazed at him silently for a while.

"I've scared him, haven't I?"

"Absolutely shitless."

"Yeah no," said Brigid finally. "I suppose a baby is a bad idea."

Lauren breathed a silent prayer of thanks to any gods who may have been floating around.

"The Tony factor is the truly bad bit, to be honest, but overall, yes, it's a bad idea. And half of your job involves trying to clean up after people who had babies when they didn't really want them, so I'd think that would be a cautionary enough tale."

"I'm just so *bored*. Everything is so boring. Why is life so boring? I wanted a job and then I found a job and now I'm miserable. I live in one of the world's most liveable and dynamic cities, but I may as well be a 50s housewife for all the options I have."

"What about that trip to Ireland you were talking about last year? You were so excited about that. Remember, you kept dreaming about that random stone well in Kilkenny—"

"Kildare"

"That's the one. For six months you literally dreamed about an archaeological site that you'd never even heard of. If that's not a sign of a past life, then I don't know what is."

Brigid rolled her eyes at this concept. "I didn't want to go on my own though and you were busy. And poor"

"I said you could have gone with a tour group."

Brigid shuddered. "I'm not dropping ten grand on a holiday to spend it with Karen from Lismore and her husband Steven."

"But you like teaching, don't you?" Lauren plugged on.

Brigid sighed. "I suppose. Yes. That's not the problem. It's the incompetent idiots in the job, and every other aspect of my life that I'm having issues with."

Lauren gestured to the bar. "This," she said, "is it. We're Generation X. This is our life. This is what we have left. The world is falling apart, we can't afford houses, and we've been left sitting around in pubs that serve gastro foam while we listen to a bodhrán designed to lull us into a terminal somnambulism."

Brigid shuddered and sent up a silent thanks that tonight wasn't live music night.

"We're supposed to blame our parent's generation and get on with living lives of bleak false fulfilment. They screwed everything up with their free education and no tax and cheap houses. They sucked society dry and left us with nothing." Lauren seemed to have really hit her stride now.

"To be fair, it wasn't my parents who did that. They made a passable go of opting out of society altogether."

Lauren nodded sagely. "Tax evasion?"

"Hippies. Nudists occasionally. On a commune."

There was a pause.

"How have I never heard this story? What… actual nudists? As in no clothes at all?"

Brigid nodded. "I don't really ever think about it," she said. "It doesn't come up in conversation organically."

"Did everyone just have sex, like, all the time?"

"God no. Would you want to have sex with someone when you see them eating wheat germ and yoghurt naked every morning? Anyway, the nudist thing was a bit of a phase. A summer phase to be honest. On days over 25C."

Lauren looked at Brigid doubtfully, unsure of whether she was having her leg pulled.

"Was this a commune or a cult?"

Brigid shrugged. "Definitely not a cult. No one was really in charge, and whenever anyone tried to get a bit bossy, everyone else decided to put them on wheat-husking duty for a few weeks. Brought you right down to earth, trust me. And I got to be one of the muses of this channelled imaginary friend kind of thing for a while, which was fun. Juniper decided I 'embodied the true nature of the symbiotic relationship between the soul and the corporeal body', or some such thing so he got me to talk to this pretend friend I had and—" She broke off. "Mur-arb, his name was. How odd, I haven't thought about that for years and years. And I hadn't thought about Juniper either. He was a friend of Mum and Dad's. And mine, I suppose. Kind of my mentor." She looked off into the distance for a moment. "Mentorish anyway."

"Yeah, that's not normal. The hippy bits maybe, but not the other stuff. Do you think it damaged you?" Laurens eyes lit up a bit at this possibility.

Brigid laughed. "Maybe I made it sound crazier than it was. It was just a bunch of hippies looking for a better way of doing life and making meaning of life and being together. But it didn't work so," she gestured to the pub, "here I am."

"I don't really see you as a hippy."

Brigid shrugged. "I'm not, that's kind of the point. Is there anything about me that's vaguely hippy-ish?"

"You quite like bean sprouts."

Brigid shook her head. "There's nothing like being brought up seeing carrot ice cream as a treat to put you off all that hippy shit. Anyway, the commune bit was abandoned shortly after people started to wear clothes. They kept bickering over who had the rights to the Steeleye Span records, and things eventually got a bit nasty. After it was decided that property wasn't actually theft, people began to head off into their own little groups, and then I guess we were just ordinary hippies. You know, stone ground bread and seagrass mats and goats' milk and chanting. And, as I said, Juniper invented this religious philosophy thingy and got me to talk about my imaginary friend, and that was kind of the end of it."

"Wait, what did you have to do? With this spiritual stuff?"

Brigid shifted uncomfortably. "From what I remember, I had invented this imaginary friend called Mur-arb, and for some reason people got all excited about it, and when I meditated, he gave me messages, and I passed them on. Or something. I wish I hadn't mentioned it now."

"God," said Lauren. "All I had was *Hey Hey It's Saturday* and Mum stealing my Johnny Farnham posters when *Smash Hits* came every week. And my pretend friend was a dog. It's funny isn't it, that I'm the one who's into Wicca and you're the one who hates all this woo-woo shit."

"I dreamed of *Smash Hits* posters. I smuggled one home from school once, but Mum made me compost it."

"I'm beginning to see why you eat white bread and your favourite spiritual writer is Richard Dawkins. Still, you shouldn't discount it all out of hand. If you're having a bit of an existential crisis then maybe you could put your cynicism on hold for a minute and—"

"What?"

"Come and have a tarot reading with me?"

"Or you could fuck off."

"Oh, come on, it's not the worst idea, is it? I'm having one tomorrow anyway. If it's all shit then it makes no difference, and maybe there'll be some clarity that comes out of it? What have you got to lose? I mean, you used to be an actual muse. A spiritual muse by the sounds of it. I don't know what that is, but it sounds pretty damn impressive to me and kind of goddess-like, so if anything is going to get you out of your funk, it's reconnecting with your woo-woo roots."

Brigid rolled her eyes at the absurdity, as above her the clouds crashed against each other, pushed by forces that were keen on the balance of things, and for her to have a tarot reading, if for no other reason than it would make many beings' jobs far easier. At this stage of the proceedings, the more things fell into place seamlessly, the better. Life had been rendered difficult enough of late, and while most of the middle management reapers were of the mind that things were only going to get worse, Brigid's appointment with a substandard psychic who called herself Vashti could potentially make things much, much simpler.

Three

From a seat at the opposite end of the bar, beyond the parquet area where almost entirely inauthentic Irish bands played on Wednesday nights, sat the dark, unnoticeable man. Unnoticeable, still, and surly.

Deliberately unnoticeable, that is, not the kind of unnoticeable that comes from having a weak chin, an inability to make eye contact and no charisma. This man had plenty of charisma. He prided himself on it. It was, quite literally, one of his *charisms*. Having the charisma that will entice even the angels of heaven to come down to your 600th birthday is all well and good, but when you're trying to blend into a noisy bar in Melbourne on a Friday night, it's more of a hindrance than anything else.

It wasn't as if people couldn't see him at all; he wasn't invisible. He had deliberately decided against this because having a corporeal body sit on your lap was a singularly unpleasant experience you wouldn't make the mistake of letting happen more than once. But there was a certain dimness about him. It was as if he was a magnet emitting negative energy, causing people to veer away from him when they got too near. The empty table at which he sat attracted plenty of attention as the evening progressed, but once people got to within a metre or two, they decided that they would rather stand at the bar, or go to the toilet, or head home early rather than make the decision to actually sit at it.

He sat at his table and glowered at everything around him, purely on principle. If people had been able to focus on him long enough to make out any characteristics, they would have seen a tall man, with angular features, and a Presley-esque swipe of black hair. His burgundy velvet sports coat over a green satin shirt, which would not have looked out of place in 1970s London, was worn in such a way that indicated he wasn't totally ignorant of the effect he had on others, even if those people weren't taking any notice of him at this exact moment. He sat firm in the understanding that, if he had allowed them to see him, they would be hugely impressed.

Not that he had any interest in anyone here, particularly the woman he was supposed to be observing, who was currently holding forth about the merits of carrot ice cream over brown rice pie crust as the centre dish of a twelfth birthday party.

This was not an assignment that Egragore—for that was the man's name— wanted, and this wasn't, by a long shot, his preferred way of spending an evening. But when the Great and Glorious Ruler, Mur-arb, told you to do something, in the political climate that he was coming from, you did it without asking questions.

There hadn't been a lot of context around the assignment. He had been told to "scope her out" by Mur-arb and given that the entirety of space and time and universal order, including the Great Abyss and the Heavenly Realm, was undergoing what could be referred to casually as "extreme flux and monumental recalibration" he had decided it was safer to do what he was told at this stage of the proceedings.

And if he could just get the woman to head off to this ridiculous but occasionally prescient tarot reader in the morning, then maybe his job would be easier in the long run.

Four

"And," continued Lauren, as she made an unsteady lunge towards her fourth tequila, "I read the other day that because our pineal gland is the gateway to other dimensions, the government is using fluoride to block it and stop us accessing our true potential. Did you ever hear about that when—"

Brigid stood, placing a kiss on her friend's forehead as she picked up her coat and bag. "I didn't have a single molecule of fluoride until I was fourteen, and my pineal gland is firmly locked, sorry." She waved over the bar, where Tony was trying to explain Aussie Rules Football to a group of Asian tourists. Pointing at Lauren and then back at him, she managed to convey, "I'm off home, so you'll need to stay with her because she's shitfaced, ok?"

Tony gave her a cheerful thumbs up.

A short distance away, Egragore stared at her. He stared and stared.

The noise of the bar faded into the background as a new thought came to Brigid. Maybe she should go along to this tarot reading tomorrow after all. What harm could it do? God knew she needed some fun in her life. Onward to new and interesting things, and all that. Maybe she could even rethink booking that trip to Ireland.

Egragore blinked.

Done.

"I want to know more about those prophetic dreams," Lauren called after her as she walked away. "And about this invented religion."

The fact that, by definition, every single religion conjured up throughout the history fell into that category was something that Brigid didn't really have the intestinal fortitude to get into at that moment.

As she stepped out into the cold damp night, pulling on her coat and swirling the now slightly frayed orange scarf around her neck, the door closed behind her and cut off the sound of the evening's revelries. She wasn't sure when the night had turned around and she had become the sober and sensible one, but playing that role was what she knew, so probably better to stick with it. She still had the vague feeling that she may be in the beginning of a midlife crisis, but she didn't feel the need to proposition random men anymore as an escape route, so she counted that as a win at this stage.

The drizzle had eased off, and she decided to walk the few blocks to her house. It wasn't that far, and a slight beer buzz always made night-time walking a pleasure rather than an effort. She began to walk down the middle of the foot path and didn't notice the door behind her opening and closing again quietly. While Egragore didn't strictly need to use doors, it did give a nice symbolic touch to the end of his night's work, and he always did like to give slightly more to a job than was required.

The gentle nudge he had directed towards Brigid had, he was certain, ensured she would be keeping the appointment in the morning, and after straightening his collar and adjusting his sleeves, he activated the slight switch in his perception that allowed him to propel himself back into the Heavenly Realm, and into his office to continue with his endless paperwork.

No rest for the wicked, and all that.

If he had known there were not one, but two other entities watching Brigid that night, with interests ranging from "fond reminiscence" to "possibly murderous intent", he would have been far less eager to get back to the office. There would still have been some eagerness, because Melbourne in April is no one's idea of a good time, but his commitment to his duties would have meant that he would have hung around for just a little longer to make sure Brigid got home safely.

The low grey clouds and the patchy mist gave the streetlights a mysterious, otherworldly haze, and as Brigid walked, she was heartily grateful that she was not currently trying to become impregnated in the back bar of the pub. Stepping over puddles, she smiled despite herself. She could go skydiving. Or spelunking. Something active that wasn't likely to kill her though. Maybe a bushwalk? Or trying one of the murder shows Netflix insisted on suggesting to her?

Gradually, without knowing exactly when she became aware of it, she heard footsteps. Footsteps that seemed to be almost exactly matching hers. Echoing taps of shoes that had some kind of a heel, not sneakers or sandshoes, but something a touch more business casual.

With this came the realisation that she was alone, in a dark street, in the middle of the city. Foolhardy, at best. Extremely silly and dangerous at worst. While the steps weren't close enough to be awkward, she couldn't shake the unmistakable feeling she was being followed. She had signed up for Self Defence for Women classes last year at the urging of Lauren, but she hadn't taken the radical action of attending any of them, so her eyes darted to the closest place of safety which happened to be a Greek takeaway. As she pushed open the glass door, the bell ringing through to the back of the building, she hoped she had just changed the risks she faced from "mugged and abducted" to "contracting salmonella from a dodgy crab stick".

The creature following her chuckled to himself. He sensed her fear. That was good. That was very good. If she was so easily frightened, then his job would be that much easier. Controlling her would barely be an issue at all.

He did the same little mind-switch manoeuvre that Egragore had done, and disappeared from the street, leaving a dark static filled space that people unconsciously veered to avoid for the next week.

The takeaway shop was oddly empty for a Friday night, the tables wiped clean and the bain-marie vacant except for a few sad potato cakes and a lamb souvlaki, which was paradoxically toughing up and growing limp at the same time. The bell above the door jangled as it closed behind her.

Brigid stepped quickly over to the drink fridge and squeezed in next to it, squinting out the window to try and catch a glimpse of whoever she had heard behind her. The street was well lit by streetlamps, glossy with the reflected puddles, and completely empty.

Realising that the sounds may have been the echo of her own steps, she berated herself for getting in such a ridiculous state when she became aware of the feeling that is widely known on the pantomime circuit as "he's behind you". She could feel a presence, and knew, utterly, that someone was standing silently next to her. Silently, creepily, and almost certainly dangerously. She swung around, now utterly frazzled, to find, once again, that there was no one there.

She placed one hand on the thrumming drink fridge and closed her eyes, steadying her breath, her chin firming up stubbornly. This was completely ridiculous and more than a little embarrassing. She was used to keeping thirty teenagers under control by the sheer brute force of her glare, and had no problem wading in to break up a fight between boys a head taller than her, so why was she so rattled by what appeared to be an empty street and an equally empty shop? She readjusted her scarf around her neck, placed the strap of her handbag firmly over her shoulder, and turned to face the door. A short, chubby man stood in front of it, grinning at her widely.

A wide grin is rarely a comforting expression, and unless it is a baby just learning how to fashion its face into socially acceptable expressions, it is more often associated with homicidal clowns in horror movies; unsettling and vaguely dangerous.

"Hello," the man said. His grin turned to a frown as he looked down at his own hand, and then jerkily held it out to Brigid, in a manner universally accepted as the symbol for "shake". But to Brigid it had about as much relatability as if he had held out a week-old fish for her hand holding pleasure. He quickly dropped his hand to his side and then said, "It's so good to—" but the words were too loud in the empty space and his eyes darted around as if he had startled himself.

Brigid took a step back, her eyes wild, and the man's face took on the expression of someone who was rapidly losing control of the situation, even if the situation was one he hadn't had much of a handle on in the first place. He too took a step back, as if in sympathy, and collided with the door behind him, which seemed to further confuse him and he half turned, extending his hand again.

While Brigid knew that one could not use someone's appearance as a measure to judge their ability to kill you, wrap you in an old carpet, and hide you in the boot of their Cortina for a month, the man's befuddled demeanour did give her a chance to get some clarity on the situation.

The man was, as she had initially noticed, short and chubby. She was 5'6", and he was quite a bit less than that. He carried most of his weight in his middle, the buttons of his red tunic (the absurdity of which she made a mental note to get back to later) pulled at the seams, and his black trousers were made for comfort rather than style. His face was round, his head bald, and a full chestnut coloured beard covered his chin.

He wore one large, hooped earring which screamed "mid-life crisis", but his age was indeterminate. He could have been anywhere from mid-forties to mid-sixties. Before she had a chance to notice anything else, he had yanked the door open and hurled himself out into the night, leaving Brigid staring after him in a state of shocked amusement that was worlds away from her initial fear. Her eyes darted around, hoping someone had appeared behind the counter, someone who she could compare notes with about what had just happened. Also, she wouldn't mind buying the last, lone souvlaki.

But after a few moments standing alone in the very deserted shop, she stepped out into the street and headed home; reasoning that the odds against meeting another very, very odd man that evening were stacked in her favour.

And she turned out to be correct.

Five

The *Tantric Om* was a shop Brigid had passed many times, but she had never felt the urge to step through the fog of incense and push open the beaded rainbow-coloured curtains.

It could have been the hand painted "Open for Hugs" sign which projected halfway onto the footpath that put her off, or the rack of tie-dyed parachute pants hanging limply outside, or the promise of "good vibes with every purchase" on the door, but mostly it was her dislike of anything new age that had kept her away.

Now though, she pushed her way through the salt lamps and amethyst pendulums that crowded around the doorway and stepped into the dim interior. It was a narrow shop, but long, and while it seemed to be a catch all for every bit of metaphysical rubbish dreamt up in a hippie's most psychedelic nightmare, it appeared that Feng Shui was the one school of woo the shop owner didn't subscribe to. There was no way every item jammed into the shop could facilitate the flow of anything, except, of course, money into the owner's pocket.

Lauren was supposed to be here five minutes ago, but by the looks of it she had not yet arrived, so Brigid self-consciously browsed the shelves near the entrance, praying in a non-denominational way that a) no one would offer her assistance and b) she wouldn't see anyone she knew. Generally speaking, she was happy to admit she had a bit of a set against new age paraphernalia. She liked to say it had nothing to do with scars from her unconventional childhood, and everything to do with a mind that valued scientific rigour. She also had a mind that disliked shoddily made handcrafts which often took the form of dream catchers made with factory farmed feathers by a girl from Nowra called Sheree, who thought she was communicating with her ancestors because she had once dreamed of a crystal bison while high on clove cigarettes on a budget trip to Bali.

As Brigid ran her fingers through the tubs of chipped gemstones, she mulled over why she was here at all. Probably, like most things in her life, because she had no better option, she reasoned. She had become a teacher because her scores were just reasonable, and she had a half-hearted desire to make teenager's lives a bit less shit. She had her friends because they had seemed to like her and invited her to things, and no one expected her to throw parties or stay out too late during weeknights. She had her hobbies because, well, she didn't really have that many hobbies. Every January her friends shared their lists of twenty things they wanted to do this year, and she could never think of what to put down. She usually just fell into things. Which was why, she thought wryly, she was at a tarot reader, in a dodgy, scammy little shop at 11.00 am on a Saturday.

Lauren bounded up to her with the energy of an excitable puppy, narrowly avoiding knocking over a display of activated charcoal miracle cream. "I can't believe you came."

Brigid shrugged. "Nothing better to do, to be honest."

Lauren took her arm and dragged her to a small room curtained off from the rest of the shop, waving to the young man behind the wide counter as she passed him.

"He's in love with me," she said. "Be nice to the poor thing."

Lauren worked here part-time, and Brigid felt no guilt in the fact that she did not support this decision in any way at all.

As she passed through the satin curtain, Brigid looked around the small space, surprised at the fact she felt a little disappointed. "I thought it would be a little more—"

"Were you expecting an actual crystal ball?" joked Lauren, stopping when she saw Brigid's face. "Come on, seriously?"

"I just think that if you're paying good money, then you should get the full Harry Potter experience."

An older woman who had been sitting at a card table covered in a velvet cloth, emblazoned with gold embroidery, and scattered beads, stood as they approached, then stepped forwards to embrace Lauren.

Between her buzz cut, turtleneck sweater and the lack of crystal ball, Brigid felt a little cheated. She might not be buying into any of it, but she would still have liked an authentic vibe.

"Vashti," Lauren said, returning the embrace, then turning to gesture to Brigid. "This is my friend, Brigid. Would you be able to read for her today instead of me? She's never had a reading before, and she's feeling a bit lost at the moment."

"Of course." Vashti smiled, gesturing to the chairs surrounding the table. "Do you want to stay while I read for her?"

"Is that alright?" Lauren said.

"Fine," said Brigid. It would be a shame if the only person really committed to the event wasn't even there to see it.

Glancing at the woman again, Brigid frowned slightly. "Do we know each other?"

Vashi smiled. "I've been working here for a while."

"No, that's definitely not it."

Vashti laughed, a noise cultivated to sound, Brigid suspected, deliberately deep and throaty. No one sounded like that unless it was on purpose. "Perhaps. Life is long; our paths may have crossed many times, in many different—"

Brigid clapped her hands together. "I know, class of 2003. Tremont McClean."

Vashti's smile became tighter.

"Tremont McClean, God I'd forgotten all about him. How is he? You were Kylie back then, weren't you?"

Brigid could see Lauren out of the corner of her eyes, tersely smoothing down the velvet of the table.

"I remember now. Gosh, you started up the Gifted and Talented program at school just for him, didn't you? You were such a great mum, advocating for him like that. Even when he was in year 12. How is he going? Doing something amazing I bet?"

Brigid was slightly disappointed to learn he now worked as a real estate agent. She was always disappointed to learn that her ex-students had become real estate agents. No one deserved that kind of future.

That conversation out of the way, Vashti turned to the shelf behind her with palpable relief and lifted down several boxes. Laying them on the table, she lifted their lids, exposing various decks of cards. "Do you have a preference as to which deck we read from?"

Brigid looked to Lauren. "I don't care. What do you think?"

Lauren leaned forwards and peered at the deck in front of them. "Maybe a beautiful Guardian Angel deck?"

Brigid, who hadn't realised that she had any preferences at all when it came to tarot decks, shook her head. "No, I don't like those pictures much."

"How about this then? Unicorns and fairies."

"God no." She shuddered. Another one was suggested, this time with cats, but she somehow felt that if she was supposedly charting the future, then perhaps cats wearing amusing hats weren't appropriately serious.

"I'm wondering . . ." Vashti frowned then looked at Lauren. "How about the Hermetic?"

Lauren drew in her breath. "Really? Are you sure? But it's her first time. Is that appropriate?"

"What?" asked Brigid, her interest piqued despite herself. "What's that?"

"It's a serious deck dealing with serious issues," replied Vashti. "I very rarely use it for people who aren't deeply activated and in tune with their higher selves." She narrowed her eyes and looked carefully at Brigid. "What kind of reading were you wanting today? Because if it's about whether a guy likes you or not, then one of these decks would be more appropriate. But if we're looking at—"

"What?" asked Brigid again. She had gone from being largely uninterested to being offended that her personal issues might not be significant enough to merit these cards.

"If you're interested in the greater karmic forces at work in your life, then we could look at using this deck. For more mundane enquiries, it isn't appropriate."

"I think we should look at what's happening on a higher plane of reality." The words came out of her mouth before she knew what she was saying.

Lauren clapped her hands together excitedly and leaned forwards. "You're so brave. I always stick to the unicorns."

Vashti, with a glint in her eye, removed the boxes from the table and lifted the chosen deck from its box. The cards where black and white, but decorated ornately, detailed designs intertwined with what Brigid assumed were metaphysical symbology and esoteric designs. Vashti took the deck between her hands and began to shuffle the cards with an expert ease.

"So, what is it you'd like clarity around? Are we going with karmic forces or something a bit more specific? The energies surrounding you both above and below? Tracking the karmic thread that you'll need to understand to propel yourself into your soul's next stage of empowerment and embodiment of your divine feminine?"

"Hang on," said Brigid, stalling. She hadn't understood much of what Vashti had just said, but passionately hoped the mention of the divine feminine didn't mean that they were going to be getting out hand mirrors to embrace their yoni when the reading was over. "Shouldn't I be shuffling? On account of my . . . energies?"

"If you want to," Vashti said, "but it won't make any difference."

"Really?"

"That's just showmanship and window dressing if you ask me. But you're more than welcome to. Be my guest." She held the cards towards Brigid as Lauren looked at her expectantly.

"It doesn't matter then," said Brigid.

"Right," said Vashti. "Karmic forces, is it?"

Brigid nodded. Might as well go for the big guns. The really boring sounding big guns.

Vashti cleared her throat and closed her eyes. The drawn curtain and lack of windows made the little space feel almost cave-like, and for a moment Brigid felt a shiver of expectancy.

"Let it be known that we are seeking clarification surrounding Brigid's karmic forces, and the energies currently acting upon her. Give her the empowerment to understand what she should be preparing for, and how she is best placed to deal with these demands." She opened her eyes and winked at Brigid. "Window dressing," she grinned, before shuffling the cards once again. Drawing four cards, she lay them face down on the table in a triangle arrangement, with one in the middle.

Brigid and Lauren sat forward; eyes fixed intently on the monochromatic cards.

"So, in the middle, we have the card that symbolises you," explained Vashti, "then around you we have the three cards that are impacting on your spiritual body—the past, the present and the future—and how your physical body is integrated within the great vortex of being."

Once again, Brigid didn't understand a word that had just been said, but felt it was a nod to her maturity that she kept that to herself.

There was quiet, as one by one, Vashti turned each card so they faced upwards.

"Huh," said Lauren, her head tilted, her brow furrowed. "That's . . . a lot."

"What?" asked Brigid, leaning forward. "What's a lot?"

Vashti sat with her eyebrows raised. "It is, isn't it. Maybe . . ." Her voice petered out.

Brigid focussed her attention on the cards. In the middle was a picture of a woman. Representing her, she supposed. Appropriate, given that she, indeed, was a woman; although the fact that the figure was holding a severed head gave it a certain lack of relatability. Surrounding this representation of her were cards on which were written the words Death, The Devil, and The Tower. Brigid reminded herself she didn't believe in any of this one bit, which was just as well, because there seemed to be a worrisomely large amount of death and destruction before her.

"This looks cheerful," she said.

"There's a lot happening here," replied Vashti. "A lot of, let's say, confronting imagery."

They stared at the cards. Beyond the curtain Brigid could hear the noises of the shop, a woman asking what crystal she should use to get a promotion at work, someone else asking why the salt lamp he had bought last week seemed to be melting, another voice complaining of an invisible creature that sat on his back and poked him in the face. The jingle of the bells of the door and the low hum of traffic outside. All of this was distant, as if in another world.

"So, what are we looking at?" she said finally.

"Yes," said Vashti, shaking her head and firming up her jaw. "What you need to understand when we see a spread like this is that the cards don't literally mean what their titles say. That's just symbolic of the bigger picture. They're embodiments of energies, or certain forces of the whole general vibe of life."

"Death doesn't actually mean death," clarified Brigid.

"That's right. Death is about change and the end of old ways. It's an incredibly positive card. It's about freeing yourself from the shackles of the past."

Brigid picked the card up and looked at it closely. "Quite a lot of skeletons for a card that isn't about death in any way. Look at them all. They're positively capering."

Vashti conceded that she had a point.

"And that knife going through the skull there? That would indicate?"

"Transformation," said Vashti, her voice lacking some of the confidence it had possessed earlier.

"Right." Brigid crossed her arms. "And out of interest, what does the kitten deck have on its death card?"

"I think that one has a ball of wool that's rolled away," offered Lauren.

The next card had "The Devil" written across the top, and on it was drawn the usual horned, scaly winged, flaming imagery you would expect; bats, a horned being of some sort, suffering minions.

Your usual, common, or garden basic demonic business.

"So, this would be describing?" enquired Brigid, one eyebrow raised.

"Not the Devil, obviously," confirmed Vashti.

"Of course not. That would be ridiculous. Why else would you name it the Devil, if not for indicating its total lack of connection with anything demonic?"

"It's about your shadow side," started Vashti. "Your subconscious and the parts of you that you don't want to--"

"And this one?" Brigid interrupted, pointing to the final card. "This one that portrays a building literally exploding and . . ." She peered more closely at it. ". . . oh yes, people literally plummeting to their deaths in flames. This one is about my need to be liked or something like that, I'm assuming?"

"Well," said Vashti, in a last-ditch effort to wrench back control of the situation. "It's more to do with the demons of anarchy and despair being released from their shackles and—"

"Right." Brigid stood up, grabbing her bag and bumping the velvet cloth, scattering the cards on the table. "I think we're done here."

She batted dream catchers out of her face and very nearly lost an eye to a stray pendulum as she strode through the shop to the exit. Behind her, she could hear a muttered conversation between Vashti and Lauren.

She stood outside on the street, breathing through her nose to calm herself. Her face felt hot, and tears threatened to well in her eyes.

This was stupid, she thought. Why was she so upset? This was all a pile of rubbish, so why did she care what the cards said?

Maybe because her life's representation looked like the keynote address at a demon convention, a small voice said in her ear.

Lauren emerged and looked around for her friend. She placed a hand on Brigid's arm, a worried expression on her face. "What's wrong? You didn't even stay for the important bits. Vashti had some things to tell you about what the cards were—"

She stopped when she saw Brigid's face.

"What the fuck was that all about?" snapped Brigid. "What kind of a shit show does that idiot run? Why would she think someone wants to see all that rubbish?"

"I'm sorry," said Lauren. "I can't help but feel partially responsible for that."

"Why, because the whole thing was completely your idea?"

"I'll admit that was a shit load of demons. It's lucky you don't believe in any of this stuff, isn't it?"

Brigid swung around to face her. "Do you really think that's the point?"

Lauren frowned at her, taken aback. "I rather think it should be, actually. Yes, it *should* be the point. If you don't believe it's true, then it shouldn't be worrying you in any way. If a random wino came up to you and announced that you were the Irish Goddess Brigid, the Exalted One of the Fiery Whatsit, just because you've got red hair, you wouldn't get so upset."

"But that happened to me."

"Exactly why I'm using the analogy. If a random wino came up to you and told you that you were Brigid, Goddess of the Flame and of the Well, Divine Mistress of Spring and New Growth, Font of all Inspiration and Creativity, down here for a spot of mortal and earthly incarnation, would you take it to heart and have a mini crisis about it?"

"But that did happen, so why are you talking hypothetically? A random guy came up and ranted that I'm a goddess and told me I had angels about me. You were with me."

Lauren nodded patiently. "That's the point. Did you get angry and upset about it?"

"No, I told him that a Celtic goddess is hardly going to have any truck, or indeed need, for Judeo-Christian angels and that he was getting his mythological wires crossed. Then he got annoyed at me and went off to yell at a lamppost about Harold Holt's disappearance. Then we had a laugh and then went for a curry. Remember?"

"Yes. That's my point. Why are you upset about this rather than that, when you allegedly don't believe in either of them?"

"Don't say *allegedly*. I *don't* believe either of them, thanks very much. But you have to admit that being likened to a sexy and mysterious Celtic queen is a bit more appealing than being told you're surrounded by a shitshow of death and destruction."

Lauren suddenly sucked in her breath. Grabbing Brigid's arm, a look of excitement jumped to her face. "Did you do devil worship in your religion thingy when you were a child? Could this have a connection to Satanism do you think? The skulls and the blood? Maybe you have a repressed traumatic memory."

Brigid pulled her arm away. "No we did not "do" devil worship, and would you please stop trying to dig out a repressed traumatic memory?" She straightened her coat and shook her hair away from her face. "Anyway, you're right. It's no different at all from that goddess thing. And we laughed about that."

"We laughed a lot. It's one of my favourite stories now. I tell it all the time. And it was weird he got your name right though, wasn't it? I've always thought that was weird."

"Na," said Brigid, taking her friend's arm and steering her down the street towards a café that looked like it primarily sold turmeric lattes, but if the odds were in her favour would have actual caffeine too. "Half the redheads I know are called Brigid. And the more I think about it, if some kind of otherworldly being wanted to enlist me on a quest, to add a little spice to my life, then that's something I wouldn't discount out of hand. It's probably the only way I'm going to get any excitement. Bring it on, I say."

In every far flung and distant corner of the Other World, from the stereotypical yet accurate puffy clouds of the Heavenly Realm, to the officious and austere board meetings of the Shadow Lands, to the plunging despair of the Great Abyss, as well as the lesser known and rarely traversed expanses in between, reality shuddered a little, and began to prepare itself.

Six

Mur-arb, the recently ascended Great and Glorious Ruler, was bored. And irritated. And he wasn't at all a fan of his new title.

Or the underlings who had started using the title in the first place.

Or any of his underlings now he came to think of it.

For as long as he could remember, however long that was, the majority of his daily life had involved having to make his own dandelion tea, thinking up new things to do with kombucha and trying to write a dictionary of llama facial expressions. But now, ever since he had been brought, nay, wrenched here, there were helpers popping in and out at all times of the day and night.

They didn't, as far as he could see, do much helping, and while he was loath to create any negative vibes, the tone of voice they used when they called him by what he supposed was his new title wasn't especially reverential. So, the Great and Glorious Ruler of the Heavenly Realm, the Shadow Lands and the Great Abyss sat on his throne, alone and bereft, surveying his domain.

The word "domain" might involve a little poetic license, truth be told. Domain brought to mind, what… an expansive territory? A special area that uniquely belonged to a ruler? Something definitely awe inspiring.

It was less often used to describe a smallish, boxy-ish, concrete-ish chamber that looked like a cross between a waiting room in an underfunded public hospital and a cold-war era elevator. It was painted what was supposed to be a relaxing eggshell blue, but looked to the casual observer like a sad selection of paint remnants had been tipped in the same can and called good enough.

Which was, in fact, exactly what had happened.

And he didn't "survey" his surroundings as much as he looked around nervously in the hope that something interesting would happen, or someone would appear and tell him what he was supposed to do.

But still, despite the unpleasant colour, the too small room, and the largely unhelpful helpers, he was now the Great and Glorious Ruler, and he—

Now he thought about it, he felt pretty uncomfortable about this, and he wished that someone would walk up to him and tell him this had all been a big mix up, and that he could pop off and have a bath or a lie down if he wanted, as he was no longer needed.

This stubbornly persisted in not happening, and his confusion and sense of being utterly lost was mounting by the second.

The Great and Glorious Ruler shifted on his throne. Once again, it had been presented to him as a throne, and he supposed that it was, in theory, but it was not a plush and comfortable throne, the kind that would typically come to mind when you hear the word. It was more of a pointy and bony throne that seemed to have been built to inspire fear and abject dread, but only succeeded in making the being sitting in it shuffle around in it as if he was developing a nasty case of piles. After it had been presented to him, he had asked for some cushions to pad it out a little, but this seemed to make people frown at him and talk behind his back even more, and after all that they still didn't give him any cushions.

So, Mur-arb sat on his throne and waited for something to happen. If Brigid had been there, rather than where she was—which was arguing with a waiter called Symon about whether she could get a shot of caffeine in her matcha tea—she would have recognised him as being the very odd little man who had so unsuccessfully tried to shake her hand the night before. He was still feeling awkward about that incident and was embarrassed, but not surprised, that the fateful meeting he had been playing out in his head for so long had not at all gone the way he had hoped.

Finally, he heard footsteps, and he eagerly looked down the narrow corridor that ran off the throne room. He held high hopes that someone may have had an idea of some kind and might at this very moment be heading towards him with a grand plan.

The figure who strode towards him was tall and haughty and wry and cynical, and Mur-arb wished he had just a touch of the charisma this man had. He also wondered why, given he was now an important, possibly omnipotent being, he couldn't iron out some of his more embarrassing character traits. But questioning this, like the cushions, seemed to be doing him no favours with all the other new and interesting species of beings with which he now had tedious and largely useless meetings.

Egragore stopped in front of Mur-arb, and inclined his head almost imperceptivity, in what Mur-arb hoped was deference.

"My dear fellow." He smiled widely, supressing his suspicion that Egragore thought he was an absolutely incompetent twat, and decided to be grateful that he had someone to talk to. "Are you here with exciting news of my "domain"?" He attempted to make his eyes twinkle, to indicate to Egragore that he was jocular and relaxed and put little stock in such things.

"We nearly have her," Egragore said after a moment's pause, perfectly designed to convey contempt. "She has almost offered to help."

"Excellent," said Mur-arb, clapping his hands delightedly. "That is absolutely splendid news. Just splendid. Who?"

"The Prospective Mistress of the Shadow Lands. We've discussed this. Ad nauseum."

He looked into Mur-arb's eyes, hoping for a glimmer of recognition. Honestly, the man had the retention of a toddler. A not very smart toddler at that.

Egragore forged on.

"She has cried out for our assistance and now we, of the aforementioned Shadow Lands, are free to welcome her to our mission. We must now balance the tenuous road between using her powers for our own good, and melding them seamlessly with yours so that . . . I'm sorry, is that a souvlaki in your hand?"

Mur-arb glanced down briefly at the now very worse for wear snack, but paid it no attention. "I do wish you would speak more plainly, old fellow. I barely know what you're referring to half the time. Maybe a touch more than half now I come to think about it. I don't know who you're talking about or even who these Shadow Lands fellows are. Are they these chaps in black who flit around here and there calling me "Great and Glorious"? Because I hate to be one to complain, but I don't really feel as if they're helping me at all, if that's their role. Unless they're supposed to be forming an abyss or some such? Someone was telling me about that the other day. If I just had a bit more of idea about what—"

As was so often the case when he became enmeshed in an impossible to avoid conversation with Mur-arb, Egragore felt a headache begin to prick behind his eyes. Of all the things that he was currently in charge of, this was definitely his least favourite.

"The "Shadow Lands fellows", as you describe them, is everyone who you are having contact with at the moment, and The Prospective Mistress of the Shadow Lands is your counsel. You know. The one you've asked us to find."

Mur-arb frowned for a moment, and then his round face broke out into a smile. "Oh, do you mean Cosmic?"

"Yes, that's right, Cosmic. The one you seem quite fixated on. She appears to be going by the name of Brigid now, but yes."

Mur-arb sat back in his chair. "Oh lovely. Good on her. Make your own truth. Subvert the dominant paradigm, and all that. Why stick to the name foisted on you at birth? Go Brigid, I say. So, she has offered to help has she? You managed to activate her sight thingy, did you? Because I saw her last night, and she didn't seem very interested in me. Or in fact even recognise me in any way at all. I was quite hurt, now I come to think about it. I mean, I know that I never literally appeared before her eyes when she was a child, I was more of a whole 'meditative vibe' but still, I had expected there to be *some* recognition. I was under the impression that I was quite important to her."

"You saw her?" snapped Egragore, his eyes flashing. "What do you mean you saw her?"

"Well," said Mur-arb, self-consciously shifting in his supremely uncomfortable chair, "I just popped down to earth, and—"

"You just *popped* down to Earth?" His voice rang out in the small chamber. "Of course you did. That's where that souvlaki came from, isn't it? She couldn't possibly have recognised you as we haven't activated that bit of her consciousness yet. She doesn't recognise you because she never actually thought you were real. Remember? She thought that you were simply her imaginary friend."

The look on his face said that no, as a matter of fact, he didn't remember.

"All that was supposed to happen when that substandard psychic gave her a reading, but she didn't stick around long enough to get to the good bits. She was supposed to be endowed with a moment of perfect clarity where all this knowledge flooded into her, but oh no, why would anything happen the way it's supposed to? Why would anything, absolutely anything at all, go smoothly?" Egragore knew that he was ranting now and could see that he was a heartbeat away from losing Mur-arb completely. "Have you listened to anything we've been discussing? And look, I'm sorry to circle back to this, but what do you mean you just "popped down" to Earth? Your Excellence, we have discussed the demarcation regarding who goes where, and it does not, at this stage, involve you *popping* down to Earth."

"Yes." Mur-arb dismissed this line of discussion with a wave of his hand. "I was just down there on other business, which I believe I should be allowed to have, should I not? Given that I am the Great and Glorious Ruler and therefore your superior? If, er, that's all right with you?"

Egragore suppressed an eye roll.

"But look," continued Mur-arb. "That isn't important. What I'm interested in is you saying she has called to you. Has she?"

"Er . . ." Egragore's eyes shifted.

"Did she agree? To help us. To, and I need to stress this exactly, help us in our new endeavour? Because it's been made very clear to me that she can't come and help me until she agrees to it, and if you haven't noticed, I'm positively floundering here. We need her consent."

Egragore looked out of his depth for the first time. "She said she wouldn't dismiss it out of hand. In theory. It was inferred, anyway."

"Oh, seriously, Egragore." Mur-arb rubbed his sweaty forehead. "That's the best you've got? I need her, and I need her here, with me. Otherwise, I can't really *do* anything, can I? I'm a Great and Glorious Ruler who can do absolutely nothing except ask middle management tempters to get me cups of tea, and even then, if they arrive at all then they are stone cold. I need you to go and do whatever needs to be done to convince her to come and work with me. With us. Activate her whatsit or offer her something she can't refuse. Whatever needs to be done, do it. Please."

Egragore sighed. "I'm going to have to take matters into my own hands then I suppose. Do it myself."

"Whatever has to be done. If you can't do it, then I'll get someone who can."

Egragore had been working hard to ensure that the ruler was too intimidated by him to question or direct his movements, and for the first time he felt all of it slipping away. The ruler's lightning-fast mood changes, vacillating between amusingly forgetful and belligerently obstinate, were something he needed one of the wraiths to compile a report on as quickly as possible. He found Mur-arb irritating and vapid, but also unnervingly irrational and unpredictable; a fun combination considering the man had been thrust into the position of ruler of everything, against his wishes, aptitude, and seemingly all bounds of good sense.

"I will deal with it straight away," Egragore finished, tight lipped, and he turned on his heel. "May I just ask though; why do you insist on all of this?" he gestured to their surroundings: the concrete block, the hospital-blue walls, the retro elevator chic.

"What do you mean?"

"Why is this your choice of throne room? Why didn't you design something a little more impressive? Or comfortable?"

"Design?"

"Yes, design."

Mur-arb looked puzzled. "It was like this when I got here. When I . . . popped in, as it were."

Egragore frowned. "I don't think so. I don't think this space is one the Cosmic Engineering Officer would have brought about, do you? I don't feel as if it's exactly His taste."

Mur-arb glared at him. "It was just here, waiting for me. There's no need to bring up the last CEO."

Egragore adopted a conciliatory tone. "No, no, of course, I quite understand. However, it came about, or whoever created it, it doesn't have to stay like this though, does it?"

Mur-arb looked as if he was trying to solve a quadratic equation in his head. "I'm not sure I quite understand what you're getting at."

"Let me try to clarify," said Egragore slowly, already regretting that he had started this conversation. "As the ruler of essentially everything, you can create your own reality, so far as it relates to your will alone, yes?"

"Um—"

"You can design whatever you want, with regard to your own surroundings. Even without your. . . counsel. Brigid. Cosmic. I know that I've explained this to you."

"OK."

"You do have some powers currently. Not as extensive as you will have when she arrives, but some. As long as what you do doesn't damage anyone else."

"Oh good, I wouldn't like that." He nodded seriously.

"So, given that," Egragore continued, with the growing countenance of someone who has realised he has been trying to explain the rise of the European Union to a penguin and now needs to extricate himself from the conversation without offending it, "you could design a throne room however you want. You could have any room, any view, any contents. The entirety of space and time could be your inspiration."

"Oh, I say," said Mur-arb, smiling brightly. "That does sound fun."

"Yes," agreed Egragore evenly. "Doesn't it." He looked at Mur-arb. Mur-arb smiled back at him. "So, you could make that happen, couldn't you?"

"I could," agreed Mur-arb nodding. "It's just . . ." a look of concern flickered over his face. There was obviously something worrying him, and Egragore had a strong suspicion he was about to hear all about it.

"It's just . . ." he said again.

A pause.

"Yes?"

"I do feel a bit bad. About . . . you know who." Mur-arb cast his eyes upwards, grimaced and gave a little waggle of his fingers, in a way that Egragore utterly failed to understand.

"Who?"

"You know. *Him.* The Cosmological Engineering Officer," Mur-arb hissed in a stage whisper. "The CEO. I feel a bit bad about where He is now. Where He might *be*. I try not to think about it, about what has happened but . . ." His voice trailed off. "It can make a fellow feel almost a bit guilty, you know. Not that it had anything to do with me, that is."

Egragore cast his gaze around the room. "I suspect that wherever He is—wherever *they* are—it's a touch more appealing than here."

"Oh, I wouldn't think so," said Mur-arb, shaking his head with determination. "No, no, I wouldn't think so. After a shake up like we've had, I'd think it would be pretty grim from His point of view. Yes, pretty grim indeed. And it's not as if things were His *fault* exactly, were they? I mean, we've all been *thrust* into our new positions. Imagine being—" Here Mur-arb dropped his voice, his eyes darting around the room as if he expected the Previous Occupant to arrive back at any moment and bodily throw him out of his medieval throne. "Imagine being the CEO, and then *not* being the CEO any longer. Imagine the embarrassment. The shame. The fall."

Egragore smiled thinly and made mental note to avoid conversations with Mer-arb more tenaciously in the future. "Firstly, we have no idea where they are. They might be in an even better place."

"An even better place than here? Than the Heavenly Realm?"

"And," continued Egragore, "they have been doing quite a good job of keeping the rest of us in our place for the last couple of millennia, so I don't know if they necessarily need our sympathy. It's your basic boss slash worker dynamic. There's no place for emotion in it."

Egragore felt a pang of guilt at these words. It wasn't as bad as all that, and he felt that misrepresenting his old boss was doing Him a disservice. The Heavenly Realm was a delight to work under, in all honesty, and there really wasn't any "under the thumb"-ness to complain about. Everyone knew their strictly demarcated roles, and therefore everything went swimmingly. There wasn't much room for vertical movement, to be sure, but—

Mur-arb gazed off into space. "You're probably right. I mean, it's not as if I *asked* for all this. None of it is technically my fault. Maybe I have survivor guilt? But you're right, maybe we should . . . zsuzh things up a bit."

Egragore nodded in agreement. "Will that be all?"

"Do you think you could draw up some plans for me then?"

"Some plans?"

"Yes, of ideas. For a throne room. Something that I might like. Based on the Entirety of All Space and Time."

At that moment, Egragore suspected, not for the first time, that breaking into the Heavenly Realm, and then moving the entirety of the staff of the Shadow Lands up to inhabit them in the absence of the CEO might have been a very, very bad idea.

Seven

From A Concise History of the Shadow Lands, Volume 216, page 3116.

There were, at this stage, many forces working on the life of Brigid Humboldt; forces that were, for the most part, operating on other dimensions and levels than the standard ones your typical human is aware of.

The fact that she was a goddess on sabbatical on Earth was a totally separate situation from the enmeshment with Mur-arb that she had been subject to during this life. While this seems statistically impossible, in the higher dimensions this kind of thing happened all the time and most of the really top-level players paid it no mind. Of course, all humans are focus points for various cosmic, psychic, and karmic energies, and apart from finding out whether you should date Eric from accounts because you had a unicorn oracle reading, the vast bulk of these forces go unnoticed. People don't usually have any idea what kind of average they are batting until they are one day raised into the Heavenly Realm, or plunged into the Great Abyss, and if you think that that sounds a little unfair and arbitrary then you certainly wouldn't be the first to mention it.

At least, this had been the traditional way that things had gone on the planet Earth. For approximately two million years, while a subspecies of ape gloriously transformed itself into something that could effectively abuse politicians on Twitter, there had been a shift in consciousness towards monotheistic religions, and they decided *they liked the idea of One CEO who was in charge of everything and who made all the Big Decisions. They liked this idea, of course, until they discovered that they had been behaving in whatever way had arbitrarily been decided as immoral at the particular juncture, and then they were plunged into the Great Abyss where their opinions didn't really count any more.*

This system puttered along quite serviceably for all the people that mattered until the curious incident with the Large Hadron Collider really put a spanner in the works.

Funnily enough, no one had ever thought to ask how the CEO felt about being in charge of absolutely everything. And if anyone had taken the time to listen, they might have been quite surprised by the strong feelings that he held on the matter.

Eight

Unlike a quiet toddler, which is universally acknowledged as being deeply suspicious, a room of quiet teenagers is usually absolutely innocuous and not, as many would have it, the sign that someone's hair is about to be set on fire.

Whereas the lack of noise from a three-year-old may well mean that a cat is being painted, a classroom of teens is incapable of being silent if something out of the ordinary is happening. They are a kind of early warning signal for drama. So, if a student has smuggled their ferret into class and is feeding it quietly at the back of the room, or if a multi coloured penis fresco is being designed on the back of a chair, someone is going to alert the teacher to it pretty damn sharpish.

It's similar to a mob of meerkats, who loudly broadcast when something suspicious is going on, except meerkats don't then flush the offending meerkats head down the toilet at lunchtime. Of course, some teachers have perfected the art of ignoring, or at least conveniently mishearing these warnings because, as a wise man once said, "If I don't know about it, then I don't need to write an incident report about it". Brigid knew who these teachers were, and had a list allocated to them especially.

Because of this, Brigid was taken aback when she turned from writing the lesson objective on the board, to see a strange man casually leaning in the doorway. It wasn't necessarily his presence that alerted Brigid to the fact that something odd was going on. It was, firstly, that he looked suspiciously relaxed and unworried. Most of the teachers that Brigid dealt with on a day-to-day basis looked harried, and leaning nonchalantly in classroom doorways was something they reserved for student free days, if they engaged in any nonchalant leaning type behaviour at all.

The other thing that raised her suspicions was the fact that he was surrounded by flames.

That's not to say he was actually on fire, of course. That would be impossible. But he did appear to be emitting a shimmer of flames in a halo around his body.

It was quite an impressive trick if you could manage it.

She glanced back at the classroom. The students were all quietly continuing with their work. She paused, but only for a minute. You don't survive in an inner-city school for twenty years without mastering a certain degree of resilience, and the firm ability to stay unfazed.

"Can I help you?" she asked him.

The man looked at her. He smiled in a way that seemed to say, *Hi there. Don't know if you've noticed that I'm on fire, but I'm very nonchalant about it, aren't I?*

"Wondering if I could have a word when you're free," he said.

"I'm a touch busy right now." She gestured to the class. "Could we catch up later?" Two could play at the old nonchalance game.

She noticed a sudden dimming in the general fiery glory of his radiance.

She glared at him. "I. Am. Teaching," she hissed. "And what have you done to my class? Why are they so quiet?"

The man straightened himself and stepped into the room. "I've merely paused them for a moment. There is something of great importance that I need to discuss with you."

She looked to the silent class, to the man, and back again. This had to be a set up. The little buggers.

"Is this about that tarot reading? Did Lauren put you up to this?" She looked out into the corridor expecting to see her friend duck behind a door.

He spread his hands widely and smiled in a calming manner.

"My name is Egragore," he announced.

She ignored him.

"Or about that wino goddess thing? Did she tell you about that too? It's her favourite story these days so I'd be surprised if there's anyone in Melbourne who hasn't heard it, to be honest."

"I know nothing about any "wino goddess" or any story tellers. It is time for all of this to end, and your duties to begin. Mur-arb needs you."

She blinked.

"Mur-arb is struggling somewhat, and given you were such a pivotal part of his original formation, it would seem he can't really do anything without you. And, I've been asked to fix he whole thing which is just typical really."

Brigid opened her mouth.

She closed it again.

"And everything is by consensus now which is a complete nightmare of course, but we are working on that, and I have great hopes that, in time, we—
"

"Look, I'm sorry, but I really do think that you have got the wrong person." Brigid smiled calmly, although her mind was working frantically. This was obviously a person off the street with some kind of addled delusions of grandeur who had somehow managed to find his way into the building and had bailed her up at random. She was hoping that he wouldn't make any sudden moves that would require her to call security.

Of course, there were the flames though. They were an entertaining touch. Maybe he had been hired by the drama department to take some masterclasses on illusion with the grade 10s?

Egragore pursed his lips. "Do you think I'm totally incompetent? Of course, we know who you are. You're the Muse of Mur-arb.'

She tilted her head to one side and pursed her lips.

"Mur-arb," he repeated.

"Yes, yes, I know who you're taking about although mind you I really wish that I didn't have to admit that. Why the hell is a grown man creeping around a school trying to talk to a strange woman about her imaginary friend from 30 years ago? And how do you know about this? And, how do you know that I know about this? I mean, objectively, what do you think you're doing? I have no idea who you are, and I'm fairly sure you've never set eyes on me in your life."

Egragore sighed heavily, then recited quickly, "The power Mur-arb was made into a reality when the great warlock Juniper summoned him from the aether. The idea of Mur-arb existed in the aether, and just needed an actuality to make it so. You were a part of that. Please pay attention. Because I don't have time to go through this with you from scratch, and I kind of need you on board, ASAP, ok? Because he is *drowning* right now, and we need you to take things in hand."

He clapped between each of these last four words for extra effect.

She had heard of many strange and fantastical things in her life to date, primarily to do with excuses as to why a teenager had to wear leggings to school or keep their septum piercings in place during a PE lesson, but an odd man with illusionist fancies, making up fan-fiction about a child's imaginary friend, was a new one and not something that she was a huge fan of.

"This about Juniper, is it?" she asked. It occurred to her that for someone she hadn't thought about for decades this was the second time he had cropped up in conversation in as many days. "Are you a friend of Junipers? Has he been telling you some weird, embellished stories about my childhood? God, why can't people just move on and live their damn lives?"

"Not Juniper," Egragore said between tightly gritted teeth. "Please don't fixate on him. I need you to focus. It's Mur-arb I want to talk to you about. I feel as if I'm making my explanation as clear as it needs to be, but if I need to add an extra level of idiot-proof clarity to it then I . . ."

"Yes, of course I remember Mur-arb. He was my imaginary friend when I was ten. I remember that Juniper was obsessed with him and didn't want to talk to me about anything else. Looks like the tradition is continuing which is a fun development."

Egragore looked puzzled.

"Are you related to him?"

"Related to who?" Egragore was beginning to feel out of his depth.

"Related to Juniper. You look a bit like him around the eyes, now I come to think of it. Are you his son?"

Egragore peered off into the middle distance and took a deep breath in through his nose. He didn't strictly need to do this (breath, that is), but if there was ever an occasion that called for a steadying breath, this was it.

"Anyway, as I said, I'm at work . . ." Here she gestured to the still quiet students. ". . . and I can't focus right now, so if you will just go away, I'd be willing to talk about it later. Whatever 'it' is."

"When later? We really need to get this sorted."

Brigid opened her arms in exasperation. "I don't know. Tonight? Tomorrow? You're the one desperate to talk to me. Why am I the one having to deal with details?"

"Well I could enmesh you in a parallel dimension right now," he said, steadying himself, "but that tends to play havoc with causality, and if I take you by force one of the smaller connected universes may implode, so we're going to have to make this . . ." At this he gestured in a general manner, which could have meant the classroom or her or the entirety of space and time. ". . . work."

"Ok then," said Brigid, who had stopped listening at the parallel dimension bit. "Nine o'clock at my house. And use the front door like a normal person. None of this weird optical illusion flame business."

"I take it you realise that I'm not a normal—"

"Absolutely. You're not in any way normal. I'm not arguing with you on that one."

She closed her classroom door as he stepped back into the corridor, hoping that he wasn't planning to swing by the office to ask Maureen on the front desk what her address was. There was no way Maureen would give it out, of course, but she really didn't have time or energy for a full lockdown because some weird friend of her family had tracked her down to her workplace and started to wander all over the school without a Working With Children card.

As her class started to murmur and come to life again, she hoped that he had just slipped quietly out of a side door, and she would never have to deal with him again.

Nine

"I must say, this is all quite surprising."

Lauren was standing in Brigid's kitchen, looking at her sceptically.

"I know," said Brigid, holding up her hands in a surrendering gesture. "But I promise you that it happened."

"No, not that bit. I absolutely believe that a flaming being gate crashed your classroom. I'm just really surprised that you didn't close the school into a full lockdown because there was a random man on the premises."

Brigid walked across her small kitchen and filled the electric jug with water. "He was talking about the fact that I was a Muse, and that Mur-arb needed me again, so obviously he knew me from somewhere. I don't think he was dangerous. I just think he wanted to talk to me. And, he was on fire, which was a nice touch. I mean, at least he went to a bit of an effort, you know?"

"Oh my god, that's amazing," said Lauren, her eyes lighting up somewhat manically. "I'm so glad that you're a kook now too."

Brigid flicked her with a tea towel and Lauren grinned.

"Not literally on fire. It was some circus stage show trick, clearly. Good touch though. So, he probably *was* related to Juniper because he was always into spectacular yet shallow tricks. All pizzazz and no substance."

"So, this *is* connected to your childhood. I told you so."

"Yes, yes, you're the freaking Oracle of Delphi."

"I feel like you need to tell me more about this childhood religion thingy. It seems relevant now, given that someone is prepared to track you down to talk to you about it. I think its best that I know all the details. For security, you know."

"What kind of security?"

"Oh, I don't know, future police statements or magazine interviews.' You need someone to back up your story."

"It was a pretty shit religion that never really got fleshed out properly, and it involved far more weather almanacs than appealed to a teenaged girl, so it wasn't that exciting. And it wasn't really a "religion" as such. More of a faith system."

Lauren sighed. "Whatever. I don't mind. I love religions. And faith systems."

"This one would have suited you to a tee then," said Brigid. "Everyone got a turn."

"What do you mean?"

Brigid laughed. "Every faith system got a turn at being right."

Lauren opened her mouth, then closed it again. "I'm just . . . what?"

"Yep, that was everyone else's reaction too. Basically, my mum and dad's friend, Juniper, had some kind of divine revelation that there are many ways up the mountain, and every religion is correct, and he was trying to make a grand unifying system of faith where everyone was right and true and respected. A truly democratic system of universal One-ness."

Lauren smiled beatifically. "That's *beautiful*," she said.

Brigid rolled her eyes. "It's unmanageable gobshite and didn't work in any way, shape or form."

"But why were you so closely involved?"

"Part of the dream, or some such. I was the unifying principle or something. Bat shit crazy, of course, and I'm still convinced it was a way to keep me home-schooled on my own at the commune. Couldn't have me mixing with 'other' kids when my dreams were directing the direction of the community, could we? You try living a different system of faith every week. It was like living in a lunatic's psychedelic dream. The last one was . . ." she narrowed her eyes, trying to remember. "Some pagan farm one, I think. A loose collection of gods who were obsessed with rain and stormy weather patterns. I always thought it was far more suited to Northern Europe in Autumn but apparently it worked perfectly well in springtime rural Victoria."

"Where does the main guy you worked with come in?"

"Yes, there was one ultimate deity, Mur-arb, who kind of oversaw all the religions, and he was supposed to be the other unifying principle that ran through all of them, but he wasn't very good at it to be honest, and he had no idea what was going on most of the time."

"I thought you were the unifying force?"

"I had a go when he turned out to be, as I said, not very good at it."

"But this was all a dream, right?"

"Some dreams, some meditation. I think Juniper told me things and I internalised them. I was young, as I said, and everybody kept telling me I was a leader—"

"Bossy," muttered Lauren.

"A leader," continued Brigid, "so it made sense that people thought I'd take to it like a duck to water. So, I'd have these dreams or imagine that Mur-arb spoke to me during meditation, and then I'd tell Juniper all about it and he'd act on whatever Mur-arb said."

Lauren looked at her carefully. "You are *very* well adjusted," she said. "Considering."

"Yes, but don't forget, this wasn't actually *real*. It wasn't as if things were really happening. I'd just have dreams and meditate, these ideas would come to me, and I'd pass them on. I was only inventing things. Not real," Brigid said again, just in case Lauren had missed it the first time. "And the things I would come up with were where we should plant the tubers and which dung we should use to make the next lot of mud bricks. It was nothing big."

Lauren was looking at her expectantly.

"British White cattle if you're interested."

"And this guy who you met today knew all about it, did he?" asked Lauren, selecting a packet of chocolate biscuits from the cupboard.

"He seemed to. Which is odd considering it was all in my head."

"Unless it wasn't."

They were quiet for a moment as they sipped their tea.

"Obviously this guy has heard about what happened back in the day and he's got an angle on it. Maybe he's a con man and assumes that I truly believed it all. Maybe he thought I might be a gullible easy touch and wanted me to invest in a machine that photographs auras or something. Shit. I bet that's it. He's going to try and make me buy a time share or something."

"Ooh," Lauren said. "Remember those machines that took photos of leaf auras back in the day? God, I loved them. I'll have to look on eBay. That might be a fun sideline now I think about it."

"Perhaps I should have given him your address instead."

Lauren didn't look worried by that prospect.

"So, what was the god's name?"

"I already told you. Mur-arb."

"Mur-arb." Lauren repeated it, rolling it around on her tongue. "Really? Mur-arb? He couldn't come up with anything better than that?"

"It came to him in a—"

"Oh yes, a dream. You said. Sounds quite piratey."

"Mur-arb was the male force, and I was the female force, and we needed to make decisions together in order to bring balance to the universe. Mur-arb was a little flaky and couldn't make a decision to save himself, so I had to do the heavy lifting in that area."

"And your parents were ok with this?"

Brigid shrugged. "It sounds weirder that it really was. I just made some decisions when Juniper asked me what to do, and then sometimes he was in communication with Mur-arb, and then we usually just ended up adding different spices to our brown rice depending on which faith system we were following that week."

"Juniper was in communication with *your* imaginary friend?"

"You're putting way more brain power into this than I ever have, to be honest."

Lauren chewed her lip thoughtfully. "I don't quite know how to ask this but . . ."

There was an ominous silence in the kitchen.

Brigid took a bite of her digestive biscuit and decided after a few beats to put her friend out of her misery.

"No, it wasn't a weird sex thing."

Lauren put her hand out and touched her friend's arm. "You might not even remember."

Brigid squinted her eyes and looked off into the middle distance. Her brow furrowed with deep concentration as her friend toyed nervously with her mug.

"No," she finally pronounced. "I can categorically say that it wasn't a weird sex thing. That I *would* remember," she said firmly.

"Thank God for that," said Lauren. "I'm not equipped to deal with actual real trauma."

"It's okay, you're quite safe."

"Not that this whole thing doesn't sound traumatic," said Lauren quickly. "I mean, did you get to hang out with other kids at all? Did you have friends?"

Brigid ignored the question.

"You know, I haven't thought about this for years and years. It hadn't come into my head until I started telling you about it the other night. This took up quite a lot of my brain space when I was younger, and yet I really haven't thought about it in any way shape or form for, what, thirty years."

"That's not that unusual surely," said Lauren. "Lots of things that happen when we're kids fall out of our brains. And if you lived a totally alternative lifestyle anyway, it can't be like this was the One Weird Thing that happened to you?"

Brigid shrugged.

"So, were you and this Mur-arb guy supposed to communicate in any real way?"

"Not really. I had dreams where we chatted about things. Whatever we needed to, that is. There was an agenda to keep us on track."

Brigid trailed off. It was true she hadn't thought about this for many years but now it was coming back to her: the day that Juniper had told her that she had the light of the world in her eyes and she was going to help guide them into a new reality, the meditations where she connected with the truth of expansive faiths, the dreams that, as she was remembering, were incredibly vivid and real to her at the time. So much so that—

Lauren interrupted her thoughts. "And this Juniper guy just made it all up? And got everyone on board? He must have been very persuasive. Was he the one growing the weed? I bet he was in charge of the weed."

"To be fair," protested Brigid, "he said it all came to him in a dream and he was just summoning a being who needed manifestation. A middleman, really."

"It was a bloody well planned and specific dream," said Lauren sceptically. "What ever happened to the Juniper guy anyway?"

"I don't know. He was Mum and Dad's friend really. They might know where he is. I mean, it wouldn't have mattered of course but now things are—"

"Kicking off?"

Brigid nodded. "Things would appear to be, as you said, kicking off. If some random guy is trying to track me down to sell me things, then I should probably ring mum and see if she has any idea what's been going on. Whether she's still in contact with Juniper and who told this random marketing guy where to find me."

Lauren laughed. "I love the way that you've made up a whole back story about this flamey guy and now, as far as you're concerned, it's the reality. I can almost see 12-year-old Brigid coming to life in front of me, making her own existence as we speak."

"I'll be sure to send him your way when he turns up," Brigid said. "He should be arriving in an hour or so, assuming he's been able to telepathically discern my address."

"I do like the fact that you're enjoying this though," said Lauren. "It's giving you a bit of a laugh, at least. You seem to have lost some of your own fire lately."

"That's funny. Mum always told me that I had fire. That I had . . . some amazing talent and it would come to me, out of the blue one day. I mean, it's natural for people to want to build their kids up, I get that. But I've always felt it set me up to fail a little bit."

"Tell me about it," said Lauren. "They put me in the gifted and talented program when I was in primary school. Literally, the only thing I remember about it was that the principal told us not to tell anyone that we were doing it because they might punch us in the nose. But then all the adults though that I should have 'made something of myself' purely by virtue of the fact that I was selected."

"Ah, perfect."

"We were all set up to fail."

Brigid looked into the distance, an old memory stirring within her. "This old lady visited one day. Well, we had a lot of visitors on the commune, people came and went a lot. I think she may have been an aunt of mums. I'm not sure of the details, as I said, there were people around randomly. But this lady came and visited us one day and sat me down for a talk. She saw something in me, apparently, and needed to bolster my ego. There was this sentence that she wanted me to remember, a phrase. She told me that it was very important, that it was my soul's destiny, and that I would know when it would finally take on life. Its own life. Its activation or something."

"Soul's destiny,' said Lauren. "God, I love that. Why did I not have your upbringing? I feel like I would have done much better in life if anonymous women had tracked me down and told me about my soul's destiny."

"True, I feel like you would have appreciated that kind of chicanery more than me. Reason 8 million why I don't believe in any higher power. Any fairness would have had you grow up with my family."

"What was the phrase anyway?"

The words came automatically out of Brigid's mouth.

"'When the worlds tremble, stand strong; creation is in your heart.'"

There was a pause. The clock on the wall ticked into the silence.

Lauren wrinkled her nose. "I've heard better, to be honest."

Brigid shrugged. "I don't think she was a poet, to be fair. It was just a special little thing that she told me so that when I finally started school, or had to learn to, you know, meet people and take part in the world, I'd have a little thing to tell me I was strong. I don't know, it's quite sweet, really. She was a funny old thing. She said that it would mean something one day, that it would become my power when the time was right. I never saw her again. So now I come to think of it she can't have been an aunt. Just one of the people that passed through life. She did look like mum though."

"What year was this?"

"I was ten-ish. It was before the Mur-arb stuff started happening. So, 1986 I guess?"

"Huh. I'm still jealous." Lauren spontaneously hugged her friend as she headed out the door on her way to a dinner date with a new musician she had her eye on. "You would have had more fun with me around as a kid, though. Luckily, you've got me now."

"Oh, fuck off," laughed Brigid as Lauren disappeared into the night, and she shut and locked the door for what she was confident was the last time that night.

Ten

At precisely 9.00 pm there was a knock on her door, and Brigid was surprised to find Egragore, who was looking around with a hunted expression on his face, standing on her doorstep. *Bloody Maureen* she thought.

"Why do you live here?" he asked. "This is verging on the utterly disastrous. Why on earth would you choose a place like this? Do you have no sense of self-preservation at all?"

"How did you get my address?"

"You invited me, remember? 9pm. I didn't get the day wrong, did I? I did head back to work for a few hours and I thought that I managed to program the dimensional shifter correctly but occasionally I get it wrong. Did I get the wrong year?"

"You're not on fire tonight."

"I decided against it. You didn't seem to be impressed last time."

They looked at each other for a moment.

"Can I come in? It's very wet out here. And we really do need to chat. It's about . . ."

"Yes, yes, Mur-arb. I know." She sighed and decided that he was probably harmless, but she was still going to give Maureen a rollicking in the morning. Ushering him inside, she paused to glare at the drizzle that continued to gloom outside. "You're supernatural, aren't you?" she said sarcastically. "Can't you do something about it? We're all sick of it. I've had wet weather lunch duty at school every day for a fortnight and the cleaners are about to go on strike."

"You know that's all you, don't you? They're your clouds," he said as she pointed at the mat, instructing him to wipe his feet. His heeled boots harked back to renaissance France, but, like the velvet jacket, he was able to carry it off.

"Haven't you noticed it's been raining a great deal lately?" He shook his head at her blank face. "You're really going to need to improve your observational powers if this is going to work." He gestured around in a general direction, as if he were referring to everything.

"If what, exactly, is going to work?"

"This is going to be difficult. I'm not sure what you don't know," he said, sitting on the sofa and crossing his legs. He glanced around the room critically, his raised eyebrows making it quite clear that he understood, appreciated, and liked, precisely none of his surroundings. His long fingers picked a piece of cat fur off his trousers, and he frowned at it disdainfully, before flicking it into the air. The owner of the fur, Princess Twinkle-rama, had retreated to the safety of the kitchen and sat under the sink, staring at Egragore with piercing eyes, her tail bristled and twitching simultaneously.

"I do rather need you to have some clarity around your circumstances, you see, and while you're in a potential state of ignorance it is going to make both our jobs harder."

Brigid pursed her lips and decided if she was going to get offended at everything that came out of his mouth then it was going to be a fruitless, frustrating, and potentially violent occasion.

"I quite miss the flames," she said. "Could you teach me how to do it? Did you need a fire-retardant suit?"

"Oh, they're more for dramatic effect. I don't have the energy for them right now. You're going to need more of my attention than I realised, and I don't have the intestinal fortitude for both."

"Right," she said, sitting down opposite him. "Let us just assume that I know nothing. Start at the beginning, with Jupiter, and finish with asking me to buy a Kirlian machine."

"First of all," he said, as his eyes tracked something on the ceiling, and he gave a casual wave to something else that seemed to be in the corner, "your house is a portal. Did you realise that? I'm assuming you didn't realise that, given you're still here. It's like a bus station. I wouldn't last a day with all this activity going on. You must be exhausted."

"What do you need from me?" she asked, cutting to the chase.

"We need you to resume your role as co-ruler of reality," he stated simply.

"Is that all?"

He looked surprised. "Yes."

"So, when you say "resume"?"

"Of course, back in your day it was a tiny little pocket of reality that affected only you and a dozen or so people, so you weren't "co-ruler of reality", you were more in the realm of "co-ruler of an incredibly specific and isolated reality", but things have. . . expanded somewhat."

He looked at her expressionless face.

"I believe you performed this role some years ago?"

"Not really. Not at all, actually. Well, when I was a child. A bit. And it was a role in more of a theatrical sense."

"Theatrical?"

"In the sense that, it wasn't actually real."

"Ah," said Egragore, crossing and recrossing his legs. "I see the confusion. May I have a cup of tea?"

Brigid huffed into the kitchen. Thankfully, the kettle was still warm, so she threw a teabag into a cup, added water, and returned to the sofa. If Egragore didn't like lukewarm tea, then he should try being less presumptuous about people's childhood imaginary friends.

"Lovely," he breathed. "I must say, for all its utter banality, the Earth does have some redeeming features. Yes, I see the confusion," he continued sitting his cup on a small table next to the sofa. "The role you played with Mur-arb, when you were a child, was yes, I concede, not quite real. It was one of those little pocket faith systems that you humans so adorably come up with from time to time. It wasn't "real", no."

"Of course it wasn't real. That's what I've been saying."

"Yes, just a dream." He laughed, an incongruous little tinkling sound. "Of course, just a dream. I'm afraid that actual ideological and spiritual systems do need a little more rigour than the REM cycle of a stoned hippy, surely you can understand that. Except—"

He sighed. A look of deep concern flitted over his face, and he leaned forwards.

"Except. It has become real."

"What has?"

"Your, as you say, religion. Your spirituality. Your faith system."

"Which one?"

Egragore frowned. "The one from your childhood. The one that wasn't real."

"Oh yes." Brigid nodded firmly in a way that spoke of her clear and complete grasp of the situation. "That's right, it wasn't real. Made up. By Juniper," she added, by way of helpful clarification.

"Ye—eees," said Egragore with less certainty. "And now certain events have transpired that have recalibrated elements of both the metaphysical elements and the nuts and bolts, if you like, of the space time continuum, and these have—"

He saw the look on Brigid's face, not one of confusion or uncertainty as such, but more indicating that she had simply checked out of the conversation.

"Who are you, anyway?" she asked finally. "You still haven't said."

"Alright." He took a last sip from his lukewarm cup of tea and decided he was going to have to make some decisions here. He stood. "Would you like to go for a walk?"

She frowned. Again. The spectrum of frowns that had been crossing her face over the last fifteen minutes were many and varied.

"It's dark," she said.

"It is," he conceded.

"It's raining," she said.

He ducked his head and glanced out of the window. "Yes," he nodded. "It is absolutely raining. Good job."

"I don't really want to go for a walk."

He picked up a coat which he assumed to be hers from the back of one of the wooden backed chairs clustered around the dining table.

"It will help. This place is doing absolutely nothing for you. I'm surprised you're able to form a coherent thought at all, ever."

"I feel like going and walking around the streets with you at night may be the most stupid thing I've ever done."

"If that's the way you're looking at things then inviting me into your house would, technically, be the most stupid thing you could have done. I'm quite safe if you haven't noticed. And I could hardly fit a gun into these pants, after all."

"They are quite tight, aren't they?"

"Come on, come for a walk. We'll grab another drink, and you can hear me out. Then, if you want nothing else to do with me, we will be finished. I will respect your wishes and I'll be on my way."

This sounded to Brigid like the best possible outcome.

"Hang on, I don't have an umbrella," she said as they stepped down onto the footpath. "It died the other day. I keep forgetting to take a new one from the staff room."

"I know. We don't need it."

As Brigid felt her hair plaster to her face, she was about to protest that he might not bloody well need it, but just because he had been granted non-frizzy, manageable hair, he shouldn't try to dictate to other people. But then he made an odd motion with his hand, and she realised they were not standing in the rain anymore.

Or rather, they were still standing in the rain; the rain had just decided that it was no longer interested in them. She looked up, and could see it was still falling above them, and all around them, but about thirty centimetres from their heads, it seemed to veer off, and then cascaded down around them, forming the exact pattern that would have been visible if there had been an actual umbrella.

Her mind boggled. The rain wasn't touching them at all now, but there was nothing solid in the air above them, nothing that was preventing it from falling on her.

As far as she could see.

"Are you doing this with magnets?" Her voice sounded shrill to her own ears, and she deliberately dropped it an octave. "Is this like, a reverse flame thing? How are you doing this?"

He started walking, pulling her along with him. "I'm concerned about your conversational skills, or lack thereof. You have a certain reputation in the Shadow Lands already, and I'm going to feel fairly embarrassed if I present you and you look like a gibbering idiot. It's going to reflect badly on me, you know."

"I have excellent conversation skills, thank you very much," she snapped. "But you will excuse me if I am having a slightly hard time coming to terms with what is happening here, given that I don't have much of an idea about what is actually happening here."

"Getting you out of that oppressive flat will help," he said tangentially. "The Feng Shui in that place is just dreadful. And as for the ley lines." He sighed heavily. "Not many people can live in a literal sub-dimensional portal and stay sane. No wonder you've lost all sense of your true self. It's a wonder that you're not catatonic. You've been there ten years, I understand?"

"About that, yes."

"And you remember things from your younger years?"

She looked at him warily. "Yes. Of course."

"About your childhood?"

She nodded. "Yes, I remember my childhood. Doesn't everyone?"

"And your communications with Mur-arb are coming back?"

"Right," she said firmly. "What does this have to do with anything?"

"There are going to be a lot of very disappointed people if you don't pick yourself up and develop a sense of gravitas pretty quickly. Not the least, you're going to make Mur-arb's job a lot harder. Do you feel mentally ready now for me to explain some things to you?"

She nodded again. Curiously, she did feel more clarity and clearness of thought now that they were out on the street. She often felt this when she left home and had always assumed that it was the fresh air and lack of cat hair that did the trick.

"In that case," Egragore asked lightly, "how would you feel about stepping into another dimension for a moment? Just so we can talk away from all this rain and general gloom." He gestured to the puddles they were stepping their way around. "My shoes weren't made for these elements. I got them in France, you know."

"Oh, here we go. You want to 'take me to another dimension' do you? That's probably the worst pickup line I've ever heard. No, actually…asking if you can show me your etchings would be marginally worse, I've got to say. Tt's a hard pass to either of them, mind you. You think you're that good?"

He looked at her with a mix of contempt and amusement, which was a nice trick if you could manage it. "A pickup line? Hardly. I have absolutely no interest in romantic relationships with anyone, let alone a mortal."

They had reached a cafe, the bright light from the windows flinging a glow out onto the street in front of them, its welcoming warmth contrasting with the gloom of the street.

"Can we go in here then? If you're ready to listen properly then I really would like to sit down, and if another dimension is a firm no, then at least we can get out of the cold."

It was a homely, cosy café of the vegan bacon and matcha latte variety, and there were several armchairs that looked suitably plump. Brigid happily sunk into one of them.

"Right," she said, once she had a warm mug in her hand and a muffin on the way. "Here's what I've managed to understand. You want to talk to me about, shall we say, a spiritual advisory role that I was once involved in."

He nodded.

"And, according to you, you're a supernatural being?"

Another nod.

"And—" she stopped. "What does that even mean? What kind of supernatural being are you claiming to be anyway? Like, a vampire? Or less specific than that?"

"Oh, for pity's sake." Egragore shook his head. "There's no such thing as vampires. Popular culture has a lot to answer for. No, I'm in administration mainly."

She narrowed her eyes at him. "I'm sorry? Clarify, please."

"If you want to be technical, I'm a reaper."

"Jesus, like, the Grim Reaper? That is not a good way to make new friends, let me tell you."

"No, no, not at all. Why do people always think that? You lot are so narrow minded. As I said, I'm essentially in admin. I work for a place called the Shadow Lands, and I just make sure that everyone ends up in the right place."

"What place? Who?"

He made an odd little movement with one eyebrow. "I just make sure that people are correctly heading *up* or heading *down*. You know, when they . . . Shuffle off this mortal coil. And if they're heading downstairs then I can help them tweak things a little, so they go upstairs. Potentially. If I can make it work. Which increasingly I can't, but still, I persevere."

Brigid's face was blank, but he plunged on regardless.

"Of course, ever since this whole current state of flux has come about, we don't know whether we're coming or going. And if we can stop with the tangents for just a moment, it's the whole flux thing that I need to talk to you about." He eyed her cagily, as if she might randomly start talking about gerbils or puppets at any moment. "Will you be able to follow my train of thoughts for a while?"

"Not so far," she said, biting into her spinach and feta muffin. "But surely due to the laws of probability I'll catch onto something eventually. So why don't you just plug on and I'll stop you if I need to?"

"Right," he said. "What do you know about the CERN particle physics laboratory?"

Eleven

From A Concise History of The Shadow Lands Volume 50, page 5623

The idea that the European Organisation for Nuclear Research, more commonly known as CERN, changed the very fabric of space and time when it activated its Large Hadron Collider in the mid-2010s, is an idea held by only the wackiest of conspiracy theorists.

Talk of this change in the fabric of reality can be found alongside discussion of reptilian elites, and is also discussed in the same circles as conversations about the fact that the moon is a hologram, and that snow is a government plot to turn frogs gay.

Fringe beliefs, to put it politely.

The basic premise of the CERN theory is this: when CERN pressed "on" on the Large Hadron Collider, it created a quantum ripple effect. Some see evidence for this in what has become known as the CERN Mandala Effect—the spawning of parallel universes in which different realities based on familiar scenarios are continually being birthed and rebirthed. So the fact that you are sure that you had brown hair during the summer that you were ten, despite the photos that your mother determinedly dug out of a sewing box to prove that you were, blond, is because a parallel universe was created when the Large Hadron Collider was turned on so you did, in some sense, have both colours of hair as you exist in two (or, an infinity of) parallel dimensions at once.

This is, of course, ridiculous.

An alternate branching timeline was not created by the simple action of slamming subatomic particles together. Any change in the appearance of reality results from the fact that humans have abysmally short attention spans and a lack of ability to notice the most basic things that are happening right in front of their faces. Blaming this on scientists trying to use their funding before the end of the financial year is just another example of the human race essentially opting out of the reality that they themselves have, largely due to poor planning and a lack of mental fortitude, saddled themselves with.

What the machinations of the Large Hadron Collider did, of course, was to recalibrate the nature of space and time as it relates to the planes of existence that are more commonly referred to as paranormal, supernormal, or, to put it more simply, "gods and the like". And, in an extremely odd turn of events, but really, who is to say what is odd and what is perfectly normal in the burgeoning area of paranormal particle physics, the Cosmological Engineering Officer who had created the universe and everything in it had been relegated to a beach somewhere—a very nice beach, but an anonymous beach nonetheless—and a being who had been summoned and/or created by an incompetent warlock who had spent too much time reading Ginsberg and thinking about bringing down the military industrial complex was now, thanks to CERN, in charge of, apparently, everything. And he wasn't the only one who suspected that he was not up to the job.

Twelve

Brigid frowned and tried to suck the chia seeds out of her teeth. "To clarify, you're telling me that the fabric of space and time are now—"

"If I could just interrupt you there, it's not actually the fabric of space and time, it's more of a dimensional—"

She held up her hand. "The fabric of space and time *or something along those lines* has been rewritten, and out of all the hugely multitudinous options available, of all the things that could be altered, anywhere and anytime, what has happened is that my particular life path or stream or whatever, is the one that has been affected. Just mine. Out of the whole universe."

Egragore shook his head. "It's not strictly about you, you know. It's not about you specifically at all. You're just part of the flotsam and jetsam, if you like. There's quite a bit more to it than you if you were listening."

"But the bit I'm interested in is the bit that would affect me, if it were true," she said tightly. "And don't think that I'm not angry about the fact that, with all the things that could potentially have been changed, you choose something as amorphous as paranormal rubbish to spin a story about. Further evidence that the world needs an evidence based sceptical approach to everything."

"The fact that you think this is amorphous, despite the fact that part of it is directly sitting in front of you, is problematic, and indicates that our job is going to be much more difficult than I initially thought. And," he said, taking a sip from his cup, "I thought that things were adequately grim from the outset, believe me. I've seen your file."

"What file?"

"Your file. Your karmic debt, your pros and cons list. We do keep a list, you know."

"I have to admit that your dedication to this charade is positively heroic. You haven't broken character once. You really act as if you believe all of this about yourself, and I, for one, am here for it. It's very entertaining and Lauren is going to love hearing about it."

"I'm sorry if you've been under the misapprehension that you're a bunch of random atoms fused together by chance and now have evolved to the point that you can essentially exist on Netflix and food delivery services, but yes, there is such a thing as the Other World, and yes, you do owe a debt to society. Right now, the being who is in charge of things is flailing somewhat and you, according to the new set of rules, are required to be part of that."

"Well," started Brigid, "at least this is a lesson to the world. That all religions are equally legitimate and valid, and every different belief system is—"

Egragore snorted. "Oh please, don't be ridiculous. Of course, all faith systems aren't equal and valid. Some are patently ludicrous. Last week Mur-arb tried to get advice from a deity who stated categorically that if her adherents didn't wear a particular shade of blue on Wednesdays every second week then there would be the complete downfall of the ecosystems on a small island in the pacific." He shrugged. "Although as it turns out that island has been almost completely swept below the waves due to the rising sea level anyway. Completely unrelated, of course, but Mur-arb was very confused about it."

"So, he's having to abide by the rules of a different faith system every week, is he?"

"No, not at all. That was just a phase. But he's lost and he's confused and he's looking for direction. Which is, as I have been trying to say, where you come in. He needs an advisor, and according to all the information we've been able to accumulate, that adviser is you. It *used* to work quite well, from what I can gather. I'm quite concerned about his mental fragility to be honest, and he needs someone who he can trust. Someone from the old days. *His* old days."

Brigid gazed off into the distance, her thoughts seemingly elsewhere. "Even if this was all true, I would have noticed, surely? Because if there's been a re-writing in the fabric of space and time, then it's completely passed me by."

"Do you think you would have? Noticed, I mean."

"Of course, I would have noticed. This is *my* planet you know. It's my world. You can be assured that I would notice if the very nature of my planet had been altered. Wouldn't you?"

She sat back heavily and glared out the window. "And it's still bloody raining. I feel like I'm approaching my own personal low point. And trust me, there have been quite a few contenders."

"Raining," stated Egragore.

"What?"

"This is the kind of thing I've been talking about. Mur-arb has been holding counsel with a branch of lesser weather deities for weeks now. He's become hopelessly enmeshed in a debate about demarcation issues and he doesn't seem to be able to extricate himself. They think if they pay lots of attention to you, then you will advocate for them with Mur-arb, so that's why they have been feting you."

Brigid glanced out of the window, up towards the dark sky. "It's raining for me, is it? Well, they can bloody well stop now."

She waited a moment.

"Oh, surprise-surprise, still wet."

"If you're impressed by attempts from clouds to emotionally manipulate you then yes, they're raining for you. Look, Mur-arb needs your help, if for no other reason so this city can get some damn sunshine. I mean, I know I can move between worlds, but this is really getting me down. I can't imagine what it would be like to live here all the time." He shuddered involuntarily.

"Can I tell you something?" asked Brigid, leaning forwards conspiratorially and lowering her voice. "I don't believe a word of this, of course—don't think that I do—but on some level maybe there is something strange going on? And maybe I've always felt like there was meant to be more to life, like I'm meant to be--"

"Oh, I wouldn't imagine that has anything to do with it. Your life does seem to be rather dull, so it's little surprise that you feel bored."

He picked another strand of invisible cat hair off his velour pants.

"But yes," he confirmed, springing to his feet, and holding his hand out to her. "As it turns out, you do have a destiny, and there is something important in store for you. Let's go."

"Go where exactly?"

"Another plane. Of existence. Just for a while. To chat. The sooner you start the process the better."

"I don't think so, but thanks for asking."

She decided that she was ready for the evening to end. She was tired, this was weird, and she needed to walk home. She just had to extricate herself from what, against her better judgement, was the most entertaining conversation she'd had for ages.

"It's very easy. Just a step up, really."

"A step up?"

"Yes, you just kind of step up. It's hard to describe really, but we're just stepping up a level."

Brigid's face registered no comprehension at all.

"Alright, imagine there's another reality layered above this one. So, another reality with other beings, if you like, a foot or so above where we are now. And they can see you and me and everything else, but you can't see them." He paused. "Is that a concept you can grasp?"

"Would you take any notice if I said no?"

"Excellent," said Egragore. "That's exactly how it is. There is literally another plane of reality layered above this one that can interact with yours, and we need to step up to it right now."

Brigid peered around her as if expecting to see strange beings manifest before her eyes, intrigued despite herself. His utter commitment to his role was winning her over. "Ok, supposing this is all true, how do I do it? Do humans ever actually do it?"

"Yes of course. It's a perfectly natural talent. Like being able to sight-read music or finding your way around Hong Kong without a map. It's just a talent like any other."

She looked puzzled. "Which people have the talent then?"

"Mainly those who see ghosts. And those who can see auras, although that's usually just something bleeding into your reality. And most of the liminal areas of the world, such as those on ley lines and thin areas, will have breakthrough communication, but we're trained in getting people who see things all classified as whack jobs. We can't have people just willy-nilly making up the narrative, can we now?"

"Are you talking about the people featured in *The National Enquirer*? Those people really do exist, and then they're exploited and mocked?"

"Yes, a fair number of them are telling the truth, but you wouldn't know it, would you?"

Brigid had a momentary desire to humour him for just a minute more. "Let's do it then."

He took both her hands in his and pulled her towards him as they stood up. "It's easy. Just think *up*." Without intending to, she did so, and felt a blink as if her whole body was a Rubik's Cube. Some of her bits had just switched one way, and other bits had switched in an entirely different and hitherto impossible direction. After a moment of almost incomprehensible disorientation, she was standing on top of the Rialto Towers, still holding Egragore's hands, with the freezing wind biting her face and buffeting her body, which, she realised with a jolt, was disturbingly close to the edge.

"What the hell is going on?" she screamed, but the words were snatched away from her mouth before they were formed.

"We have to do this in stages." She heard Egragore's voice in her head. "If I take you straight to the top level, bits of your body and possibly most of your mind won't make the journey. Think of it as acclimatising. If you don't take it easy, you'll get the bends. Just a moment."

Brigid heard his words, but her attention was captivated by the massive cloud-like things she could see drifting all around them in the darkness. Cloudlike, but utterly solid and present in a way she had never been aware of before. They drifted out over the city at her current eye level, and with a deep knowing that she could not explain, she knew that they were sentient. Thoughts came from them; slow ponderous thoughts that made little sense but deeply, deeply unnerved her. One drifted behind them, almost close enough to touch, and from it she could sense great age, but also great antipathy towards her, and she suddenly felt very small and very stupid.

"What the hell's that?" she screeched again, this time in her mind.

"What, the Aguafies? Big grey things?" Egragore glanced around. "Just part of the macrobiome. You just need to focus on grounding yourself here for a moment. Are you feeling grounded?"

Deciding that Brigid was not someone who could decide, at that moment, whether she was grounded or not, Egragore made a snap judgement. "Alright, that's probably enough then, so again, let's step up. The sooner Mur-arb sees you, the sooner we can start to iron this whole business out."

"What? No!" She snatched her hands out of his and her thoughts resonated in his head. "I'm not doing that. What do you mean? We were only supposed to be talking."

"This is important," he snapped. "I don't have time to talk about your feelings and how you plan to negotiate all the emotional heavy lifting of being an assistant deity, alright? I need you to commit to this, and I need you to commit to it now."

"Does that kind of demanding dark eyed assertiveness usually work? Because quite honestly, you can go fuck yourself. Don't try to shoehorn me into your bloody cosmic game of chess. This has nothing to do with me, and I have absolutely no commitment to helping you, so you can fuck off."

She usually preferred not to say "fuck" twice in the same rant, but what with the roof and the wind and the dimensional shift and the still bloody unnerving weird floating caterpillars, her powers of oration were limited. Ignoring the anger in his eyes and the fuming noises going on in her head, she swung around and stomped off, ducking to avoid the aguafie that was ponderously wending its way overhead, singing an impossibly peculiar song to itself.

"You can't just leave, you fool," she felt Egragore bark in her head. "You've been lifted to a higher plane. You can't just leave and go on as if nothing has happened."

She blinked in her mind; she didn't quite know how she managed it, but once again she was fully part of the world—at least the world as she had known it five minutes ago. The disconcerting creatures were gone, the feeling of being unpleasantly intoxicated was gone, and the roof was firm beneath her feet, although that roof was far further above the ground that she was usually comfortable with.

"Just bloody watch me."

Casting around, she found a service door and threw herself into it.

The last thing she heard as she landed on the stairs was Egragore peevishly letting her know he was definitely going to be cloaking his thoughts from her, and that if she thought she was going to be telepathically getting any help from him then she had another thing coming. She tried to throw back a thought, to have the last word, but their connection was already lost.

It was the exorcisms that started it all, Fraster had decided. If not started it, then foretold it. At least, the two were now enmeshed in his brain. It had been just a week before they had moved to the Upper Realm, and things in the aether (that being the whole general jumble of universal energies that tangle together like spider webs over the surface of everything) were already afoot. Things that were out of the consciousness of any of the workers on the floor, unbeknownst to Fraster and Egragore and any of the other staff that made up the bustling metropolis that was the Shadow Lands but still . . .

Things were happening.

Fraster stared at the small blue blips that streamed across the screen in front of him; the blue blips, and the black blips that overlapped them. The red ones, and the yellow ones that were rarer but, still his problem. These blips ebbed and flowed over shapes that made up the bulk of the screen, shapes that were tediously familiar to him. Indeed, he had stared at them for the past millennia, and, given the way things were going, he may very well stare at them for a millennium more.

The shapes. The messy, impractical, and infested land masses that made up the surface of the earth. The countries upon which the vermin swarmed, the pathetic, useless vermin that had colonised the surface of the planet, taking up valuable space and energy and just . . .

Existing.

The room that he preferred to work from was dark. He didn't even call it an office; that would indicate too much commitment to the space. It was dark and poky. And dank. He didn't notice this, though, and even if he had noticed, he wouldn't have cared. He could have formed himself a new area; he had the ability to tweak his surroundings to his own desires, but concerning yourself with light, or space, or indeed whether a room smelled like four-week stale soccer gear was not his domain. Far, far too human, those kinds of concerns. The kind of petty, superficial concerns of a substandard race of beings that had been given full run of a perfectly good planet . . .

His eyes swept over the screen, the usual daily scanning that ensured everything was in order, when he noticed that one of the blips had started to move erratically. Vibrate, almost. Waving his hand at the screen above his desk, he brought the specific area into focus, and, moving his fingers, he homed in on its precise geographical area. Ah, he frowned. That again. They'd been having problems in that area. Fraster pressed one spindly finger against his earpiece, and there was a dull crackle before a voice sprang into his ear. It sounded surprisingly close, considering that the being it was most typically attached to was 5000km and, probably more importantly, a sub-dimension away.

"Mulcaydo", snapped Fraster. "Are you anywhere near Sydney, Australia at the moment? I think that we're having another issue with one of our elementals."

"I'm quite near, what's the problem?"

The blue blip in question was in sharp focus now, its wavering shape formed a figure that meant something only to Fraster's trained eye. As he pressed more buttons, trying to extricate data from it, it lit up with a ghastly green glow, like a nauseous supernova, and then blinked out entirely. All that was left was a highly magnified photographic map of an area of Sydney, that looked suspiciously like it came directly from google maps.

"Are you there?" came the voice again in his earpiece.

"It's gone," said Fraster, with bitterness in his voice. "Just blipped out of existence. Dammit, I had plans for that elemental. I was going to have it progress to a full-blown manifest haunting within the next century."

"It would be that meddlesome exorcist again. That's the second time this year. Bloody humans."

Fraster clicked out of the conversation, his face grim. The elementals on earth, a group of lesser spirits that existed just above mortal frequencies, were his area and he felt the loss when one was expunged from existence entirely.

Sadly, many of them aspired to be human. Or human-esque. They had a deep need to be part of human things, no matter how much Fraster tried to convince them that what they needed to be, on the deepest and most fundamental level, was anything but. However, typically, humans were increasingly encroaching in their spaces, and now there was even a resurgence in those trying to get rid of them entirely—exorcists.

Of course, the beings that he dealt with were all officially sanctioned by the Upper Realm. They were not, strictly speaking, evil. Humans didn't like them, naturally; they were often scared of them and, as had just been made so painfully obvious, actively worked to get rid of them. But they were essentially harmless. They might give people the willies at times, but they didn't cross the line into demonic. The demonic forces that roamed the planet were not his area at all, not his spec, not his field. He was explicitly forbidden from having anything to do with them even if there was, on occasion a certain . . . overlap.

So, he had nothing to do with them at all.

Mostly.

As he idly watched the screen, wondering if dealing with an exorcist was something that would get him in actual, real trouble, he noticed a faint blip. A blip that was not his normal variety of blips, it was . . .

Something else. It's colour and shape were different, and it had an almost 3-dimensional view to it. Fraster tried to bring it into focus.

This shape wasn't on the planet, at least not within its etheric aura. And it wasn't in the overlay that showed the ephemeral beings that flittered in and out of the dimensional vortex. It seemed to be in another layer entirely, one that was usually hidden from him, partly because it wasn't his allocated assigned area, but mostly because it was above his pay grade, which was, on his last performance review, that of *Reaper overseeing elemental, haunting, non- predatory manifestations and general ambiguous trans-physical entities, including but not confined to poltergeists, orbs and inhuman residuals (non- combative).*

The memory of this last performance review tried to push its way into his mind, the sheer smugness of that intolerable Egragore, the patronising nonchalance, the fact that the ridiculous semi-vermin thought that he countenanced any friendship . . .

He pushed it away.

Not the time. He couldn't be distracted.

And Egragore's time would come. Oh yes, his time would come.

He waved his hand again and the screen stepped out of itself, taking on a VR status. He might not love the new technologies, but they occasionally came in useful. A helpful little label was coming into focus on the screen, but even before it became clear he knew what it was going to be.

It had been thirty years. No time at all, and yet he had barely thought of it during this time. It had been a brief interest to him, but after its exile it had dropped from his consciousness.

It hadn't specifically been his area, but "summoned demi-deities of very specific sub universes" didn't have a specific oversight committee, and given he'd had a casual interest in this rather ridiculous little magician's mistake (more out of a kind of voyeuristic interest than anything else) he had always been aware of what was happening to him. He racked his brain. . . Mur-arb, that was it. An irritating little deity that never amounted to anything and was summarily exiled when he became more of a hindrance than a help. He was exiled to a vessel of some kind by the same magician. That's right. It had briefly interested him for a while. There had been some potential for something interesting, some kind of power explosion he thought might be possible, but it had come to nothing.

But now, he seemed to have moved.

Fraster frowned and glanced around him. Surely not . . .

How could he be in the . . .

But he was.

And with that, Fraster began to hatch a plan.

Thirteen

Brigid's rise to consciousness the next morning was signposted by fleeting memories.

Rain; well, ok, normal.

Café with Egragore; odd discussions and revelations.

Talk of karmic responsibilities; ugh, a feeling of abstract guilt.

Learning how to shift dimensional things; wait . . .

Enormous sentient floating caterpillars.

She jerked up into a seated position, relieved at least to be in her own bed. She didn't *feel* hungover, and her memories of last night had an air of clarity around them, however bizarre and improbable those events were, not the vague disjointedness of too many bevvies.

Odd.

Making the decision to just start the day as if everything was normal and go about her usual business with a can-do attitude and the option to duck and weave, if necessary, she left her room and headed into the kitchen. Despite her open and accepting attitude she was quite taken aback to come face to face with a massive and otherworldly angel standing majestically in her front room.

"Good morning." She said this more out of shock than good manners.

"Oh, good morning," stammered the angel, who seemed more shocked than she was.

Brigid had always thought of angels—if she did think of them at all—as being slightly kitschy, sweet, girly looking little creatures, loved by Hallmark cards and nativity scenes. She had never pictured them as looking like this enormous flaming muscled creature that could twist your head off without breaking a sweat, if he decided to, rather than utilising the hefty and jewel emblazoned sword next to him. Despite this, she immediately recognised him as an angel, even given the fact he was standing in her front room at 6.30 on a Thursday morning.

"Who are you?" she asked.

"I'm your Protection Angel."

"And what are you doing here?"

"Protecting you."

"From what?"

He shrugged massively. "From whatever turns up."

"Did you just start today then? This protecting thing?"

"Oh, no. It's been a pretty regular gig for the past forty-ish years. This is kind of my job. Well…it actually *is* my job."

He gave her an awkward little wave. "Hi."

"You're not doing a spectacularly good job of it," said Brigid, turning on the jug to make coffee. "There's been a damn interfering reaper on my back for the past few days. It didn't occur to you to protect me from *him*, I suppose?"

"Not my area, sorry," he said in his deeply resonant and mellifluous voice. "I'm more of a "muggers and murderers" kind of protection angel. Reapers are another department. And he wasn't trying to hurt you, was he? I mean, they aren't supposed to bother mortals at all, so I don't know what's going on there. But the fact that this place has such shit energy means I'm pretty preoccupied a lot of the time and some things might slip past."

"Slip past?" She turned to look at him. "A murderer might just *slip past*?"

"I'm doing alright so far, aren't I? You're looking pretty healthy."

"Reapers do seem to be a bit more pressing than murders at the moment, to be honest. Coffee?"

The angel declined.

"Hang on, there was something following me the other night, I think. Were you watching me then?"

The angel nodded. "I was. And look at you, not murdered."

She eyed him suspiciously. "Was that going to happen?"

"Na. It was just another reaper checking you out. Fraster, I think his name was. You have been getting some weird attention lately. Very weird. I've been meaning to memo someone about that actually. He didn't stick around for long."

"He scared me."

"A bit of fright is good for the soul."

Holding her mug, Brigid wandered back into her bedroom to get dressed. She kept one eye on him, making sure he wasn't trying to catch a peek at her as she put on her bra, but he continued to stare fixedly into the middle distance.

"Do you have any idea why I can suddenly see you?" she called out while pulling on her stockings.

He thought for a moment. "Good question. Have you been meditating deeply lately?"

She grimaced. "Hardly."

"Taking Ayahuasca?"

"Can you even get that in Melbourne?"

"Yes, but I'll take that as a no."

"Could you have raised your vibrations somehow? That does sometimes result in realities crossing over."

She opened her mouth to reject this idea too, but another memory started to surface. Could the Rubik's Cube shift she had so improbably felt last night have something to do with it?

She asked him.

"That would be it," confirmed the angel.

"My friend," she said awkwardly, "called it a "dimensional shift" or some such."

The angel shrugged, causing his gold breastplate to catch the morning sun as it came in through the front window, cascading brilliant sparkles of fragmented light around the room.

"Yeah," he said. "That's the terminology" — and here he cleared his throat as if he had been engaged in a full and frank discussion of the merits of these exact words in the not-too-distant past— "that we are being encouraged to use these days. But I'm more of a "raise your vibrations" kind of eternal being, myself. These young suits come in with their new ideas, trying to reinvent something that has been working perfectly well for millennia, but I don't need to tell you that." He grinned conspiratorially. "Not with the management in your school over the last year."

Wait. Brigid's train of thought was abruptly derailed. "Do you follow me around everywhere then? Oh my god, can you read my thoughts?"

"No, I usually just stay here." He pulled himself up to his full height. "This is my post. Unless something interesting is going on. Like if you're going to the pub or something. I usually tag along on Fridays. I can make my own hours, mainly. One of the perks."

He glanced down and answered her unspoken question. "You just talk to yourself a lot. And you have very boisterous arguments in the shower too. Cogent talking points too, I'm always impressed."

"Does everyone have a, I'm sorry, what is your actual name?"

"You can call me Michael. It's kind of a general, catch all name of us Protection Angels, but I think it has a quite nice ring to it."

"As in, St Michael the Archangel?"

He glanced around and lowered his voice "Well, we're supposed to be moving away from the whole Judeo-Christian aspect of things, so I really shouldn't tell you this but, yes."

He winked at her. "Don't tell anyone I told you."

"This must have something to do with the job Egragore told me about," she mused out loud. "The fact that I have such an obviously important guardian. Is that what it means? That I have a special angel?"

He shook his head. "I exist outside space and time, so I can do this for thousands of people at once. Sorry. I mean, yes you are very special and worthy and amazing, but no more so than everyone else."

"Will I be able to see everyone else's angels then, now that I can see you?"

"No idea. I'm still a bit surprised you can see me. There are no hard and fast rules in this area, you understand. You might be able to see other angels. You might not. But I can tell you that you'll—"

Realising the time, Brigid gasped. "Shit. I'd best be off. So, you don't come with me then?"

He shook his head. "Not today."

"You have a good time doing whatever it is that you do."

"You too."

He stepped aside to allow her easy access to the front door.

"And believe me, you are in for some fun today. Those vibrations. I don't imagine you'll be able to turn them on and off at will yet." He whistled. "I look forward to hearing all about it tonight. You know, on reflection, I think I like the fact that you can see me now. We're really not supposed to engage with our subjects, but I've always assumed that means we're not meant to go all poltergeist, you know, pushing pens off tables and turning the telly on and off. I don't see how talking to you now that you can see me, can be a problem."

Brigid wasn't really listening; she was weighing up whether there was any point locking the front door given the circumstances, and then trying to find her phone in her bag. It took till she was well down the street to raise her head, and at that moment, her whole world exploded.

Fourteen

"You didn't *get* her?" Mur-arb stared at Egragore. "You mean she isn't here?"

Mur-arb snatched his new fisherman's cap from his head and twisted it anxiously in his hands. "You had *one* job; to bring her back here to me. That's it. That's all I wanted."

"One job?" boggled Egragore. "What gave you the impression I had just one job? I'm carrying this entire show right now if you hadn't noticed. And given the fact that you seem singularly incapable of—"

He stopped himself, took a deep breath and pasted a tight smile on his face. Temper. He must keep his temper. At this precise moment his most important task was to keep things light, to keep things breezy, and to keep this ridiculous, tubby, barely functional poor excuse for a deity afloat. He ratcheted his smile up another octave.

"I realise you're upset, sir."

"Dude." Mur-arb sulkily tugged the hat back onto his shining head; crooked. "I want everyone to start calling me dude. That's the vibe I want from now on. You guys are all so un-hip. We need to get things a bit more mellow and less . . ." He gestured to the beings who could be seen busily working through the now translucent walls of the throne room. ". . . less whatever that is."

"I realise you're upset . . . dude," said Egragore, very nearly choking on the word. "But you know how women are." He tried out a wry smile in an attempt to get Mur-arb onside, but it was clear that the Great and Glorious Ruler was having none of it.

"Can't you just kidnap her and bring her here?"

"Ssshh." Egragore's eyes darted around the room. "Don't say that. Don't even think about it. You know we can't do that. There are still *rules* you know. You can't just go around kidnapping mortals willy-nilly. And you explicitly said you don't want it to happen that way if you remember."

"But I'm in charge now, so I make the rules," snapped Mur-arb peevishly. "And I've changed my mind."

"Yes, but we still don't quite know exactly what you can and can't change," said Egragore, equally peevishly. "There are some of our best minds working on this at the moment who are firmly of the opinion that too much flux and alteration will cause the entirely of existence, on *every* dimensional plane, to implode into a black hole. So, if we could just stifle talk of kidnapping humans with free will—which, I remind you, is something that the CEO was *very* clear about—then I think it will be better for all concerned."

Egragore decided to try a different tack. Thrusting a very poorly prepared, unstable, and theologically very limited deity into this role was always going to be a challenge. He had hoped Mur-arb would live up to his reputation as a middle aged, peaced out hippy, but unfortunately the weight of responsibility and command seemed to be getting to him more quickly than had been envisaged. Not that he was *doing* anything that would cause him to buckle, Egragore thought bitterly.

"You need a break. Dude," he added. "All this, er, heaviness is getting you down. Would you like to spend some time in the garden? Or do some . . ." His mind darted around looking for a suitably soporific activity. Bread making? Weaving? His mind drew a blank. Even trying to compile a list of such activities nearly put him to sleep.

"Drumming," said Mur-arb. "I need my tribal drums."

Egragore's expression took on the demeanour of a very patient but almost entirely frazzled, maître d', who has trained at Michelin star restaurants but was currently waiting tables at a Hog's Breath Cafe.

"Get Gerald," he hissed to a passing wraith.

"I don't want *your* people, I want *my* people," said Mur-arb. "No one here gets me. I need people I can relate to, people on my level."

"May I remind you, sir, that you don't *have* any people. When you arrived here, you had been living in a yurt with a llama for company for quite some time. Having things to maintain a conversation with is still quite a novelty for you, if I remember correctly."

But Mur-arb had been distracted by the appearance of a set of bongo drums, and ran off in their direction.

"How's he going?" asked Gerald, sidling up to Egragore. Casually dressed in jeans and a flannelette shirt, his carefully cultivated beard and tousled hair made him look like someone's slightly less well-off younger brother.

"Unravelling," answered Egragore, glancing at Gerald. "I like the new head."

"Thanks, I thought I'd give hipster a try. People seem to hate them, and I do find triggering people on Earth to be entertaining."

"Didn't you start the whole hipster trend?"

"I did," Gerald nodded. "That I did."

"And now you're using it against them." Egragore stepped back and surveyed the mid-level tempter in front of him. "That's quite clever. That kind of low-level annoyance really separates the wheat from the chaff. I think you'll have great, great things in front of you. But for now," he gestured towards Mur-arb. "Can you please do something with him? I have no idea what he's going to ask for next, and I don't like it. It makes me uncomfortable. He needs some serious handling, and that touchy feely bullshit that you've been trying out might possibly work with him."

Gerald nodded. "So, what are we going for? Comfortable, but not too comfortable? Cognisant of his power but not interested in using it? Should I get him stoned maybe?"

"I don't really give a damn at this stage. Keep him drumming for a few weeks. Get him some Shaolin Monks. That should keep him busy. But don't get him stoned because he will follow me and talk to me about the nature of reality, and I'm not going to be responsible for my actions if he puts me onto the fifth plane of existence again to try and "chill my vibe". Those Dryads absolutely did my fucking head in last time, and I'm still trying to get the moss off my purple velour pants." He shuddered at the memory.

"Has he noticed it's just us here?" asked Gerald, looking around at the wraiths and reapers and mid-level tempters that could be seen through the translucent walls of the throne room. Heavy on the black suits, none were dressed as theatrically as Egragore, or as casually as Gerald, but all looked frightfully on-task. Those with a humanoid, or roughly humanoid, form were carrying dossiers or files, and those who didn't have limbs capable of carrying still projected demeanours of extreme efficiency, and you could tell that thoughts of projected growth rates and building a reliable infrastructure were filling their minds.

"He's noticed but I think he assumes it's normal. I don't think it's crossed his mind that any angelic beings should be around. And that's the way it's going to stay if we do our job properly."

"Duuuuuuuude," bellowed Gerald, hurling himself forwards and embracing Mur-arb, who looked at him with the fretful eyes of a puppy who has just realised there is a chance he will be allowed to sleep on his master's bed tonight. "Where did you get those righteous drums? Let's jam, baby.

Egragore shuddered and, trusting that the job would now be well in hand and not his responsibility for the time being, stepped through the translucent wall of the throne room and into the business area of the complex. The hubbub of administrative efficacy thrummed off the modern furniture and the reception desk that had been designed exclusively to emit the image of rigorous clear thinking and administrative excellence.

"Right." Egragore clapped his hands together, and the well-dressed beings who had been milling around the reception area looked eagerly towards him. "Let's get down to business."

The meeting room was excitingly modular and curved. The attendees who were biologically designed for sitting took their places in the seats scattered around the table, and those with other appendage arrangements placed themselves where they would have the ability to involve themselves in the discussion, while not floating off through the ceiling or oozing onto the dynamically patterned carpet.

Egragore took his place at the head of the table, glancing appreciatively at the layout of the room. When he had arrived, it had not been an actual room, so much as it had been a section of a forest somewhere in the Amazon. He wasn't exactly sure about the specifics, but something about the temporal mechanics meant that the last CEO had been able to watch over this singular patch of endangered forest by keeping it in some kind of bubble. There was a particular species of frog that had apparently held the future cure to cancer, and the staff of the Heavenly Realm were intending to keep it safe until the humans realised they needed to conserve the forest rather than burn it down for agricultural land. So, the CEO had kept the few hundred acres lovingly protected, safe and ready for the new dawning of consciousness that was slated to occur soon in the human race.

Of course, as soon as the Shadow Lands crew had gained occupancy of the Heavenly Realm, they had reconfigured the coordinates and the land had become available immediately. It had been burned and planted with soybeans within a matter of months, with the spotted Frey-wing frog safely extinct and out of the equation as a cure for cancer.

This area was a much, much better use of space. Not that Egragore cared much either way, and getting rid of cancer probably would have been a lovely development for the souls stuck on Earth, but ho-hum, not his circus not his monkeys.

Egragore reflected on the fact that it really did seem to be the case that if you *acted* as if you were in charge then people treated you as if you were in charge, then, ipso facto, you were in charge. He had always suspected this was true but had not had the opportunity to experiment with it until the recent turn of events. So far though it had been working quite splendidly for him.

"Right, thank you all for your attendance. I know you're all busy, or at least if you're not I want to know the reason why." Some of the younger attendees tittered politely at this. "So, I don't want to take too long, but I need to touch base with you all to ensure we're capitalising on this time as fully as we're able to. As you all know, we don't know how long the situation, if we can call it that, will be in our favour, so time is of the essence. If the, er, previous occupants suddenly appear again from wherever they have gone, they will ask us to return to our own space, and I think that we can all agree that they would be within their rights to do that."

He noticed that, down the table on his right, Fraster was glowering at him, solidly staring in his direction as if he was weighing up every word and storing every comment to assess at a later time. Egragore knew that if anyone was going to hold him to account it was Fraster. His friend, his mentor.

The look on his colleague's face was anything but supportive. He briefly wondered if it was something that he should be worried about but dismissed it. If Fraster was annoyed, then it was his own fault for not acting sooner. There was no time for weakness, for delay, and survival of the most assertive and most determined was just the way things were. Fraster knew this as well as anyone, and Egragore knew that deep down he would be pleased for him, the happiness of an old king as his son began to take over the reins of the kingdom.

He assumed.

"Amber, do we have any updates on where the CEO and his staff may have disappeared to?"

They all looked down the table at the amorphous blob who was surveying a table of information that had appeared in the air in front of her. Her dulcet voice was projected into their heads telepathically, and the table vibrated gently with its modulations. It was a nice trick if you could manage it, but when you were essentially a blob of putty trying to convince others that you were a competent executive, you needed all the tricks that you could fit up your non-existent sleeve.

"Certainly," she started. "I've had some of my statistic bods crunch some numbers, and we've projected some data and looked at the past-future projections."

There was a rumble of approval from around the table. This sounded absolutely like the kind of work that would get results sooner rather than later.

"And what we can conclusively say is that he isn't here. Neither he nor any of his staff are here."

There was a pause.

Egragore raised his eyebrows. "And?"

"Well," she continued hurriedly, "I mean, we hadn't conclusively decided he wasn't here somewhere. You know, around."

The attendees at the table glanced up in the air and then around the room.

"I'm sorry, can I just stop you there?" interrupted Scelion, a lesser tempter who had been temporarily promoted to the position of Acquisitions Manager. "You're saying you were not sure whether the creator of all existence, who breathed the universe into life, was here or not? You needed to check that he wasn't still here. Didn't the fact that we have all moved into His offices without any resistance give you the hint that he might be absent?"

Amber made a low humming noise, in what was both an irritated and irritating manner.

"You wouldn't consider the fact that a bunch of mid-level tempters and reapers are currently occupying the engine room of the universe a bit of a giveaway, at all? It's not a bit of a bloody hint?"

Egragore raised his hand to silence them. The irritated buzzing was filling his headpiece.

"If I can continue," snipped Amber, "we didn't have the *actual data* on the situation, and I thought it needed some clarification. I'm sorry, but if we're just going to carry on as has been happening in the past, making snap judgements based on what we assume, then are we in any way better than those who were here before? My brief was very clear, as I think were the rest of yours."

There was a murmur of agreement from around the table.

"If we don't get things on paper," Amber plugged on, "as it were, signed in triplicate and with the appropriate cross-checked data, then I, for one, don't want any part in such an amateur operation. We have a chance to make some real change now, and I don't want to muck it up."

"No, look, Amber, you're quite right," hastened Egragore. "You are absolutely right and, Scelion, I sincerely hope we're all on the same page. Our main task here is taking over the reins and tightening up what has, to be frank, been an absolute mismanaged nightmare."

An undersecretary down the table choked back a bitter laugh. "You would not *believe* the mess of receipts found in the archives. I don't know who's been doing auditing for the past few millennia, but they should be struck off. It clearly hasn't been a priority for quite some time."

A rumbling voice came from further down the table.

"Perhaps, Egragore," offered Fraster, "you could clarify for everyone present your *vision*." He spat out the word as if it were a unpleasant and unexpected mouthful of aged crustacean. "There seems to be a lack of consensus about what we're actually doing here, and I know that I, for one, work better when leadership makes things . . ." he thought for a moment, ". . . foolproof." His smile crept up the sides of his face as if the same crustacean, though horribly maimed, was trying to make a break for it.

Egragore narrowed his eyes. Their conflict and their sparring were an age-old performance now, as natural to them as slipping on a loved pair of slippers. Still, it couldn't hurt to re-establish some boundaries.

"What exactly are you not clear about, my friend?" asked Egragore. "Are you struggling with something of note, or is the whole rich tapestry of our current situation too much for you to handle?"

There was a nervous titter at the table.

"Clarity," said Fraster simply. "I think that we could all do with some clarity. I know that your mind works slightly differently from ours, slightly more . . . human, shall we say, but even given that, I think we could do with some explanations." He glanced around the table and was buoyed by the nodding and noises of agreement that came from most of the attendees. "Clarity around what we are actually doing to solidify our position here and to ensure that there is no repeat of the events we have just been part of—have capitalised on, if you will. I would hate for the same thing to happen again, and for us to be the losers this time. You have expressed your willingness to step aside if they return, which I think is a worrying utterance from you, at the very least."

Egragore leapt up and with the touch of a few buttons, data and projections appeared at the front of the room. He was no fool. This had been prepared for just such an occasion. It wasn't every day that one walked into a position of such leadership, and he was in no way planning to let it go. He pressed another button that opened communications with the rest of their pod.

"If anyone is interested in hearing an update on our current position and growth trajectory, they're invited to come to the central pod immediately. In the interests of full transparency and an open, vigorous, and honest dialogue, I welcome any who would like to sit in." He saw Fraster surveying him with a suspiciously raised eyebrow. Good. Let him wonder. Serves him right for trying to undermine him.

With a wave at a few buttons, the room was expanded to accommodate everyone who wanted to attend: a mix between mid-level tempters, reapers, wraiths, some aspiring angels who hadn't quite managed to finish their training beforehand and had applied for a position with him instead, and a smattering of other beings who were mainly amorphous and tended to have difficulty keeping their forms. The atmospheric density seemed to be slightly different up here from their offices downstairs, and while their scientists had done their best to even things out, some of the more unstable life forms had to occasionally dip down to the now cordoned off realm of the Shadow Lands to steady themselves before heading back up.

"Welcome to you all and thank you for your interest. I know if one being has a question then many of you probably do, so I'd like to give Fraster a big round of applause for his initiative in seeking my expertise and guidance to clarify matters, and the respect he has paid to my position in seeking out my wisdom."

Egragore smiled at the smattering of applause, noticing Fraster's glowering had notched up a few rungs.

He began.

Fifteen

At first, Brigid was so enthralled by the colours dancing before her that she was unaware of anything else in her line of vision. Her world was filled with an entirely new spectrum. Not merely variations on the colours she was already aware of, but utterly new and impossible to describe hues flooded the damp and ordinary street, causing what would have once seemed brilliant, like the blooming wattles, seem wan by comparison.

Trees had layers of reality punctuated over the top of them, visions that supplanted the traditional greens and browns, which had seemed so adequate up to now. Clouds glowed from within as if an LED light had been inserted into their hearts, and even the annoying yappy dog next door seemed to shimmer with an other-worldly blue heat.

She realised that the light headedness she was feeling came not from the utter glory of what she was experiencing, but from the fact she had totally neglected to breathe for the past thirty seconds, and so she took a sudden deep gulp of air. As she did so, she realised she could see the soft pink air glowing within her as it filled her lungs.

Brigid closed her eyes, overwhelmed, and considered running back inside to the safety of her room, but realised quickly that a chatty angel was potentially more work than some new colours, so she decided to take her chances out here.

She counted to ten, opened her eyes, and started walking. It's just colour, she reasoned. This is obviously part of the vibration thingy. I'll probably get used to it. It will be like free Wi-Fi. Once upon a time it was the most exciting thing on the planet, and now no one ever noticed it unless it wasn't working properly.

As she walked down her street to the bus stop, she concentrated on a steady gait and a fixed smile. Nice and normal. Nothing to see here. Glancing up into the sky in front of her she realised that a huge Aguafie floated below the clouds just above her head, and it was at that moment she realised that, truthfully, she was quite overwhelmed by all of this, and she turned tail and fled straight back into her house.

Slamming the door behind her she leaned against it, breath catching.

"What the hell is going on out there?" she whispered, eyes wild.

"Colours?" asked Michael.

She nodded.

"An entire new ecosystem of life?"

She nodded again. "Aguafis, anyway."

"Just Aguafis?" Michael frowned, clearly perplexed. "You should be seeing much more than that. You're seeing the 2nd element I'm assuming? Of course, you've got no idea, but this is my area, you see, and trust me, you should be seeing quite a bit more than just Aguafis. Let me think."

He laid down his sword and started ticking things off on his fingers. "You should be seeing fairies, for a start. And wraiths. Possible bluncors, depending on how they're vibrating. Tremoirs, Chicains and Ursuans. And then just all the normal microfauna and flora that's hardly worth describing. That's if you are at the 2nd element, that is. And as I said, whether you see other angels is hit and miss. I can't make any predictions around that one."

"Wait, fairies?"

Michael was staring off into space.

"I mean, you couldn't have stepped up to 3rd, surely. He wouldn't have allowed you to get there and then let you wander off to your own devices. That's just negligent. He'd get in trouble for that. It's not safe for either of us.

Not that I'm worried for myself, of course, but with my stellar track record I don't want some Buncor swooping in and . . ."

He trailed off, seeing the look on Brigid's face. "No, I'm sure he wouldn't have done that. Mind you," he continued muttering to himself, "knowing the specific reaper in question, he very well could have just abandoned you. But he's not supposed to, that's what I'm saying. There are rules, and he's supposed to abide by them, no matter what else is going on. Not surprised though, given his history. I mean, reapers aren't evil at all. It's not like they are tempters or even—" and here his voice dropped "demons. But facts are facts, he is a reaper, he's more interested in his bottom line and his tick boxes than any nuance or genuine emotions, so yes, on reflection, he very well could have just abandoned you on the 3rd element . . ." His voice petered out.

"Just out of interest," ventured Brigid, "do you get to have many conversations with people? Or, I suppose, beings? Of any kind? Ever?"

"No, never. This is the first proper chat I've had in 556 years."

She pulled back the blind and searched out the front window. The world was still full of the indescribable colours, but they had almost begun to settle into her consciousness, and she had the suspicion it wouldn't be long until she took them for granted.

"So, what you're telling me is that I should be seeing other things too. A microcosm, you said?"

"Or a macrocosm. It depends on your perspective. You're insignificant to some of the beings in the higher dimensions. But to others you're huge and they rely on you for their very existence. The fairies, as I said. None of them are particularly enamoured with you humans though. You've become an invasive species. Oh no, *I* don't think that," he hurried to confirm. "It's just that some do. Others. Not me." He shook his head convincingly.

A memory niggled at the back of Brigid's brain. What was it Egragore said about a bus station? Or a portal? She glanced around the room.

"I'm sure Egragore said my house was a portal of some kind." She stared into a few corners, pointedly. "But I can't see anything."

"Do you want to?"

"I might as well. Given the circumstances."

He gestured to her green, overstuffed sofa. "There are some tricks I can teach you if you really want to see. By the sounds of it I'd say Egragore did an abysmally half arsed job, and—"

Brigid held up her hand. "It doesn't matter at this point. If you can do something about it though, let's try. I'm getting creeped out by the fact *things* might be watching me."

Michael glanced around the room, his eyes lighting on a spot just below a windowsill. "Alright, look at that area there." He pointed with one massive finger.

She looked.

"What am I looking at?"

Michael narrowed his eyes and moved his head around. "What I need you to do is look at it, but not really look at it."

Brigid tilted her head and attempted to peer out from under her eyelashes. She felt the stirrings of a headache coming on.

"Anything?"

"No"

"Ok let's try this. Have you ever read a Magic Eye book?"

Brigid nodded uncertainly.

"Right, so you know you have to kind of, look through the picture to see the hidden image? You have to see the page but not see the page, if you know what I mean."

"How do you know about Magic Eye books?"

"I'm a protection angel of a forty-something who seldom moves beyond a 15km radius. I have a lot of time to kill."

Brigid drew her attention back to the spot and blinked a few times before letting her eyes drift away, while still fixed in the same position. Her vision crossed a little, things became blurry and then, gradually, she began to see a bright light in the very space where she was staring. With a little shift in her focus, this bright light sharpened somewhat, took on a more solid form, until she could see a long gold snake with a misty halo of orange around its middle, wending its way across the middle of the room. It twisted and turned, weaving slowly onwards, until its head disappeared through the solid wall.

"Did you see it?"

She nodded. "Thanks for showing me a snake first up, by the way."

"Keep looking around though. If that worked, then you should be good to go."

He was right. The whole room was filled with life, although she quickly realised she could easily shift her vision to see, or not see, the things that were scattered about depending on her capacity for weirdness. There was a slowly spinning vortex above her head, through which sprinkles of glitter-like matter burst every few seconds. These sprinkles flew off in different directions, disappearing through walls and windows as rapidly as they had appeared.

A group of tall, dark beings that looked like spaniels but with crocodile tails were gathered around the front door talking. One held a beige suitcase in his talon, and after shaking hands with each other they all disappeared through the closed door.

A waterfall of blue light cascaded directly through the room and continued into the wall of her bedroom. It pulsated and shimmered and various beings seemed to be swept up in its continuous movement. They were swept away out of her sight, and Brigid noticed that a family of small, squirrel-like dragon creatures seemed to wave at her as they careered by.

These sights filled her heart with wonder and excitement. Her house, full of all this life. But her gaze was quickly distracted by something over at the fireplace: a dark mist emitting tentacles, stretching out, growing. As she watched, the mist—as deeply black as she had ever seen—coalesced into a figure that struck a deep, visceral fear into her heart. A huge, cloaked presence that drew itself up to its full size, filling the whole room with a fear that she—

Brigid withdrew her vision. "Right, that's enough for one day," she said briskly. "It's probably better not to know what exists in here, come to think of it. I'd never know where to sit down."

"You should be able to do that trick at will now," said Michael. "I mean, the other stuff that you activated by stepping up is probably going to be tricker to unsee, but you'll get the hang of it."

"I don't mind the sparkly things. It's the other stuff that I don't want catching me by surprise."

She shivered at the dark presence. Was it still filling the room? Glancing out the window something else drew her attention. A nondescript man was walking down the street, dressed in a worn blue suit, and carrying a grey umbrella. He was talking into his phone, which was on speaker, and by the look on his face and his whole demeanour, the conversation he was engaged in was not one that was bringing a great deal of joy or satisfaction to his life. His brow was furrowed, and he was using the hand that also carried the umbrella to make poking gestures as he walked, as if to punctuate the great import of the words he was saying.

It wasn't this that caught her eye, though. Irritated city guy on the way to work wasn't worth expending any energy focussing on. What had grabbed her attention, and now held her, wide eyed and staring, was what was on his back. Laying against him, like a dark and impossibly creepy backpack, sat a creature. Its arms were wrapped around his neck, in the same way a small child would hold onto their father when he was giving them a piggyback ride, but there the similarity with a bright-eyed toddler ended. This being was scaly and sinuous, with a forked tail and a serious underbite. It wore an incongruous red beanie on its head, and its hands were firmly placed around his neck. Every few steps it lifted up its fingers and jabbed them into the man's cheek which seemed, to Brigid's eyes, to match the moments when the man's own fingers jabbed into the air in front of him.

As the man passed the window, the creature raised its head into the air, as if it had heard something that had grabbed its attention. It raised its flat nose up and seemed to be sniffing, eyes darting around. With a jerky movement redolent of a reptile swinging its head towards a prospective prey, the creature locked eyes with Brigid, and the yellow gimlet eyes lit up with recognition. A cavernous smile broke out on its squat face, and at the same time as Brigid jerked back from the window in horror, the creature raised one of its arms from the man's neck and waved at her.

"Oh my god," she gasped, flinging her hands up to cover her face and falling back heavily on the sofa. For some reason the mixture of creepiness and revulsion bothered her even more than the cowled figure had.

"What?" Michael moved forwards and ducked to see out of the window. "What's the matter?" He surveyed the street.

That . . . thing. On the man. Ugh." She shivered in revulsion. "It was disgusting. I think I'm going to be sick." She staggered over to the kitchen and rattled around in the fridge for a bottle of coke. "I need sugar and caffeine," she muttered. She turned back, ashen faced. "Is that what I'm in for? A demonic world of evil?"

Michael frowned. "Ok, look, can we just . . ." He awkwardly took her hand and settled her onto the sofa again, managing by some trick of physics so shoehorn himself onto the seat beside her.

He looked deeply, soulfully into her eyes, and Brigid felt a strange stirring within her.

"You're going to need to toughen up," he said.

The stirring went away.

She opened and closed her mouth in a way that did nothing to increase Michael's confidence that she was able to deal with her new reality.

"That," he said, "was a fairy."

She narrowed her eyes. "I think there's been some confusion."

"Yes, yes there has been. The confusion has stemmed from your modern storytellers and their complete inability to relay universal truths faithfully."

"What?"

"Alright, let's take a step back. What do you know about fairies?"

"Well," stammered Brigid, "I suppose I know that they're magical. With wings. Disney." She cast about for the appropriate description. Surely "fairy" was a somewhat universal concept.

"Oh, *Disney*," spat Michael in disgust. "Bloody *Disney*. Don't get me started on Disney. That company has single-handedly undermined the strivings for the rights of magical and/or mythological creatures. They have perpetuated a thorough misunderstanding of their reality and responsibilities in the history of this planet, including..." Here he clenched his angelic fists together so that tiny blue sprints of electricity could be seen "...and I am including, do you understand, Richard Dawkins."

"Fairies," he said simply, "are bastards. I'm sorry, I know that angels aren't strictly supposed to speak so plainly, but they are. They're nasty piddling little bastards that like to ruin people's days. But that is all they are. They make a bad mood worse. They make an argument go on for longer than it needs to go on. They distract you so that you miss the last parking spot in the car park on Christmas Eve. But that's all."

Brigid frowned with uncertainty. "But that thing was—"

"And they're ugly. But honestly, Brigid, they're very mild low quality annoyants. Not worth your emotional energy. You need to save your anguish for things that are worth it."

She bit her lip nervously. "And will I see things that are worth that level of anguish?"

He nodded. "I think so."

"Why?"

He shrugged. "Because the universe has been thrown off kilter, and you have been swept up in events in a way that none of us could have ever expected. Just the normal way that people's lives are usually turned upside down."

Smiling, he extricated himself from the couch and stood. Brigid felt the low-level humming that had been resonating through her body die down a bit. She briefly wondered how she could possibly have been living in such close proximity to him for all these years without once sensing it. How many other things had she been similarly blind to?

"You know," he said, lacing his fingers together and stretching them above his head, somehow miraculously not bringing down the ceiling. "I feel like taking a stroll. And it's not as if there's anyone overseeing me at the moment. No one to tell me off, anyway. Would you like an escort?"

Sixteen

As the data danced in front of his eyes, Egragore turned to the expectant room.

The story so far. The words flashed up in the air in front of them.

In Garamond.

He flinched and waved his hand at a few more buttons. The words disappeared.

The story so far. This time in Gotham. That was better.

Showtime, he thought. He knew he looked good, and he wore bravado like a second skin. He pivoted slightly to show off his best side.

"As we know, recently, the Heavenly Realm—"

There was an early murmur of concern from down the table. Scelion spoke up.

"Look, I'm sorry, but I, and I feel I'm not alone here, am going to have a problem with this. I deeply feel we need to work on relabelling the bulk of reality as we know it. If we keep using the old terms, doesn't that mean we'll be trapped in the original paradigm that has caused all these problems to begin with? A completely new way of describing reality is needed for us to truly throw off the shackles of our oppressor and to begin our new bright future."

Egragore paused the PowerPoint.

"I really don't want to get bogged down in semantics, but at this stage, in order for us all to understand what the other is saying and in the absence of any other agreed frame of reference, then yes, I'm afraid we will have to . . . to," he cleared his throat, ". . . utilise the language of our oppressor. Traditional nomenclature if you like."

There was a murmur of disgruntled acceptance from the room at large.

"As an aside," said Egragore, "do most of us feel that the last CEO was our oppressor, as it were? Because I personally feel that they were fairly magnanimous and don't—"

There was a hum of voices from around the table and a shaking of heads or headlike appendages. Apparently Egragore was in the minority. It was so easy to lose a room.

Far, far too easy.

"Of course, they are our oppressors. Remember what Fraster said? They have always kept the nice offices for themselves!" came the voices.

"Yes, and they get casual Fridays. Have we ever had casual Fridays? No. It's clearly a case of corporate oppression."

"Can we get on?" asked Fraster impatiently.

Egragore marshalled himself again. "As I was saying, recently, due to certain events brought about by the humans—and no one is more surprised that they managed to bring about real, actionable change than I, namely, the turning on of the one particle accelerator in the Great Hadron Collider . . ."

He was very happy with the diagram that was unfolding in front of them; lots of retro graphics and simulations of pistons going "boom" and lovely chunky labels.

" . . . *Somehow* we came to find that the physical space that makes up the Heavenly Realm was unoccupied, except for one minor deity—Mur-arb—who, from what we can tell, was yanked out of the pocket universe inhabited by llamas and jazz musicians, and seated—" here he used his laser pointer to direct the room's eyes to the floating stylised representation of the different Realm they were discussing, "—here. He is now, from what we can tell, in charge of the universe as a whole and the fate of everything in it, but he doesn't seem to have fully conceptualised that yet. Really big ideas seem a bit beyond his cerebral reach, and if we manage to have our own way then that is, in fact, the position he will continue to enjoy. He is also, and I'm sorry to have to relay this as I know it might bring about some concern, dangerously unstable and unreliable."

Fraster rose his pale spindly hand as if to speak, and Egragore pretended he hadn't noticed it.

"As luck would have it, or of course fate, I happened to catch wind of these monumental changes shortly after they occurred, and I was able to step in and render much welcomed assistance to him who you now know to be our current leader; Mur-arb. And of course, seeing as I was first on the scene, I have had the honour of taking on the adviser role, if you will, in the power vacuum that resulted in the absence of the, er, previous occupants."

"Catch wind of these monumental changes? Would you care to share with everyone how you came to step in so fortuitously?"

Egragore glared at Fraster, who smiled at him oilily.

"I just had this overwhelming sense that—"

"You found a door open, isn't that correct?"

Egragore felt the momentum slipping away from him again.

"You found a door," said Fraster, "that had previously always been locked. You slipped through it like a common thief and discovered the whole place vacant. Like a metaphysical Mary Celeste."

It was true.

He had been finishing up his work on a Sunday evening. Shadow Lands record keeping was vital, and he was doing the tediously awful job of triple checking those souls who were being allowed to lodge an appeal against their allocation. He was having a break, pottering around, giving his eyes a rest, and waiting to see if any of the souls would add some supporting documentation before he made final decisions, when he happened to find a door ajar.

A door that had always, in his experience, been locked.

It should be noted that the development of the whole Heavenly Realm/ Shadow Lands/ Great Abyss region was piecemeal, like a very old city that has grown beyond the constraints of what its founding fathers envisaged, and there were strange pockets of accessibility all over the place. These tended to be largely unknown, except by those who made it their business to know potentially useful little titbits of information.

He had seen the door open and had casually glanced in. Usually, he would have been stopped by a gentle force field pressing against his body in a polite but non-negotiable manner. He had felt it before on occasion; not enough to make him feel bad about himself, but just a vague sense that he wasn't quite good enough to be there. Like a particularly judgemental bouncer at an upmarket restaurant, letting you know you would not be dining on their fillet mignon in the near future—not with those shoes, or that hairstyle. Although in Egragore's case it was more a sense that he wasn't quite up to their highly exacting standards. He was a lovely chap, the force spoke into him, he was doing awfully well, but you're not quite . . .

One. Of. Us.

Anyway, it wasn't the Realm's way to judge him too harshly, so he was usually just left with the vague sense that he really could do better, if he put his mind to it, and wouldn't he just like to try being a slightly . . . better version of himself?

Usually in the past Egragore had been able to shake off this sense of discomfort within a few hours, but a strange sadness stayed with him for longer, a sense of missing out on a really, really good party that everyone who was someone was invited to.

But this time he had felt no such resistance, no deep deficiency stirred in what had once been his soul, and he found himself stepping through into a spacious hallway. Wide, rounded walls curved away from him, the plush forest green carpet hugged his feet, and the smell of grapefruit mixed with vanilla hung in the air. He stood for a moment, eyes darting around to see if this was some kind of joke, but he could see no one else around. The only movement was the swell of the tropical ocean that he could see just outside the half-windows that contoured around the walls.

His heart leapt at the thought he had been granted access, that they had once again seen the essential goodness within him, and that they were welcoming him into their fold. But this ridiculous notion disappeared when, on further exploration, he came to the conclusion that the place was completely deserted.

He wandered through endless rooms, entire ecosystems, habitats and forums. So lost was he, in a place that felt so quintessentially "good", so utterly inviting, that time seemed to have no meaning. No lists to be curated, no decisions to be made, no budgetary measure that he needed to convince anyone of. An absolute feeling of peace.

It wasn't until he was making his way back to the door he'd entered that there was the first sign of another being. Everywhere he'd gone, everything seemed normal, except there were none of the heavenly beings that one would have expected to find. No other beings at all and, (and this was, he thought, the biggest giveaway of all) none of the unmistakable presence that was the CEO. He had been within the presence of the CEO just once before, but once you'd experienced it, you didn't forget it in a hurry. And while he couldn't put his finger on exactly what it was, after walking around these expansive rooms for a few hours he could say with certainty that the CEO was nowhere nearby.

Gradually he became aware of a strange keening noise coming from a small area off the main tropical rainforest biome, and after he had made his way to it, he met the being who he would soon come to know as Mur-arb.

According to the little man's story—which he was exceedingly eager to share with someone else— he been minding his own business learning the finer points of weaving llama fleece in his yurt, when he had found himself sitting in the middle of a strange room. There was some rambling talk of not being in a pot anymore and a mention of a conversation with a tall man in a suit, but it was days before he could form a coherent thought or remember peoples' names.

And the rest, as they say was history.

Egragore's quick decision making, and summation of the situation meant he moved the entire population of the Shadow Lands through the door in double quick time, and they had taken over within the week. They rapidly began to rejig the surroundings to make them far more suitable to their purposes. He had soon realised that Mur-arb was the key to change, the only one capable of making massive reality altering changes, but that he was essentially impotent until they could enlist Brigid's help.

Of course, the whole situation with the Large Hadron Collider was discovered later on, thanks to one of their bods-on-the-ground, but as to where the occupants of the Heavenly Realm had got to, there was no intel at all. They had people working on it, certainly, but the business at hand kept them all very busy and the first order of duty had been streamlining processes and increasing profit margins. Something that had clearly been atrociously overlooked in the past. The less useful biomes had been converted into offices, and condos for the staff, and it was all coming along nicely.

"Yes, I found a door," snapped Egragore. "And I think we're all the better for it, don't you?"

There was another murmur from around the table.

"*We* are now in charge, and we have set about immediately putting to rights the mismanagement and negligence of the past. Only now are we able to see the enormous potential of this planet, and really work on getting as many souls up to the level of the Heavenly Realm standard as we can. Not, of course," he added quietly, "that we know quite what to do with them yet. Or where to put them."

"That's all very well," countered Fraster, "but why don't you tell everyone about how much of a liability this new so-called "Great and Glorious Ruler" is? How much of an absolute wild card he really is, and how he is functionally useless without his—"

"I am working on it," hissed Egragore, glaring at Fraster. "I am working on getting her here within the appropriate regulatory guidelines, and when that happens—"

"The fact is," Fraster announced, turning to the rest of the room and instantly commanding authority, "Mur-arb is only half a deity, and not even an officially sanctioned one at that. No one has any idea where he came from, or what he stands for. We can't do anything of real lasting value regarding the human souls or their puny lives until his co-ruler arrives. Have you told everyone about that pertinent fact, my friend? Or have you been keeping that tasty snippet to yourself?" Fraster smiled inwardly. A masterful performance, if he did say so himself. No one would have suspected that it was he who had found Mur-arb and had led him up here. The more he derided the nitwit the less anyone would suspect the role he was forming for himself.

Egragore clicked off the screen, resigning himself to the fact that his meticulously prepared PowerPoint was not going to be appropriately appreciated. He sat himself lightly in the chair at the head of the table. "It's by no means a secret, really, it's just that we have certain constraints."

"We can't do anything at all without that human you've been fraternising with, am I correct?"

Gasps rang around the table, and someone knocked over their water. A flurry of activity mopping it up gave Egragore a moment to collect himself.

"It is not *a* human, as you so dangerously state. It is a specific human who, we understand, has worked closely with Mur-arb in the past. We aren't just randomly casting around for the closest available human everyone, calm down."

"Has he worked in the past? He seems singularly unsuited to work of any kind."

"From what we can tell," continued Egragore pointedly, "she and Mur-arb have a certain metabiosis. One cannot exist fully without the other. They have, from our reports, been living a kind of a shadow life for the past few decades but bringing them together will increase Mur-arb's powers, and also stabilise him somewhat."

"So, get her," hissed Fraster. "Just go down and get her."

"Don't be ridiculous. You can't just say "get her". We can't take a non-consenting human and drag her up here. It's against the fundamental laws."

From down the table, Scelion raised a bulbous hand. "We don't know what else has changed, so maybe that has changed too?"

"Don't be ridiculous. We can't just take her, and you know it. It would be foolhardy and dangerous."

"If you're not committed enough to do it, then I know plenty who are," rumbled Fraster.

"Really? Here? Plenty who are?" Egragore cast his dark eyes around the table and was thankful that none were willing to meet his. "Careful, my friend, you sound like your motivations are coming from a lower place than the one on which you have been assessed to belong. It's a dangerous game and you know it."

As if on cue, there was a nervous knock on the door and the front reception wraith, Cashion, shimmied her constantly changing essence to the room.

"Excuse me, sir, but Mur-arb has said he won't sign the overtime reports unless he's allowed to ride on a dolphin, and I've tried to tell him that we concreted the atoll last week, but he won't be told."

"Oh, for pity's sake. Isn't Gerald with him?"

"Um," she glanced behind her. "I think he's quite keen on the dolphin idea too, to be honest."

"Right." Egragore stood. "Is there anything else, any questions? I'm afraid I didn't get the chance to cover everything, but please make sure to look through the PowerPoint that I'll send out later."

Fraster flicked his fingers dismissively. "We have achieved absolutely nothing here. What we *need* is the human woman, and the last thing that we possibly need is a human woman, so we are in a difficult position, are we not? And given the fact you are woefully unable to come up with any other solution, I think the most logical course of action is to open your position to tenders. Let's see what others can come up with. I, myself, have been thinking of ways to eliminate the woman entirely from the equation."

"You mean eliminate the need for the woman entirely."

Fraster raised his eyebrows.

"May I remind you," said Egragore, gathering up the dossier of papers he hadn't been able to distribute, "that we are not actually the evil ones. We are not the doom dwellers, the malignant tumours, the lovers of misery and horror. We are *not* the bad guys here, we simply have a job to do, so it would serve us all well not to act like them."

Amber vibrated more quickly. "But we're not exactly nice, are we?"

"We aren't supposed to be "nice" either."

Egragore suddenly realised there may have been a breakdown in communication between the trainers and his people on the ground. "We are neither here nor there. We aren't lovely and light filled beings, but we also aren't evil. That is our whole *point*, assuming that we have one. Don't you understand? We have been freed from the constraints that so beleaguer the existence of those above and those below. We are the lucky ones. We can get on with the business of getting things done, without the hindrance of being responsible for the minutiae of people's souls. We don't have to be good or bad anymore; we can be *effective.*"

"Poppycock," interjected Fraster. "That was never the design, and you know it. You're changing the truth to be what you want. I don't blame you specifically though. This bastardisation of our role has been happening for quite some time. You're only the newest in a long line of managers who have totally lost sight of who we're supposed to be. And on that note—"

Fraster motioned in the air with his hands, and his own display appeared at the front of the room, much to the irritation and unease of Egragore.

"As we all know, the idea of "purgatory" has gone decidedly out of fashion over the past few hundred years, to the extent that the word itself is rarely, if ever, used."

An over-the-top picture of a fiery abyss with angels pulling naked people out and demons pushing equally naked people back in burst into life in front of them.

Egragore rolled his eyes.

Amber sighed. "Oh, I *miss* those times. They were good days."

A bristle of agreement sounded around the table, comments of "*those were the days*" and "*I just loved having a clear purpose*".

The screen blinked out and was replaced by a pyramid diagram, divided into three levels. At the top sat stylised angels sitting on clouds and playing harps, and in the middle, a battalion of official looking men in suits carrying clipboards (the fact that they were sitting around a desk not unlike the one that they were currently sitting around was a detail that did not escape Egragore's attention), and at the bottom, a variety of decidedly demonic looking activities were taking place.

Fraster pulled out a laser pointer and directed everyone's attention to the middle level.

"*This* is not who we are. We have created generations of snowflakes who need trigger warnings at the slightest mention of eternal torment; they're becoming soft. It's a horrific bastardisation of what our intended purpose was. Humans think that they are *good* as a default. It's disgusting. They need to understand they are foul pestilence and only through our refinement can they be made pure."

He was leaning forward now, his fingers punctuating his words, jabbing into the desk repeatedly.

"I'm sorry," said one of the lesser wraiths nervously, "but I haven't been here as long as most of you. I personally was never given a clear outline of duties, so I feel as if I may have misunderstood my role, such as it is."

"Exactly," interrupted Egragore. "This is what we are moving towards. Clear outlines of duties, EOIs, transparent processes." He felt a headache pricking behind his eyes and saw, out of the corner of his eye, Mur-arb gesticulating excitedly in the corridor. He wasn't sure if it was good or bad gesticulating, and that made him nervous.

"Let me clear something up for you," said Fraster, turning to the wraith. "We are meant to be purifying the humans. With fire."

Conversation broke out around the table.

"Fire? What are the Occupational Health and Safety ramifications on that? What training would be needed to be completed to oversee—?"

Fraster continued. "There is *supposed* to be a vast swathe of humans who are not good enough for the Heavenly Realm, but not bad enough for the Great Abyss. Where to put them has been a question for the ages. For millennia we have given them a thorough cleaning. Painful, but what they deserve. Lately though, because of several generations of mismanagement, they have all been let in upstairs, with the bare minimum of screening. There has been an open border policy." He hissed these words. "Have you been slightly good; helped an old lady across the street, *not* advocated for neo-Nazi rights? Up you pop then. No faith at all? No trouble, head in. Have you been nice to kittens? Eternal happiness in the Kingdom can be yours! No ifs, buts, or maybes. The CEO will welcome you with open arms. It's disgusting. How dare *everyone* be happy with no effort at all? How dare it be that easy? No, what we need is a tightening up of security, a far harder raft of policies. Not even a raft of policies, as a matter of fact. Just one. Plunge them into fire. The bulk of humans, 99%, are unworthy, vile, and repulsively servile, and must be made to suffer."

"But," ventured the wraith somewhat tremulously. "Does it really make a difference? I mean it's not as if it can get full up, can it? It's an infinite space as far as I understand. It's not as if there are special dimensions to consider . . ." The wraith's voice trailed off as it saw Fraster's stony expression.

"Why are you here?" he asked.

The wraith boggled nervously. "I applied for the position so—"

With a flick of his fingers, Fraster dismissed it from his presence.

"The point is, if we are not happy with the way things have been done, we can change them. We have been following the Heavenly Realm's orders, which we have been powerless to defy, but now they have walked out of their duties—"

Egragore tried to protest but Fraster raised his voice.

"Walked out of their duties. Then we can make any changes that we see fit. And I, for one, see fit to make very many changes, and if the murmurings that I can hear mean anything, then I am not alone."

"We may be occupying the area, but we are a long way from being in control," clarified Egragore. "And until we get Brigid—I mean, the human— then even the very worst of your ideas are just pipe dreams. Oh, we can plan and design and conceptualise, but we can't *do* anything. Not until they're together."

"What I think I meant," spoke the wraith again, "I think that what I meant is that it doesn't make any difference—"

"The problem around here," said Fraster, now working himself up into a decent rage, "and I include you as being at fault for this Egragore, is that no one *means* anything anymore. Everyone is scared to have an opinion, to say what they mean. It's all so PC. This is not a safe space," he yelled, his face growing a worrying shade of scarlet. "What's *wrong* with telling people that they aren't good enough? That they have to suffer? And WE have to help them do that. That they have to *do better. We have to set fire to them until they learn how to become better people.*"

There was a sudden sharp explosion of blue sparks, the smell of sulphur, and a noise that gave the impression all the air in the room had been sucked backward into a balloon that then exploded in the room next door. Fraster disappeared, and all that remained in his seat was a bedraggled but also very angry looking cane toad.

Silence filled the room.

"And *that's* what you get," announced Egragore as he lifted the toad carefully and called out the door to Cashion. "Cash, can you please come and get Fraster and take him back to his office? He's imploded again."

Egragore swiftly lifted his jacket off the back of the chair. If he moved fast enough, he could head this dolphin business off at the pass and still check in with Brigid's recent movements.

"I think, if anything, this meeting has shown us that the old ways are short sighted, band aid measures that simply aren't sustainable. Becoming overly emotional," he gestured to Fraster's chair, "ends in an absolute loss of productivity. He won't be good for anything until tomorrow now, so if you had a meeting scheduled with him, you'll just have to cancel it."

A few hands went up around the room, but he ignored them.

"Now, I'm off to see a deity about a dolphin."

As he left the room, he heard a welling of conversation beginning again, and his mind briefly lit on the possibility that finding that open door may not have been the best thing to happen in his exceedingly long existence.

Seventeen

The man sat on the beach, gazing off into the distance as the orange sun gradually sank over the horizon. If he had thought about it for a minute, he would have known that it was the western horizon, because that was where the sun set. But he wasn't interested in compass points, and he wasn't particularly interested in the sunset either. He has seen sunsets, the glorious and the mundane, those that cast a glow on newborn babies, and those that lit up the horrors of genocide. He had been there for all of them.

Quite literally, all of them.

The man was worn. He was deep brown, and he wasn't so much wrinkled as crevassed. His hair was stylishly matted, in a way that indicated he had spent a great deal of time in an expensive ashram rather than, for example, the streets of a megacity where the impoverished headed to climb the ladder of capitalistic success and inevitably ended up living in a box outside a rich man's office. He wore few clothes, just a sarong around his waist, and a pair of sandals. He had had quite a giggle when the woman in the shop had told him what this type of sandals were called. He liked the way his feet felt in them. He liked the way the sand felt as he pressed his hands into it and grasped it loosely with his battle worn fingers. He liked having nothing to do, or worry about, or think about, except run the sand through those fingers, and think about where he would go to sleep that night.

Sleep. He really, really liked sleep. He felt a little sad he had taken so long to realise how wonderful it was, but his new motto was "better late than never", and it was at this point he decided it was time for a piña colada. He stood and stretched his wiry arms above him. Walking down the beach, he kept an eye out for somewhere comfortable where he could fashion a bed for the night. He was utterly and deliciously enraptured by the fact that it was the only problem he had to deal with, at all.

Eighteen

Stepping out of her house for the second time that morning, Brigid felt comforted by the enormous presence of Michael by her side. She had been aware of this new reality for about twelve hours, had not yet had a nervous breakdown, and was striding out into the world with a protection angel at her side. She felt pretty impressed with herself.

"Think of me as your tour guide," Michael said as he hunched down and sidled through the door. "Your tour guide to all things spectral and otherworldly and terrifying."

"If you could lose the spooky voice that would be great, thanks." She glanced down the street. She hadn't immediately seen any of the creatures Egragore had opened her to, and quite deliberately didn't do the Magic Eye trick Michael had taught her, but that didn't mean things weren't lurking just out of her line of vision.

"Are you sure you're allowed to come with me? I wouldn't want you to get in trouble. I thought you said you are supposed to stay in the house most of the time?"

"Technically I am geographically confined, but it's not a law as such. More of a tradition. It's a matter of demarcation. And numbers too; having two angels on at once probably isn't a wise use of personnel."

"Wait, two angels?" She turned to look at him, puzzled.

"It's so your guardian angel doesn't have to—"

112

He saw the look on her face and smacked his hand theatrically onto his forehead. "But of course, you haven't met Guindaline yet, have you? Oh, you'll love her. She's hilarious. You have to get to know her, it's true, but she's great really. And she should be here about now." He glanced over to see how far they'd walked from the front door.

As the words came out of his mouth, Brigid heard the tiny tinkling of bells in the air above her right ear. A curious sensation came over her, as if a train was approaching and sucking the air out of a tunnel. The bells quickly became louder, until the train tunnel sensation came to a crescendo and then, standing in front of her, was a figure; a figure that was exactly what Brigid would have described if she had been asked to describe her idea of a guardian angel.

The flowing white robes that shimmered with what she intuitively felt was starlight, the thick blond hair that cascaded to below the angel's shoulders, the wide, friendly face smattered with a sprinkling of freckles; all were absolutely Guardian Angel 101, in Brigid's opinion. Guindaline stood in a mint green haze that expanded and contracted rhythmically around her. She glowed with love and compassion, and Brigid felt an overwhelming urge to wrap her arms around the angel and confide in her all her dark secrets.

She opened her mouth to speak. "What the hell are you doing out here? It's not Friday."

Michael also opened his mouth to speak but before he could get a word out, Guindaline noticed that Brigid was staring straight at her, and by the look on her face there could be no doubt she had been seen.

"Shit. Shit!" Guindaline slammed her hands onto her hips and glared at the both of them. "Shit, Michael, what are you up to?"

Michael waved his hands lamely, first in Brigid's, then Guindaline's direction. "Yeah, so, Brigid can see you now."

"Yes, *obviously* she can see me, *Michael*." She glared at Brigid then turned her attention back to him. "Why?"

"Our best guess is that a reaper raised her vibrations last night, but I'd kind of assumed that you would have known that. She went out with one last night, so I thought you would have, you know, been with her. Since she was out with a reaper and all."

"Oh, yeah, that." She flicked her hair back and surveyed Brigid with pursed lips. "I knocked off at seven o'clock because she *never* goes out after nine, so I didn't think there was much point just hanging around. You never go out," she insisted, glaring at Brigid.

Brigid felt a sense of indignation rise in her. "Yes, I do, as a matter of fact."

"Tell me the last time you went out after 9.00pm?"

"I don't think it's either of your faults," Michael interjected soothingly, in a voice that could be used to tame rabid ferrets. "I think we can all agree we should place the blame firmly with Egragore."

Guindaline's eyes lit up, and a small grin appeared on her perfect lips. "Egragore? That changes things. Now I'm interested. How hot is he?" she asked rhetorically, turning to Brigid. "And what do you mean by "out"?" She winked, far more lasciviously than Brigid felt appropriate for a halo-enabled angel.

"So anyway," stammered Michael, "Brigid can now see all of the 2nd dimension biome, and from what I can tell a fair whack of the 3rd, so I thought she might be better off with me accompanying her, for the time being at least." His voice trailed off as he saw the look on Guindaline's face.

"You think I can't do it?"

"No," he said somewhat weakly, thinking for a moment. "No." he stated again, his voice becoming firmer. "Of course, you can do it. It's just I know you have a lot of things on your plate, and a lot of—"

"Irons in the fire?" suggested Brigid.

"That's right, irons in the fire, and I just thought you might appreciate me doing the heavy lifting, if you will, this end. I mean, you're used to just hovering around Brigid while she does her thing, which, the be honest, isn't that stimulating. No offence Brigid. And you're often double booked. So, I thought I could step in and help out, so you could attend to your other responsibilities without the extra workload."

"It's true that I am fairly busy," agreed Guindaline.

"She has some really top-level clients," confided Michael.

"Can't say too much. Need to know basis. But let's just say that a lot of people try to kill him. A lot. I have to keep on my toes."

"But can't you do that "lots of places at once" thing that Michael can do?" asked Brigid.

Guindaline shrugged. "In theory, but I'm also a Myer-Briggs ESFP, so I don't like to be bored. This," she said, gesturing to Brigid, the house, and the street, "isn't enough for me."

Brigid had never realised you could be socially snubbed by your own guardian angel, and quite frankly she wasn't a fan of it.

"And there is this demon that I'm kind of seeing and that's keeping me busy."

"Well then," concluded Michael, "if you want to . . . pop off, and do your other things, I'm happy to hang out with Brigid and teach her the ropes because I know it isn't really your area.'

She crossed her arms and surveyed them both.

"Alright, that sounds fair enough. But you have to call me if Egragore comes back, alright? Promise?"

Brigid nodded.

"Because if he's hanging out with you then I need to know."

And with that, she was gone.

"*That* is my guardian angel?" Brigid was flabbergasted. "She's awful. You said she was great. She hates me. How on earth did she get the job?"

"Oh, get away, she doesn't hate you, I promise. She just finds you a bit dull, that's all. Admit it, she's pretty funny. Funny-mean, anyway. She's much cleverer than I am. And, you know, it takes all types. She's excellent value in a flap."

Brigid continued to stare at the vacuum recently vacated by the angel. "Surely, they're meant to be a bit more loving and kinder instead of just nasty. How am I not dead yet?"

"That would mostly be down to me if I'm being honest. I do often have to follow you round when she's out consorting with demons or whatever. I know it's against the rules, but I have learned just to cobble things together as I go along."

"That's one of the good guys, is it? One of the angelic realm, as it were? *That* is what's supposed to be guiding me through my ups and downs? That explains a fuck tonne about my life."

Michael shrugged. "As I said, things have been a bit funny lately. Some wires are crossed, or something. Things are in flux. New possibilities are opening up for all of us apparently, and old ways are . . ." His voice petered out.

"Apparently? Don't you know what's going on?"

"Not really. There's just been gossip and transitory thoughts passing through the aether. But obviously we know there has been some sort of change of management." He rubbed a hand across his impossibly handsome face. "It shouldn't really affect those of us who are boots on the ground; those of us at the coal face don't really get involved in top level stuff. We're actually, you know, working. But even we have been aware of . . . jiggles in the continuum. Flux, as I said."

Breaking off, he lifted his head. His eyes narrowed, as if listening to something on the wind. He started walking, and Brigid ran after him, two steps to each of his.

"Where are we going?"

"We need to get over there." He gestured to a small recreational park, visible in the distance. It was wedged awkwardly in between a betting shop and a discount pharmacy, a patch of emerald green in between decidedly un-picturesquely aged constructions. "Quite quickly if that's ok."

"Why? What's the rush?"

Michael glanced up, then sideways, frowning. He seemed to be looking deeply into the air in front of them. Brigid stared in the same direction, expecting to see something jump into life, but it seemed as if whatever was happening was on a frequency with which she had not yet made contact.

"I have a sense something is about to happen." He lifted his hand level with his eyes as if measuring something or weighing the mass of the air. Then he stepped backwards, stepped forwards again, frowned, and continued forwards in a little dance that only he knew the steps to.

"Why the park? What's there?"

"Ley lines."

"What do you—?"

"Be quiet," he hissed, his eyes darkening. Deep lines cut into his forehead; the weight of ages obvious on him for the first time. His arm slid automatically to the sword that hung at his side but just rested lightly on it. He seemed taller, broader, and Brigid momentarily wondered how on earth she could have ever regarded him as a slightly comic, brotherly figure. What she saw before her now was something she could very well imagine standing tall at the gates of heaven, fighting on behalf of the heavenly hosts.

Responding intuitively to his alert, she glanced around nervously, and with her new senses she could feel a palpable static in the air. The smell of electricity seemed to be descending on them from above, and she felt her legs dissolve into weakness, as if they had turned completely to water.

"Hold on," he grunted, and before she knew it, his arm had swung around her waist and after a momentary feeling of weightlessness, they had moved closer to the park area. She couldn't tell whether he had flown, or engaged in a kind of angelic floating manoeuvre. She had just opened her mouth to ask what he thought he was doing when she saw that silver lines, which she swore were not visible two minutes earlier, were drifting up from the grass, steaming up as mist does from the dew on an icy morning. She hardly had time to register the fact that the lines were projecting upwards, forming almost a barrier around the border of the park, when her body jolted to a stop, and she found herself swung around behind Michael. The size of both his body and his armour meant she couldn't see what was in front of them, but the sound of his voice caused her to freeze in her tracks.

"Fraster. And friends, I see. What is your purpose here? This is not your domain."

His voice sounded nothing like the genial, brotherly timbre she had become used to. Gone was the smile, the playfulness, and the genuine eagerness to help. What she heard now struck awe into her heart. She heard steel, fury, determination, and it was a sound she could imagine reverberating down through the aeons as a saviour to those in peril and a poison to those who wished to do evil.

"My dear Michael. What a singular pleasure to see you."

The voice dripped like rancid honey, and Brigid felt her skin trying to crawl off her own body to get away from the sound.

"I'm surprised to see you here, I must say. I thought that this charge would be a little . . . high stakes for you."

There was a chuckle of voices, the sound of contaminated water trickling over pebbles in a stream that was gradually disappearing from drought, laying waste to all life before it. Against her better judgement, Brigid craned her neck, daring to catch a glimpse of what horrors stood before them.

"Why are you here?" asked Michael again.

"We need the girl."

"I think she prefers to be referred to as a woman, if it's all the same to you."

By repositioning her body, and with the regained use of her legs, Brigid could see what was happening in front of them, and given the build-up she was, all things considered, a little disappointed. Terrified, obviously, but disappointed in a deeper sense, as the beings who stood between her and Michael and the park looked decidedly human. A slightly angular form of human, it was true, but after what she had been exposed to over the past twenty-four hours, something that looked even vaguely human gave her an immediate sense of relief.

The man in the middle was tall and pale, and his sunken eyes glimmered like two polished stones. His dark suit seemed both utterly normal, but also out of place. The other three men (although this was not, she suspected, what they really were), were so nondescript as to be slightly concerning. She found it hard to isolate any of their features, and as soon as her eyes slipped away from them, she seemed to lose all sense of their existence.

Fraster smiled slowly, the smile of a being who would, with utter confidence, be having his own way very shortly.

"You're not what you once were, are you son?"

Michael stood silently, impassively.

"You do yourself a disservice, speaking to me as if I am one of your serfs," he said finally, quietly. "As if I will lose myself at your words and give you the upper hand. Make your move, if you have one, Fraster. I grow weary."

Brigid briefly wondered why he was speaking like something from a Tolkien novel, when there was the now familiar "rush, pop" sound and her guardian angel reappeared.

"Hi, Guinnie," hissed Michael, without taking his eyes off the beings in front of him. "Thanks for making the time for us."

"No worries," she said, rearranging what Brigid strongly suspected was her bra and patting her slightly dishevelled hair into place. "It's not like I was busy or anything."

Glancing up at him she grinned. "Oh, look at you all heroic. That's what I like to see." Out of the side of her mouth she whispered, "He's sexy when he's like this, isn't he?" and Brigid barely had a chance to murmur a non-committal grunt when the Archangel's voice boomed out again.

"I am Saint Michael the Archangel, Defender of divine glory, Ambassador of Paradise, Invincible Prince and Warrior and—"

Next to her, Brigid could practically feel Guindaline rolling her eyes. "Does he know what a wanker he sounds when he says all that?" she whispered. Then, more loudly, so he could hear, "You know you don't have to do the full introduction thing before you kick their arse anymore, don't you? You can just wade right in and get down to business."

Michael paused. "Really?"

"It's true. Been a while, hasn't it?"

"By that ridiculous display of hubris may I take it you're not going to hand her over?" called Fraster.

Michael brandished his sword and Guinnie pulled a scrunchy off her wrist and started pulling her hair up into a bun. "Do you have a bobby pin," she whispered to Brigid who stared at her like a rabbit in the headlights.

"Is there going to be a fight?" she squeaked.

Guinnie smiled broadly and started tucking her long robes into her underpants, which looked suspiciously like the netball shorts Brigid had worn in the '80s.

"My oath there is. And not before time. Demonic arse kicking is something that doesn't happen nearly enough these days." She glanced over at them. "I don't think this lot has gone full demon at this stage, but maybe a sound thrashing is just what they need to rethink their lives and their choices. Bring it on, arseholes!" she yelled towards them.

Brigid could feel Michael positively thrumming beside her, and she took a step backwards, wondering desperately where she fitted in all of this. Was she supposed to fight? Or run? She glanced behind at the park that was now fully enclosed by the silver shield. She couldn't help but think that she was supposed to be *inside* the secure and magical looking barrier.

"Stay behind us," said Guinnie. "He's worth eight of them, and I can take at least four, so it'll be over in a tick. Bit of a heart starter and then back home for third base." She winked at Brigid's pale face.

Fraster smiled his unearthly smile again.

"Certainly," he called over to them, and in the distance, just in front of the betting shop, Brigid saw a dark shimmer begin to form. It rose from the ground, very much like the lines around the park had risen just minutes earlier, but this mist had a denseness to it, a deepness that caused the surroundings to become quickly blocked out. The mass rose, formed what at first seemed to be vague figures, then solidified into shapes such as she had only ever seen in her nightmares; shapes that made the fairy seem like the kind of fluffy thing you would find featured on the calendar for an animal shelter.

Dark shapes, horns, what looked like an eyeball with tentacles, every rank and unnatural form that could be dreamed up in a Beksinski painting. As they took shape, their number seemed to multiply until there were seemingly hundreds of them streaming down the street. Brigid looked around wildly. How could other people not be seeing this? How was it possible that the entire suburb seemed filled with unspeakable hordes, but she was the only human aware of it? She could even see people walking through them, going about their daily business as they strode bodily through the foulest creatures Brigid had ever seen.

As people got to the heart of the mass they disappeared from her sight, invisible until they reappeared again at the other end of the street, oblivious to what they had waded through, although their faces were now grim and troubled. Most were frowning, some rubbed their foreheads as if they had been struck with a sudden migraine, and those walking with others seemed unconsciously to devolve into an argument, their angry faces shadowing the demeanours of the demons through which they had just passed.

"Fuck," said Guinnie.

"Steady." Michael motioned his hand in a downward motion. "It makes no difference how many they have. We have right on our side."

Without warning, Michael stepped towards the hoard, and Brigid saw Fraster motion to his own army. With one swift movement, the angel raised his jewelled sword into the air. Fire flowed from the aether above Michael's head through his arm into the sword, and it lit up with a blaze that Brigid imagined could be seen from space. Engravings and characters visible for the first time, flashed into life like incantations from another realm. Michael let out a roar and leapt forward.

What followed was a blur, but also an impossibly detailed play by play battle. Brigid saw Michael decapitate demons, saw him grab creatures with his free hand and thrust them into each other, saw him use bolts of energy summoned from the air to lay waste to those who were out of the reach of his sword.

Guinnie had also leapt into action, using moves that were barely visible to Brigid's eye to twist in the air and use the sword that had seemingly magically appeared in her own hand. Flashes of blue and gold cut through the demonic army more quickly than Brigid could register, and as each being was hit, they seemingly blinked out of existence.

So engrossed was she in watching the battle taking place before her, that she was taken by surprise when she felt a bone like hand on her arm, and a macabre voice in her ear.

"Come on, this way," it said calmly, and before she knew it she had stepped backwards, away from Michael. As soon as she realised what was happening, she tore her arm out of his grasp, only to feel the other one grabbed by his claw like hand.

"Get away from me," she barked but felt the words catch in her throat, as if she had spontaneously come down with laryngitis. She cast around desperately seeking Michael, but he seemed engulfed by the swarming horrors, and Guinnie, who was supposed to be here precisely for moments like this, was high kicking a three-foot-long mosquito with a horse's skull for a head and looked like she had her hands full.

The creature Fraster had both hands around her now, holding her with a deathly cold grip, and Brigid twisted herself around furiously as she found it harder and harder to move. A jolt of pain shot through her head, and she felt thoughts of steely determination fill her consciousness. Thoughts from outside forced themselves into her core, thoughts trying to make her mind lift itself up to that other level, the one Egragore had been trying to persuade her to lift to last night. But there was no query here, no gentle persuasion, just the persistent angry pain that said *Go up, go up. Do what you're told, human.*

She had no idea what was happening, except that she was being forced to do something against her will, and she was suddenly very, very angry. She deliberately let her body lose all momentum and drop to the ground, the unexpected weight loosening Fraster's grip on her but still, the pain and screaming in her head was all pervasive. She grabbed her head in her hands, her face a rictus of pain, and she felt herself involuntarily curling into a ball. *Alright* she spoke, replying to the intrusive thoughts. *Alright, I'll do it.*

She began to rearrange her mind, stepping up into a new framework. She desperately did not want to do it but she was powerless against the harsh intrusive ideas and felt the otherworldly sense of lifting that signified an alteration of her consciousness.

The pain gradually began to subside, as she accepted her fate and felt the sense of herself change into another form, the voice in her head let out a cry of sudden alarm and then was gone.

She found herself able to think and move again as if the previous thirty seconds had not happened. Lifting her head, she could see just behind her Michael and Guinnie battling the now considerably depleted demon hordes. The thought of *"my god they were right, they really could take them on"* flashed through her mind but was replaced quickly by the sight of Fraster snarling at something behind her, a look of murderous rage on his face. She hauled herself to her feet unsteadily.

"Fool, why did you do that? I had her. She was doing it. We nearly had her."

Egragore answered with a sense of calm fury. "Not like that. You know it can't be like that."

"But it was her will, she had accepted it, you ridiculous man."

She was unsure whether she could hear the voices out loud, or whether the beings were speaking telepathically, and her heightened senses were picking up on it, but when she felt Egragore say, *Go to the park, quickly*, it was unmistakable. *Is it safe?* she threw at him, When an exasperated, *Of course it's safe, why would I send you there if it wasn't safe* came back to her, she turned and ran towards the silver fenced area.

The noise of the tumultuous battle, while still technically raging, was dying down a little behind her, and became almost non-existent as she put her hand out to touch the shimmering semi-transparent barrier. With the painful memory of the forced thoughts fresh in her head, and with little choice but to believe Egragore when he had said it was safe, she stepped quickly through the ephemeral silver web.

Nineteen

"Why did you stop me?"

Fraster looked disbelievingly, furiously, at his colleague. "Don't you understand I nearly had her? That *we* nearly had her?" Seeing Egragore's eyes drift away, he swung around to see Brigid disappear within the safety of the park.

"You fool," he snarled. "Has your only purpose been to constantly get in my way? What actual use are you at all? Do you realise that your ridiculous ideals mean that you risk jeopardising all that I have worked for? What do you want?" he spat, beginning to pace backwards and forwards before Egragore. "What is it you want? Because I feel as if we might be working towards very different purposes and, trust me, my purpose is completely in line with the purpose of the Shadow Lands."

Egragore laughed humourlessly. "Rubbish. You have no sense of purpose at all. You're trying to form the Shadow Lands into another version of the Great Abyss and that seriously concerns me. You have no belief in redemption or love."

A creeping sneer leapt onto Fraster's face. "Oh my," he laughed, "redemption and love? Are you serious? Oh, please. Wait till we get back to the office. This is perfection. This is the best thing I've ever heard. A reaper who believes in redemptive love."

"No, you're the one who's forgotten where we came from," snapped Egragore. We aren't demons, we are reapers, you forgot that in your obsessive search for status and cynical point scoring. And you're the one who's always been drawn down to the baser level of our kind. All that time supervising the elementals has had an effect on you. Oh, I know that they're not evil as such but still, I have my doubts. Believing in redemptive love is no more counter intuitive than your vision of fiery pits. Neither of us want—"

What we have been given, he was going to say. But he bit back his words.

Behind them, with a mighty bellow, Michael cleaved the last head off a white lizard type dragon which spewed forth a mighty gush of ink-black viscous fluid, and then all was utterly quiet. He saw Michael and Guindaline high five each other and then look around for Brigid.

"We will speak more about this later," said Fraster, "and I have a feeling I will enjoy it immensely." With that he was gone.

Egragore swept his dark hair out of his eyes and cracked his neck from side to side. Putting his hands on his hips he looked around him, breathed deeply, and assessed the situation.

"Heeeeeeeeeey, sexy." Guinnie skipped over to him, pulling her hair out of its messy bun, and shaking it out so it cascaded like a golden wave down her back. She gave him a peck on the cheek. "Did you see that? Did you see my moves? I'm pretty flexible you know."

Egragore grinned despite himself. "Hey there, Guinnie. Yeah, you did a good job with that lot. You have moves."

"I do." She nodded to confirm the fact. "I do have moves. You know, I'm pretty sure they were actual demons. I don't mean your lot, the basic wet non-committal half-hearted thing you Shadow Lands guys do. I mean actual demons from the Great Abyss. Do you know anything about that?"

"You know I have nothing to do with the Great Abyss. I'm as far removed from that as you are."

She looked at him suspiciously and with a fair degree of disbelief.

"Fraster is one of yours though, isn't he?"

"Yes, of course he's one of ours. What are you saying?"

"There's something highly dodgy about him. I think you need to look into that. I'm pretty sure that he enlisted that lot's help. Unless they just spontaneously sensed the disagreement. It's happened before."

He ignored her words. "Good job of protecting Brigid," he called to Michael, who was walking towards them, occasionally stopping to peer into the air, or make strange gestures over different patches of ground.

"What are you doing?"

"He's eliminating principalities. Healing any . . . rifts in the . . . flux. Or something." Guinnie shrugged her shoulders. "He knows what he's doing, ok?"

"What's that?" asked Michael, as he made his way over to them.

"I said, good job of protecting Brigid."

"Thanks." Michael smiled. "Hang on. Shit." He looked around wildly.

Egragore gestured over to the park. "It's ok, I sorted it."

"What do you mean you sorted it?" Guinnie asked. "Why are you being helpful? You're a fucking pen pusher. You're not invested in any of this."

"I'm getting really fed up with this. I'm a reaper; we don't just file papers all day, you know. I'm sick of people always assuming the worst of me. Have you never heard of assuming positive intent? Why does everyone think I'm as good as evil? You go around shagging actual demons and no one questions your position as a gorgeous and heavenly guardian angel. Oh, nooooo." He waved his hands around in the air in what Guinnie considered to be a decidedly unattractive manner. "The double standards are just breathtaking."

"All right, all right, calm down, I get your point." She peered at him through her long lashes, sizing up his current outfit of leather pants, satin jacket and red cravat over a black shirt. "You're much hotter when you don't talk, by the way. Are we done?"

Michael nodded. "I can't see why not. The dimensional rift that allowed them to populate this sector has disappeared, but I've got no idea how it opened up at all. You head off and we can catch up later, if needed."

Guinnie blew Egragore a kiss and was gone.

"She's really hard work. It's not just me, is it? It can't be just me. She seems like really hard work." Egragore looked to Michael for confirmation.

"Yeah," confirmed Michael. "But she can really fight, and I needed all the help I could get just now. There was a minute when, hang on, what are you doing here anyway?"

"Fraster was forcing Brigid to step up a level, trying to get her to connect with Mur-arb against her will, and I sensed it, so I stepped in." Egragore shrugged. "It's unacceptable for him to do that."

"Mur-arb?" Michael frowned. "I don't think I know them. Tempter or reaper?"

Shit. Egragore realised Michael had missed some fundamental points along the way.

"You don't know who Mur-arb is?"

"I just said that. Sounds like a pirate."

"Do you know that my lot has moved up to the Heavenly Realm?"

"What?"

"And all of your lot up there have disappeared?"

"What?"

"This is not good. What have you even been doing? Do you know anything?"

"If you hadn't noticed, I know how to kick a demon's arse."

"Fair point. There have been some changes you really need to know about. I'll fill you in."

They started walking over to the park where Brigid was sitting, idly swinging on the rusted swing. "In short, it was the human's fault, of course. Some science thing has thrown everything to shit."

"Fucking humans," said Michael.

Twenty

Brigid had, meanwhile, been learning about New and Interesting things. She'd decided she needed to reframe the current happenings in her life as "new and interesting things", otherwise she may have a nervous breakdown which she really didn't have time for. Apparently, all her efforts were currently going to need to be directed towards keeping her body safe and not abducted, so self-indulgent mental health issues were going to have to take a number and wait in an increasingly long line.

On arriving at the park, she had stepped through the silver fence, and had been surprised to see a beach in front of her. Not a little cordoned off pool with sand, for instance, but a beach, in its entirety, stretching out before her. Luxurious, warm, and expansive. Quite far removed from a tiny, one block sized park in suburban Melbourne, boasting a swing from the 1970s and a rubbish bin with a Keep Australia Beautiful sticker with a dick drawn on it.

Screw it, she thought. At least it's not raining. And so, she stepped in.

The heat of the sun was the first thing that hit her. Warm, yet not burning. Odd.

Glancing up with shielded eyes, she noticed two suns blazing in the sky. Odd.

Not Earth, she decided casually.

Far down the beach she could see a figure reclining in what looked like a deck chair, and she decided that heading towards this figure was as good an idea as any.

On the way, she removed her shoes.

When she reached him, the figure on the deck chair beamed up on her. He resembled nothing so much as a leather bag; worn, sinewed, but with an open face, and a smile that restored your faith in all things you may have lost faith in.

"Brigid," he said.

She wasn't surprised that he knew her name.

He gestured to the spare deck chair next to him that had not been there twenty seconds previously, so she sat down.

"How are you?" he asked. And because he sounded like he really wanted to know, and because she had the inexplicable feeling that he already knew a fair bit about her, she told him.

After that, they sat for a while watching the tide come in. Green fish that looked a little like kittens leaped out of the water, and occasionally tumbled up the shore towards them before rolling back down and diving into the water again.

She may have napped a bit.

After a while he began to talk again.

"Bubbles upon bubbles," he said.

A pause.

"I'm sorry?" she said, more politely than she strictly felt necessary.

"It's just bubbles upon bubbles. With some of the bubbles joining up occasionally and forming bigger bubbles."

"I—"

"And then, and I do especially like this bit, a little bubble can join up with other bubbles, so they are like a whole—"

"Look, I think I should—"

"Ooh, a corridor. Or a tunnel. But probably more of a corridor. That's what they're like. Like a corridor. So, things can come and go as they please."

Brigid stopped interrupting and decided to ride it out.

The man sat back in his deck chair, smiling contentedly. "I did like that bit. The connecty bubbles. Such a lovely feeling of expansive oneness."

He laid his head back and let the twin sun's rays warm his ancient face.

Brigid waited a few beats, wondering if he was going to start talking about bubbles again. Despite the fact she had been thrown into a whole world of unpredictable conversations of late, this one was definitely testing her.

Something suddenly occurred to her.

"Hang on, are you saying . . ."

He opened his eyes and looked at her piercingly. He seemed to be able to vacillate between doddery old man and gimlet-eyed eagle with no effort at all.

"Are you saying that all of these bubbles are separate universes? And that they all exist in conjunction with each other, but also quite independent and separate, and sometimes, in certain circumstances, the membrane between them, the veil if you will, thins out to allow contact between each universe? And that—"

The man shrugged his bony shoulders. "I don't know. I really don't." He tapped his head wryly. "Things aren't what they once were up here, you know. Trying to fit an omnipotent brain into the constraints of a biological evolutionary process, well, something had to give, didn't it? It's up to you young ones to make the great theological and philosophical leaps now."

Some of the kitten creatures had found a jellyfish looking thing the size of a small car on the sand and were trying to pull it back into the water. When they couldn't get a good grip on it with their teeth they decided to roll in it instead.

"What I think it is crucial for you to understand," he started.

"Yes?"

"Is that we really all just needed a holiday."

She nodded calmly.

"Sorry, who?"

He turned to her, a look of seriousness on his wizened face.

"I do think though that he needs some help. The new bloke."

"What? Are you suggesting that I should go up?" she gestured upwards with her finger.

He nodded and mirrored the gesture. "That's right. I feel like it might be important. Or not. It could end terribly badly. It's hard for me to know these days." He shrugged. "As I said, I'm losing it a bit. It's quite lovely."

After a while, Brigid explained that she really must be going and pulled herself out of the deck chair. The Man waved merrily as she headed back up the beach, and she thought that his parting words, caught on the wind as they travelled to her were, *you should ring your mother.*

She waved to acknowledge she'd heard him and continued to where she hoped to find a portal to her own world, reflecting on the fact that it was a damn shame that she hadn't brought her bikini because, as a child of the '80s, she would never lose her belief that a tan was always the best look.

Twenty-one

It did not take Brigid very long to get heartily sick of the lot of them.

Michael, she understood. He was supposed to be following her around. But Egragore, that was another matter. He sat moodily on her sofa, staring out the window or scrolling through Brigid's Instagram feed, refusing to answer her requests of "so why are you here?"

Eventually, Michael beckoned her into the bathroom.

"He's having a hard time," he said by way of explanation.

"Excuse me? Is he the one being tracked by a demon horde?"

"Possibly. That's part of the problem. What do you know about him?"

Brigid thought. "Well, I know he's a reaper, and that he's been charged with getting me to help this guy I used to know, and I've made his job very difficult because it sounds like a terrible idea to me. And the fact that some demon with a horde tried to abduct me yesterday, has done nothing to allay me of that fact."

"Right."

Michael sat down on the toilet. The absolute absurdity of an angel lightly perching on the lip of a toilet would have delighted her even a week ago. Now, she had bigger fish to fry.

"That guy, Fraster. He's one of Egragore's colleagues. They've worked together for time immemorial. But now they seem to be having some professional differences about their purposes and the purpose of the entire Shadow Lands."

"Where does the horde come into it?"

"That's part of the problem. It seems they could have possibly been demonic, from the Great Abyss. And Fraster seemed to be working with them, which calls into question his allegiances. The whole point of the Shadow Lands is that they're supposed to be impartial. They do extra paperwork to decide if souls are supposed to be in The Great Abyss or go up into the Heavenly Realm. It's like a kind of extra assessment process for people who weren't quite good enough for up, or quite bad enough for down."

"So, I take it this Fraster shouldn't have been working with the Great Abyss to try and enlist me then."

"That's right."

"But if he shouldn't be working with the Great Abyss, then should Egragore be working with you?"

"It's a bit of a tricky one," said Michael, tearing a piece of toilet paper up into tiny bits and letting them drift down onto the tiled floor. "He's not actually working with me obviously; we've just been drawn together because of our mutual interest in you. But the fact that he consciously stopped you being taken up is also a problem, as some up there see it as a case of the greater good and all that."

"When I was on the beach, I think I began to understand a bit of what's been happening. He explained it like . . . like all these universes exist next to each other, and sometimes there is crossover, and sometimes they're quarantined. So, I'm thinking that the whole Heavenly Realm may have moved themselves to another universe."

"Been moved, more accurately."

"Been moved then."

There was a pause.

"Why didn't they take you when they left? And Guinnie?"

He looked nonplussed. "Maybe it all happened so quickly. I don't know, I wasn't there, but Egragore says the place was totally deserted by the time he got a chance to look around."

"Snoop around," she said wryly. "But why is he still here? In my house, I mean. Doesn't he have a job to go to?"

"Partly, I think he wants to keep an eye on you, and partly because . . ." He thought for a moment. "He's scared. I think he's scared of what he'll find when he goes back up."

"He can't just sit here for ever. I need my phone back for a start."

She went out into the lounge room.

"Why are you still here?"

He looked up from her phone. "To keep an eye on you of course. Nothing useful can happen up there until you decide to come with me, you know. We're all just marking time."

"And I'm not coming up until I know more about what I'm getting myself into."

"Let me see if I can explain—" he started.

"Michael says you're scared."

Egragore sat in front of her, and an impossible stillness came about him. "Michael doesn't know what he's talking about," he said quietly.

"An archangel, one of the pinnacles of the entirety of creation, doesn't know what he's talking about?"

"For a pinnacle, he's pretty out of the loop. And no, he doesn't. He doesn't know what he's talking about, because he doesn't understand human emotions because he's never been human." His voice caught in his throat.

"What is that supposed to mean?"

Egragore stood and nervously moved around the room.

"How is your masking practise going? Are you getting better at blocking the dimensional fauna out of your vision? We need to work on your supernatural hygiene if you're going to be able to integrate your new understandings with your normal life."

"Were you human?" Her voice was soft.

Egragore stared at her. She saw the weight of the centuries cascading through him, impossible grief and unstoppable tides of hope and dismay. The full impact of every thought he had ever had was transmitted through one look, and she realised what she had seen in his eyes was a remaining spark of essential humanity. His thoughts were her thoughts, and she felt she understood the essence of him, and he her. She felt her breath stop in her chest and . . .

Her phone rang.

"It's your mother," said Egragore, handing it to her, and the moment was gone.

Twenty-two

Brigid wouldn't want anyone to think that she had a bad relationship with her parents. Quite the contrary. They never fought. Whenever they spoke things were perfectly amicable. They asked about her job, she told them. She asked them about their online shop where they sold water that had been activated by infusing it with quartz under the light of the full moon and managed not to laugh out loud while she did so. It was all perfectly amicable and surface level, and that was just the way Brigid liked it.

Not because they were bad people; they were utterly lovely. Everyone said so. It was just hard to become your own person when your parents were such forces of nature.

From the hippy commune, from being arrested at blockades, and building their own house out of wine bottles and mud; they had strong feelings, strong passions, firm values and they liked to make them very clear.

Quite hard to know your own mind when your parents had so many. . . opinions.

No one could say she wasn't a good daughter. It was just that she was frightfully busy, and this was just the way life went. You grew apart from your parents. Healthy and normal boundaries were absolutely essential in the development of the self. As a matter of fact she was pretty sure they were the ones who had taught her that. If you had asked her, she would have told you she was very happy…nay proud…of the way she had constructed her own world view, forged her own beliefs and made meaning of her existence in general. It just so happened to be very, very different from that of her parents.

Well, it *had* been different.

Now she wasn't so sure.

So, when the phone rang, hot on the heels of the strange-man-on-the-beach telling her to ring her mother, well, it was quite a surprise.

She self-consciously snatched her phone out of Egragore's hand, and he turned and walked into the kitchen. She sat heavily back onto the sofa and took a deep breath before accepting the call.

"Hi, Mum. What's up?"

"Is this a mobile number?" Her mother's voice managed to sound tinny and far away, as if she was calling from 1987.

"Yes, Mum. You've called me on the mobile."

"Do you have a plug-in phone I can call you on? A land line? You used to have one. What happened to it?"

"I got rid of it, Mum. I didn't need to pay two bills."

"I don't want to be complicit in you getting brain cancer."

"Mobiles don't give you brain cancer, Mum."

"You know if you wear tourmaline earrings, they can modify the electromagnetic energy coming out of the phone. Or a tourmaline phone case. I feel like I would have already told you this. Have I told you this? Actually, that's an idea. Frank!" she yelled off into the distance, as Brigid closed her eyes and sighed. She turned the phone to speaker so she could lay down and prepare herself for the conversation.

"Frank, write this down. Tourmaline phone cases. Embedded with chakra crystals to identify the mood of the person you're talking to. Oooh, that's good. Right, so, we're worried about you."

"That's nice, I appreciate it. Is it the fluoride in the water?"

"Don't be silly; we're big fans of that these days. My teeth have never been better. No, Dad had a dream you were being chased by demons and you weren't doing a very good job of standing up for yourself, which we thought was odd seeing as you've always been so assertive, so I thought I should call you to see what's been happening."

Suddenly alert, Brigid swung her legs back over the side of the sofa and sat up.

"What?"

"Yes, there was a horde of demons, or some kind of physical manifestation of 5G towers is my guess, attacking you. An angel was fighting them on your behalf apparently, so Dad is a bit worried he's being inculcated by the Judeo-Christian paradigm, because apparently the angel was St Michael. However, he's been communicating with his Buddhist spirit guide, Vairochana, and he's assured him it's just his patriarchal need for domination manifesting in his dreams. Dad says that's all very well, but it was a very real dream, and he wanted me to ring you to check you're alright."

There was a pause.

"So, everything alright?"

Keeping her voice light and breezy, as she always did when her heart threatened to beat itself out of her chest, she asked, "Do you remember anything weird happening? Back when I was little?"

"You'll have to narrow that down a bit, love. What kind of weird do you mean specifically? Because a lot of strange things happened when you were little, and a disproportionately large amount of them were concerned with mung beans."

"Can I come and visit?"

The words were out of her mouth before she had a chance to realise what she was saying. Something was coming towards her. She didn't know what it was, but just maybe her parents had some answers.

Her mother's voice took on a seriousness Brigid hadn't heard for a long time.

"Yes, yes, I think that's a good idea. We do need to talk to you, actually. If you're interested, that is. If you're opening your mind. Are you opening your mind, dear? Because in the past you—"

The conversation was interrupted by Frank's voice in the background.

"Your father is reminding me that my two-minute time limit is up. I don't want to be responsible for you using a mobile phone for any longer than that. Unless you're wearing tourmaline. Are you wearing tourmaline?"

Given that she was not, in fact, wearing tourmaline, her mother terminated the call, but the tone in her voice made Brigid realise she was excited for her only child to come and visit, and she would probably be breaking out the afghan throws and the good mead for the occasion.

Twenty-three

Egragore was scared to go back.

Maybe "scared" was too strong a word. "Trepidatious" was what he had been feeling ever since he had come to terms with the fact that yes, Fraster had enlisted *literal* demonic forces to kidnap Brigid. He was both horrified at the blatant disregard of basic rules that had been set down at levels far above their pay grade, but also somewhat impressed at the sheer bloody-minded determination displayed by his colleague.

Now *that* was leadership.

Clearly leadership that was utterly unsuitable for the Shadow Lands, where consensus, and clear impartial thinking were the order of the day, but for other, more chaotic or dictatorial Realm? Perfection. He would tell Fraster that when he saw him, Egragore decided. Obviously, there would be the need for some kind of censure, given that he had blatantly ignored directives, but there was no reason why praise couldn't be sandwiched between some pointers as to appropriate behaviour going forward. Perhaps he could wait until his next performance review. No need to jump the gun.

It took Egragore a while to realise something was amiss in the Shadow Lands. He had quietly manifested himself back into his office and had caught up with some outstanding assessment paperwork. It didn't matter what else was happening; what tricky political deals needed to be negotiated or what personality deficiencies needed to be balanced, there were always souls that needed to be given a second chance (or at least a fighting chance), at redemption.

He had spent an invigorating few hours setting an ex-far-right wing politician (ex because said politician was dead, not because they had reconsidered their views, it should be noted) a range of tasks that included eating a vegan diet for two years, becoming an advocate for gender fluidity in public bathroom use, and volunteering in a mosque. He set up a parallel mini-universe for this to occur in (they still ran most of these as offshoots of their old work space; it was still there to be used, after all, and the delivery bays and reticulated eclipse machine would be hard to set up from scratch again), and doubted that she would get through all the "challenges" as he liked to call them, before spontaneously bursting into flames and plunging into the Great Abyss for all eternity, but one had to give them an opportunity, at the very least.

Egragore considered tasks such as these much more difficult to withstand than Fraster's literal and frightfully old-fashioned flaming inferno. They involved far more self-growth and soul searching than a decent roasting ever had. The herculean efforts that he was asking should be seen as the harder path, he thought to himself as he finished off for the evening.

It was the lack of activity outside his office that eventually drew him out into the foyer. There had been a muffled thudding noise going on for some time, which faded into the background as he had been working, but gradually it became harder to ignore. As he stepped into the open area outside his office, his feet sinking into the pristine white carpet of the foyer, the flashing *"Welcome to the Shadow Lands"* sign was the only movement his eyes could detect. The faint thudding noises continued, and if he really strained his ears, he could hear a vague cheering that swelled up after each thud.

Checking in some neighbouring offices, he continued down the hallway in the direction of the sounds. Looking in on Mur-arb's wing, he called a hello through the door.

"Helloooooo." Mur-arb appeared eagerly from within the depths, a solitary figure carrying a flask of some sort. "Would you like to sample some of my new hemp Kombucha? I think I've finally tweaked the recipe so that it can be kept down."

Egragore promised he would swing by for a sample on the way back and walked on. He felt pulled by the thuds and cheers but wasn't specifically heading in one direction. Soon he found himself in an area he had never seen before, although whether this was because he had simply missed it or because it had only recently spontaneously appeared he did not know (this did happen with alarming regularity, and a task force had been commissioned to look into it). Large doors, like those of a sports centre gymnasium on steroids loomed before him, and behind them was the unmistakable source of the noises that had pulled him here.

He shouldered the heavy doors ajar, a fierce swathe of heat shot out through the gap, and with another push, the massive doors opened to reveal an immense space; one that would have been impossible to exist within a building of typical temporal constraints. It appeared that a Conjoinal Vortex had been fashioned for the occasion. Had Fraster done this? Or had he enlisted Mur-arb's help? It seemed more expansive than the kind of things that reapers could usually do.

How it existed was not, at this precise moment, important. What was important was that it existed at all, and this fact was causing his eyes to bulge unnaturally in a kind of enthralled horror.

During the recent meeting that had culminated in Fraster turning into a cane toad, Fraster had advocated for his ideal version of the Shadow Lands. One that involved the complete dismissal of all advances in thought, theory and practise that had been made in Practical Redemption over the past one thousand years and a return to the bad old days of traditional, old fashioned gratuitous punishment-centred purgatory. By the looks of it, Fraster had made great inroads in making this an actuality. What lay in front of him, massive and monstrous, was a cavern sunk into the earth; a gaping open wound cut into the ground. Its jagged edges projected up, forming crags and ridges. From deep down within this fissure came an impossibly intense heat; a blood red glow with the occasional lick of flame vomiting out of it, roasting the monolithic rocks that layered the sides of the cavern.

Egragore knew now where all his staff were, why the halls and offices and meeting rooms had been vacant. They were all here and, most absurdly of all, they were dressed as if it were a frighteningly realistic Halloween party. Some wore devils' horns and tails and carried pitchforks, capering around as if they were dancing a Scottish reel. Others were dressed in flowing white robes with halos and wings.

He knew they were not, in reality, angels, of course, they were his staff, but they floated and dipped and manoeuvred clever little pirouettes in the air, swooping down, arms extended, to the teeming multitudes of naked souls who filled the cavern, climbing and falling back, desperately trying to claw their way out of what must have been unbearable, excruciating heat. As each person came close to touching the hands of an angel imposter, the flying figure would snatch their hands away and make a *whoops* expression with their face, and this, Egragore realised finally, was the source of the cheers. Every time a desperate human fell back into the pit, there would be rapturous cheers and cat calls from all those enjoying the show.

The doors closed behind him, and he stepped forward despite himself, knowing what had happened, but not wanting to consider the implications of this fact too deeply. Fraster must have taken matters into his own hands; this plan that Egragore had so clearly vetoed was happening right before his eyes.

He noticed one of the more gaudily dressed characters sweeping towards him, and as it drew closer, he could see it was Fraster. He came to a halt in front of Egragore, and Fraster's nun costume was on full display, a sexy nun's costume at that. A costume that, to Egragore, looked jarring at the best of times, but here, on his colleague, looked utterly absurd and horrific.

"I'm sorry, I only have a Popeye costume left. Would you like that one, or would you prefer to go without?"

Egragore stared pointedly at Fraster's habit. "I take it they didn't have any toad outfits?"

Fraster's eyes glinted, but he turned and gestured to the spectacle that lay, apocalyptically and glowing, beyond them.

"I'm dying to know. What do you think? I've been mulling it over in my mind for a while now, and then when you decided not to turn up for a few days I thought, why not? Nothing ventured, nothing gained. I read something recently when I was down on Earth, in a house of one of those creatures you seem to relate to so well."

He lightly brought his fingers together into a diamond shape and thought for a moment. "I believe it said, *if it's important you will find a way. If not, you'll find an excuse.* Isn't that wonderful? So, a little vortex manipulation, a few invitations sent out, cracked into the props cupboard downstairs and voila." He held his hand up majestically. "Dream it and you can do it."

"This is barbaric."

"Yes, I *know.* I'm so glad that's the message you got from it because it really is what I was going for." Fraster seemed almost giddy with excitement. "I really feel it connects us with our forefathers, don't you? Oh, and this is a touch I know you probably won't appreciate ." He drew Egragore closer to the pit, "Dante is *actually* down there somewhere. How wonderful is that? We had to pull him out of limbo for the occasion, but that's really the point, isn't it? I pulled some big names just to create a profile, as it were. Create a bit of a buzz. Stirring up interest." Fraster almost crackled with excitement and demonic pleasure. "And everyone's loving it. Just look."

"Well, not quite everyone," observed Egragore dryly. "The souls are having an ordinary time by the looks of it."

As if inspired by his words, a great grey dragon-like head emerged from the cavern. Covered with glistening scales, eyes blazing a sickly green, it towered above the cavern, tilting its neck to take in the enormity of the horror and despair that its very existence was causing. Throwing its mouth open, it reared up to its full, gargantuan expanse, its shining scales reflecting the faces of naked horror that undulated below, until finally, it snapped its jaws shut, crunching and ripping the bodies that had fallen into its mouth.

"Ooh," grimaced Fraster, shivering a little with delight. "That's quite nasty. I surprise myself with my inventiveness."

"But what *good* is this?" asked Egragore. "I can see that people are suffering so yes, technically yes, well done, this is how we perfect souls, but all we're doing here is creating suffering. Where's the good that's being done? I have the strong suspicion you don't understand our job description in any way at all."

"What good?" Fraster spat out the words. "Why, there's no good at all. You and your obsession with higher purposes. It will be your undoing, mark my words." He shook his head in mock exasperation. "These people weren't "good" enough, and that's the whole point of this. They failed at being the humans they were supposed to be, and they have to be punished until they're sorry. Soundly punished. Severely punished. Stop trying to inject your own agenda into it."

Egragore saw a man scrabbling around on a burning rock, blindly trying to find his head so he could reattach it to his flaming body. "I'd say he looks quite sorry now, wouldn't you? Has he had enough, would you say?"

Fraster seemed to be distracted by the screaming that reverberated off the walls, as the dragon came back for a second round. "You know what, this is ridiculously loud. Let's talk outside."

With relief, Egragore stepped back out of the room of horror and the door closed, masking much of the sound.

"That's better." Fraster removed his headpiece, confetti flying everywhere.

"Did you have to make it all quite so . . . festive?" asked Egragore.

"These beings have been working hard. They need to unwind. You do have many good qualities, but looking after staff welfare isn't one of them," critiqued Fraster. "They needed to let off some steam, so I delivered. Leadership," he winked, tapping the side of his nose.

"But where's the good?" Egragore kept pushing the question. "Surely the fundamental essence of purifying people, of making them worthy, was creating good works out of their suffering. Because the Earth needs more—"

"Bah, you're obsessed with that place. Always have been. And with your ridiculous *good works*."

The air quotes and the mocking voice did show that Fraster was in a reasonably good mood, which Egragore hoped he could capitalise on. He was always easier to deal with when he was in a good mood.

"It's at times like these I see how you almost made it up there," continued Fraster pointing. "I mean that metaphorically, of course. We are up there now, aren't we?" He laughed, clapping Egragore on the back. "It's almost as if you think inhabiting this space makes up for the fact they didn't want you. Have you ever thought about that? And it was so, so close, wasn't it? So amusing we once thought it was all omnipotence and omnipresence and the like."

Egragore could tell that Fraster himself had been ruminating on this possibility quite a lot lately. "It's almost as if you're trying to make your *own* heaven, isn't it?", laughing uproariously as Egragore felt his face redden.

"Anyway, must get back in there, all the humans are going to turn into piñatas soon, and given the planning I've put into it there's no way I want to miss that bit. Yes, literally piñatas. Although it's not going to be candy coming out of them, as you may have guessed. And as far as I'm concerned, the key issue for you right now is getting that girl. We can't make any real changes until she's reunited with Mur-arb, and time is ticking away. Tick tock."

"You certainly seem to be making some big changes," said Egragore limply, gesturing to the fiery inferno within, and regretting the words as soon as they were out of his mouth.

"It's not really a change though, is it," said Fraster. "It's exactly how we used to do things. It's just a return to the good old days. Days that you, my friend, would do well to remember."

Fraster disappeared back inside through a crack in the door, and Egragore heard him call to him, *"Remember, suffering is good for the soul."*

As Egragore headed back through the building to keep his appointment with some god-awful kombucha, he reflected on his increasing suspicion that cleansing souls wasn't at the forefront of Fraster's mind at the moment, but for the time being he was powerless to understand exactly what he was playing at.

Twenty-four

"So, remind me why we're here?"

Lauren started collecting minties wrappers from the floor at her feet, and, twisting around, looked for the lid of her bottle of coke. "I mean, I know in theory, but what should be my main talking points if I'm asked?"

"You can't bring that rubbish inside, for a start. They won't want toxin wrappers in the house. Although that was Mum's main obsession last time I was up here. She might have moved on, but I'm in no frame of mind to risk it."

Lauren held the handful of rubbish up in the air towards the back seat. "Can you please magic this away for me, Angel?"

"I do wish she wouldn't do that," protested Michael. "It's not magic, it's science, and that kind of comment just plays into the stereotype."

"He says it's not magic, it's science, and I think you're annoying him."

"Can you science it away then, please?"

The rubbish disappeared from Lauren's hand.

"That's amazing," she said. "I'm so glad you're all woo-woo now. It's the best thing ever. I hardly have to lift a finger. I'm all special and important just by association."

"I'm glad my life crisis is enabling your idleness. I'll be sure to write that in your karmic record."

"Can you do that?" Lauren looked momentarily worried before moving on. "Anyway, do we have a safe word? Something that will tell me to stop talking, or start talking about whelks or global warming or something? I'm going to try really hard not to get you into trouble, and I don't know if I can stress this strongly enough, I can't promise anything."

Brigid thought for a moment, the familiar landmarks from her childhood passing by like a visual timeline. Although they had moved away from the commune, they had stayed in the same area; the land was subdivided and sold, but they had managed to buy some at a reduced rate.

"God, I don't know. Everything. I'm increasingly feeling that my sense of reality is tenuous at best. Most of the things I need to talk to people about at this stage have a high probability of getting me locked up somewhere. Or getting funding to open my own distance Reiki clinic."

She saw the lake on the right where she'd broken a canoe as an eleven-year-old and had tried to hide it in the bulrushes, too scared to tell anyone it had been her. The cemetery where it was general knowledge that disembodied orange lights floated in the dead of night. The art gallery where her father had worked, briefly and mortifyingly, as a life model.

"I just need some clarity," she explained. "I need to know if anything especially weird happened when Juniper was running the commune. Was there any indication what was happening there was real? The delusions? I mean, what's happening to me now is real, and it seems to have stemmed from when I was young, so did Mum and Dad have any knowledge of what was going on? From a paranormal point of view?"

"Are we going to touch on why they let a ten-year-old become a semi-religious icon for a bunch of stoned hippies, for example?"

"I think I remember Mum said it was good for my self-esteem, or something along those lines."

"I didn't realise self-esteem had been invented back in the '80s."

"It was new. Anyway, I don't want to have to delve too deeply into things. I'd rather this didn't become a recovered memory session, so we need to tread lightly."

Lauren extracted another wrapper from under her thighs and held it up, smiling smugly when it disappeared. "It's funny," she said, "because I never got the impression your life had been damaged at all. I mean, I didn't even know about this whole palaver until recently, and I certainly would never have labelled your life as "damaged". You seem to be doing ok."

Brigid thought for a moment. "I think it's more a question of it stopping me from being what I might have been. It stunted me."

"You think you're stunted, do you?"

They drove on in silence for several kilometres.

"I should probably just let you know," said Brigid as she pulled the car off the highway and slowed down to a crawl as it bumped over a cattle grid, "that my parents might not call me Brigid, and I don't want you to be caught off guard."

"What do you mean they might not?"

"I mean they know, technically, but they sometimes forget. Mum does, anyway."

"And that's because?"

"It's not the name I was born with."

"I don't think it's possible for me to express how excited I am about what I'm about to hear." Lauren turned to her friend, grinning widely. "So, Brigid is not the name your radically hippy parents named you. I am stunned."

Brigid bit her lip. "I don't feel as if you're supporting me in the most appropriate way at this very difficult moment in my life. I just always felt that my name was supposed to be Brigid, so I changed it when I turned eighteen."

"Tell me. Please, please tell me. What's your birth name?"

"Cosmic Peace-Ruby."

Lauren's laughter had almost subsided by the time they pulled up in front of the mud brick cottage that Brigid's parents called home.

"Your father is seeing the Deshas again. Remember them? Those spirit being things that used to hang around the house telling us that you needed to go to mainstream schooling. They're back" said Brigid's mother by way of greeting as they walked up the cobbled stone path. "I personally think it means something untoward is afoot, but he won't be told. He keeps discussing politics and the European Union with them."

Brigid glanced behind her at Lauren who was manoeuvring a few bags with difficulty through the solid old door. The house had been fashioned from mainly salvaged materials from an 1800s furniture emporium that had been demolished to make way for the brick and tile sensations that were the '80s, and apparently Victorians were considerably smaller than current day bodies. She grabbed one of the suitcases to prevent Lauren from knocking a large chunk of mudbrick out of the wall.

"Alrighty then," she said amicably. "Hi, Mum, how are you?" She kissed her on the cheek, noticing how the wrinkles were deeper than the last time she had seen her.

"Hello there, love, it's so good to see you. He hasn't seen them since that business with Juniper and that silly Mur-arb, so it was quite a surprise when they just popped up out of thin air the other week, wasn't it Frank? And now you're here, so something is obviously going on. My pendulum is being no help at all, bloody thing. Although it did tell me it's time I remembered your decision to be known by your chosen name, and it's very disrespectful of me to forget, so that's sorted then."

Brigid looked around the room, but her father didn't seem to be in it.

"Frank," Pat called again. "I said, you haven't seen the Deshas since they started telling you we should move out of the commune years ago, isn't that right?"

Her father wandered into the room, drying his hands on an old piece of flannelette sheet that had been ripped into a rag. "Hello, sweetheart", he said, hugging his daughter. "They visit me, you see."

"Do you remember them, Brigid? You must remember them. It would have been a good six months that they were visiting with him back in the day. Six months, was it? They sat around telling him that he needed more roughage in his diet and suggesting that we should move you to the local high school; that Juniper's friend was just taking too much energy out of you." She called after her husband's retreating back as he left through another adjoining door.

"I didn't appreciate their advice at the time though, I must say. I was putting plenty of wheat germ in your rice muffins as it was. Hello, dear, you must be Lauren. I'm Pat."

Lauren was kissed too.

"You shouldn't have taken it personally, love", came a man's voice. "I think they knew that I was buying takeaway fish and chips on the side and they weren't happy about the cholesterol. They were supporting you, actually."

Her father reappeared and took a mug down from the cupboard. "I liked the fact I could sit down and have a chat with them. A friendly chat. They were always so chatty. And they *did* give us some good advice, remember?"

"Yes, well a stopped clock is always right once a day," conceded Pat, pulling open the oven door. "Or is that twice? Scones, girls?"

Lauren dropped the bags she was carrying on the floor and eagerly helped herself to a scone, and within minutes she and Pat were discussing recipes, and cream/lemonade ratios.

Brigid looked around, reacquainting herself with the home she had never lived in, but that, on the occasions that she took time to make the journey down, instantly relaxed her. Her eyes were drawn to the wooden staircase that led to the upstairs bedroom: a curving set of steps that had been taken from an old department store. The heavy steps were worn with age, and vines from the philodendron that her mother grew, crept around the bannisters. These were only one of the multitude of plants that grew in the room; a monstera reached the high ceiling, ferns lined the windows and peace lilies covered the top of the fridge.

Not for the first time, Brigid reflected on the fact that here, you felt you were in a jungle of some kind; the whole dwelling was an earth ship, made of mud brick and wood, and barely any modern materials graced the presence, except for the usual kitchen appliances and a large radio that sat on the solid wooden table. Leadlight windows looked out onto an overgrown garden, and through bannisters that ran along a mezzanine area, Brigid could see thick woven rugs lining the upstairs walls.

She raised her levels a little, just a little, and sure enough, there were five Deshas sitting on the staircase. Roughly human sized but with wispy bodies that drifted away into nothing (as far as Brigid could see; those bits may have been on another level), their elongated heads and large smiles made them look like Muppet characters. Brigid gave a half smile, and the Deshas waved delightedly at her.

Michael was standing by the door, displaying his typical Protection Angel persona: regal and steady. Brigid assumed he was trying to impress the Deshas with his angelic gravitas, which, for some obscure reason, irritated her slightly. Who was he trying to impress? She noticed her father wink in Michael's direction and narrowed her eyes suspiciously.

"Why were you winking at the door?" she snapped.

"Wink? No wink. Must have been a twitch."

Michael glanced at her guiltily and shrugged his shoulders. "I don't know why you're so on edge," he said to Brigid. "This is a nice thing. Family together again. Most people would be happy." Ignoring Brigid's glare, he stepped forwards and held out a massive hand to her father.

"Hi there, Frank. Good to see you again."

"G'day, mate." Grinning, he wrapped his arms around the angel. "It's so good to see you. Did you say hi to the Deshas?"

Michael waved at the staircase, and again the Deshas merrily waved back. They seemed to be having an absolute ball of a time.

"Look, I have to say, this is unexpected," admitted Brigid who had personally considered herself approaching the Realm of the unflappable and was slightly disappointed at being caught off guard. "You can see him?"

"Of course," they both answered. The two men had let go of each other but were still beaming.

"Can I grab a cup of tea?" asked Lauren who seemed to be loving the whole scene playing out in front of her, even if she was only seeing one side of it.

"Of course, love," said Pat. "You'll get used to this after a while. I've learned to ignore half of what he says these days. And given I miss half anyway, I only really understand a quarter. Have you smudged yourself lately?"

Lauren admitted that she had not.

"We'll have to get on that. I'll activate some later tonight. You'll need to keep an eye on your spiritual hygiene if you spend time with my daughter. She's like a paranormal Petri dish."

"So, you can see other things too?" Brigid asked, turning back to her father. "Why didn't I know about all of this?"

"Yes, of course I can. Michael and I have been friends for years, haven't we? Since you were about five at least."

Michael grinned, clearly ready for some intense reminiscing. "It was that tab of acid you dropped, back in what, '84?"

Her dad nodded. "That it was, that it was. I came down and you were still there. Best moment of my life. Everything opened up to me then. I was never the same."

"That was uncoolly late to be dropping tabs, Dad," snapped Brigid testily. "But you can't see anything can you, Mum?"

Her mother shook her head. "I've never had that kind of sense. My gifts lay in other areas. I use the spirit board to do most of my communication. Lauren, do you like crystals?"

"Do I *love* crystals?" She brandished the black tattoo on her inner left arm, which showed a large crystal surrounded by herbs and native plants. A large moth with sickle moon markings floated above the scene. "I got this when I was inducted into my coven a few years ago. I'm a Wiccan."

Pat raised her eyebrows. "And you're Brigid's best friend?"

"I know, right? I must have always known she had it in her, all this metaphysical stuff. Did you hear about the visit to the tarot reader?"

"You got her to visit a tarot reader? How on earth did you do that? She thinks all that stuff is mumbo-jumbo."

Pat peered at Brigid, then back to Lauren, staring intently at the two of them. "This friendship was part of your destiny. I can feel it. Lauren was sent to open your heart and your third eye chakra, to open you up to your—"

"Lauren was sent from the relief agency during the flu outbreak of 2008 when we couldn't get any qualified teachers," Brigid snapped again. She may be coming to terms with the fact that the world wasn't quite calibrated in the way that she had always assumed...nay hoped, but she was buggered if she was going to buy into every crackpot idea. Her chakras would stay firmly closed, thank you very much, and any destiny that she was being called towards would be, quite simply, on her own terms.

Twenty-five

An early evening walk was a routine that her father had committed to thirty years ago. It was by no means Brigid's idea of a treat but given that her other two options were joining Lauren and Pat while they wove hemp necklaces as pouches for crystals, or listening to the Deshas talk about the Green Party's latest decisive election loss and how humanity continued to vote against their own interests, she decided that a walk was the lesser of three very irritating evils.

They wandered down the overgrown path that led from the house to the surrounding paddocks, and climbed over fences until they reached the slow, darkly green river that murmurated through the surrounding fields and hills. As they walked, companionably silent, hands thrust deep into pockets, Brigid looked out over the river like she was seeing it for the first time. She noticed how the willows nodded down to the water, creating eddies and ripples as the branches touched the flow which slid away, forming and reforming as the tiny waves travelled off into the distance. The surface sat glassy in the gathering darkness, interrupted by the occasional bubble rising to the surface. Fish? Platypus? Jenny Green Teeth? Out of curiosity she rose her levels, just an inkling, but she could only make out a few whisps of sentient mist playing catch and kiss amongst the willow branches. They reminded her of kittens, except damper and less likely to give you a blood infection with their claws. She watched them for a while, smiling, wondering if Frank could see them too but not bothering to ask. By the sounds of it, he had been aware of this ability longer than she, so it was probably all old news to him anyway.

A stream of light passed over her head, and as it cascaded through the evening, she felt a graze of grateful and unconditional love sweep through her. The moving light was roughly bird shaped and as it moved on towards the mountains, she realised that she may well have just seen the source of that odd, ephemeral feeling of happiness that descends on people seemingly out of nowhere.

"I've got a bit of a problem I was hoping you could help me with. Or at least I could tell you about. You don't have to help. I don't know really."

Her dad put his arm around her shoulders and hugged her to him briefly. His wool lined, bulky coat smelled like her childhood, and it occurred to her again that maybe she had underestimated her parents. Tears pricked behind her eyes, and she wondered what else she had been wrong about.

"Let's see then. Tell me what you think I need to know, and we'll go from there."

"Remember Mur-arb, the guy Juniper said he was in communication with back in the day? Who I used to meditate with, or about, or whatever it was? Apparently, he's come to life somehow, and he's become the Ruler of Everything or some such. I know how it sounds but he needs me to help him rule," she finished with a rush, the words sitting uncomfortably as they came out of her mouth.

"Really?"

Her father chewed on a green stem of bulrush he'd pulled from the spongy bank of the river and looked off into the distance. He had a habit of thinking for a few moments before he spoke; it annoyed Brigid no end when she was younger but now, she decided that it may well be the secret to sounding wise. Maybe she should try it.

"Ruler of Everything, hey? That's quite a turn up. The first thing I'd want to know is how that happened. He couldn't rule his way out of a paper bag when I knew him, and I can't see how he would have been able to improve that much over the past thirty years. He was just a bit needy. And baffled. He seemed baffled quite a lot."

The sun was low over the horizon now, silhouetting the gumtrees on the distant hill, dark against the vivid red. The crispness in the air spoke of the approaching winter, and Brigid pulled her mother's hand-woven alpaca wool poncho around her, glad that Pat had made her slip it over her coat as she left the house. It smelled musty in a familiar way, and Brigid felt herself falling more into the comfortable familiarity of childhood.

"You talk like you knew him?"

"I communicated with him a bit, like you did, when we were meditating. The theta brainwave patterns were the best bet for finding him. I always found that and the vibration of the crystal singing bowls. He always liked them. Does he still? But yes, I guess I did meet him once, on this level. Plain as day, he was. He was in the kitchen of the old hostel, remember the one that had electricity because it was hooked up to the water wheel? I got up one night to make a cup of tea and there he was."

"In the kitchen? What was he doing?"

"Making a cuppa of course—like me. Nice fellow, I have to say. A bit vague and doddery, I thought, but he seemed nice. We chatted for a minute, and then I went back to bed. Of course, shortly after that the Deshas told me it wasn't good for you, this co-dependent relationship you were having with him, so we took you away. I mean, it was around then that Juniper banished him anyway, so we could have stayed, but it was time for you to go to a mainstream school. No 14-year-old wants to spend all day with their mum and dad. But I don't know. Maybe you were both good for each other? The more I see of the dealings of the other dimensions, the more I realise I don't have any idea what's going on. For now, we see through a glass darkly and all that."

Brigid frowned, wrapping her arms around herself more firmly.

"I don't remember much of that. I don't know what was real and what I imagined. Or what I was told."

"You were young. And you weren't that interested in it. You had your horse and your books, and I always got the idea it wasn't something that you vibed with. I didn't realise you even took that much notice of it. I'm sorry if it had an impact on you. It sounded like an exciting thing, being a spiritual muse. We felt like it would benefit you."

"Benefit me? It's hard enough being young without the added pressure of people looking to you for ultimate answers. I felt as if I had to solve things for everyone."

"We were young. We made mistakes. So, what are you supposed to do for Mur-arb exactly?"

"Help him, from what I can tell. I think I'm expected to go to this Heavenly Realm place and help him with whatever it is he needs help with."

"So, is that place basically Heaven?"

Brigid shrugged. "I suppose so. It's meant to be for the really good people and the angels and that kind of thing. But I can tell you, from what I've seen, just because you're an angel doesn't mean you can't be incompetent. Not Michael," she explained hurriedly, glancing over to see whether he'd heard. "Other ones. They're much grumpier and sassier than we've been led to believe."

"Angel nature is the same as human nature, then." He sighed. "I'd be a bit disappointed if the whole Judeo-Christian God theory proved to be right though. I've spent a fair bit of time arguing against that."

"I don't think so. At least not specifically. There seems to be a general hodgepodge of ideas as far as I can tell. Many ways up the mountain, and all that."

Frank contemplated this idea.

"Anyway, it sounds like a blast. Are you going to do it?"

"Really?" Brigid swung her head around to look at him in surprise. "Do you think it's a good idea? Aren't you worried it might be dangerous or something?"

"Everything's dangerous, when you think about it."

"Yeah, I think that this is a niche of "dangerous" that normal life hasn't prepared me for."

"You don't think you could do it?"

"I don't know what I expected from our conversation here, but I feel as if I was going for "wise counsel" rather than "yolo"."

Frank chuckled. "What does Michael say?"

"Michael? I haven't really asked him."

"Don't you think you should?"

Brigid shrugged her shoulders noncommittally.

"I would have thought that asking your protection angel is probably one of the first things you should have done. Most of us don't get to communicate directly with ours."

Brigid suspected her father would be heartily disappointed at just how every day and humdrum the reality of a protection angel ended up being.

"Do you ever see yours?"

"No, I never have." He sighed. "But I don't see as much as you do, anyway. Must be on a different frequency or something. I've told you; I don't know how any of this works."

Brigid felt tears come to her eyes. "I don't know how it works either. I'm not in control of any of this. I don't know what's happening and I hate it."

"Well, you were never really a fan of unpredictability. You always wanted to know exactly what was happening and when it was going to happen." He took her hand. "Being a muse probably wasn't the best thing for you, on reflection."

"No," she protested. "It was fine."

"I'm sorry," he said.

"You and Mum didn't do anything wrong," she said, realising it herself for the first time.

"We were young," he said. "We were making it up as we went along too, you know."

"I know you were."

"And look at the life you've made for yourself. It's a good, solid life."

She laughed. "It's solid alright."

"Are you happy?"

She shrugged. "What's happy? I'm secure. I've been in the same office for twenty years. My job is to make fourteen-year-olds sit in silence. I know what I'm eating on a two-week rotation. I know where I'll be every Friday night, and I know what time I'll be in bed every night. That's what makes me happy. Predictability makes me happy."

"Does it really?" He looked over at her doubtfully. Given that, you seem to be coping very well with . . . all of this."

He gestured to Michael who was sitting a respectful distance away from them, his gentle glow visible in the now dark air.

"You know what though?" she began, feeling the ideas that had been percolating in her head for weeks coming together. "The night before this all started to happen, the night before Egragore came to see me, I was having a kind of mini breakdown about how bored I was. About how this life I have built up for myself just isn't enough. Do you think I knew? Do you think that somehow, deep inside, my intuition was telling me that this was all about to start?"

Her wise and gentle father smiled at her. "Could be, love. Could be. Or it could just be the totally natural response to the fact that you're a forty-four-year-old woman in a boring, stagnant routine who was made for much, much more than the mind-numbing tedium of controlling the behaviour of teenagers."

He stood, stretching the kinks out of his back.

"Come on, let's head back. The lentils will be cooked, and while I know you probably don't want to hear it, your mother might have some useful insights into what to do."

Gathered around the heavy wood dining table, the four of them worked their way through deep bowls of lentil stew with dumplings, served in hand thrown pottery and garnished with herbs from the garden. With the wood heater giving warmth and light to the room, Brigid felt the tension in her body unknotting for the first time in weeks.

"You seem to be a better cook than you used to be, Mum," she said after several minutes of silent eating.

"Or maybe you've just developed better taste?"

"You usually eat microwave meals, so of course this is going to taste better," giggled Lauren. She and Pat clinked glasses of homemade rosehip wine and grinned at each other.

"Fabulous. So, you two have bonded I see?"

"We have."

Lauren lifted up the chunkily woven piece of jewellery she was now wearing around her neck. "This is a Lemurian seed crystal from the Himalayas."

"Very rare," interjected her mother.

Lauren nodded. "It is. It's very rare. It will protect me and connect me with the ancient wisdom of my foremothers. A strong ancestral maternal influence is something that I've been lacking in my life."

"Lauren is potentially a very talented light worker, but that city and its noxious energies is masking all of her power. You need to move," she said as an aside. "Possibly to Nimbin. And if she follows the ladders within the crystal, it will connect her with the divine."

"Jesus Christ," groaned Brigid. She called over to Michael who was chatting quietly with the Deshas. "Will this random hunk of rock help Lauren connect with the divine?"

Michael raised his hands in a gesture universally translated as "I dunno".

"There is literally a divine being over there who doesn't know what you two are talking about."

Her father leaned over and placed his hand on hers. "Why don't we get your mother involved with the quandary you're dealing with? And try not to come from a place of ego, OK?"

"I'm not trying to come from a place of ego, I'm trying to come from a place of humour," she muttered, but feeling her father's fingers squeeze hers, she took a deep breath. "Mum, remember back in the day, the commune had this guy we were worshipping called Mur-arb, and I talked to him while I was meditating?"

"Of course, I remember." She looked to her husband. "Why is she talking to me like I'm an idiot? Of course, I remember. I helped Juniper collect the offerings to create the evocation he used to summon him. And that ended up biting me on the bum, didn't it? Our whole lovely commune was disbanded. I swore off spell crafting after that."

"Well," continued Brigid, determined not to become side-tracked after her first sentence. "It appears he has . . . I'm sorry, but what do you mean "summoned"? I feel like there were some vital things my young brain must have missed. I was always under the impression that he was just made up. That Mur-arb came out of my imagination, or Juniper's."

"Now how would that work," laughed Pat. "You can't just invent something out of nothing. It's simple science, for goodness' sake. No, he summoned him from the Otherworld or somewhere; I'm not versed with all the appropriate terminology, but the point is, he already existed. Juniper was trying to summon an entity who would encompass the whole rich plethora of human and spiritual experience in an all-loving oneness, but things got a bit muddled somewhere and we ended up with a short, fat, quasi-deity with self-esteem issues, which was a bit of a surprise, I can tell you. Juniper's ambitions always outstripped his abilities, bless him. But you always refused to acknowledge he was real, so it makes sense you would have convinced yourself he was just an imaginary friend."

"In that case, you may be surprised to hear, by some really random turn of events, he seems to have become the new ruler of the universe, and he wants me to help him with all of that, whatever that is."

Her mother lifted another dumpling out of the casserole dish that sat in the middle of the table. "I have to say, I find that surprising. Ruler of the universe? He was always so vague and wet. He'd be an awful leader." She piled some more food onto her husband's plate, who nodded knowingly at her.

"That's what I said."

"I see how he would want your help though, love. Your get up and go would be a positive boon to him at this stage."

"That's what I want to ask you about. I think it would be a terrible idea."

"Of course, you do, because you're terrified of change," said Pat. "Your terror of change and need to be in control has always held you back."

Lauren began to choke violently on a mouthful of lentils, and Brigid took the moment to jump up from the table and grab her a glass of water. She could feel her face burning.

"Come on, sweets," she heard her father say to Pat in a cautionary voice.

"Oh no, I say it with love," her mother called over to her. "It's not necessarily a bad thing."

"You have a way of making it sound like a bad thing though, Mum."

"You have been feeling very stuck in your life though, haven't you Brigid?" said Lauren. "She's been hating everything. Haaaaaating it. My god she's been like a bear with a sore head for the past six months."

Her mother started scrawling numbers on a pad of paper in the middle of the table. "It's probably time for a growth phase for you anyway. If we look at the numerology . . ."

"I have been a bit bored," Brigid conceded. "And yes, I don't like change, and it's true I like to control things. But that's only because other people are so useless at doing things."

"There." Pat firmly underlined something on the page and dropped the pen. "According to my calculations you should be going through a deep need to be fulfilled and find true value in your life right now."

She gestured to some indecipherable symbols on the piece of paper she'd twisted around to face Brigid and pointed out what appeared to be the relevant scrawls. Lauren nodded knowingly.

"There is a tumultuous search for an authentic life, and it looks to me like the universe has deliberately turned things upside down in order to make things happen for you. And there's another factor there which is important, but I can't quite get it now. It will come to me."

"You got that from maths, did you?"

"She wanted to get pregnant," whispered Lauren as an aside.

"Oh god, no, don't do that. Terrible idea. Having a baby just makes everything worse. Avoid that move at absolutely all costs."

"So, can I just clarify, you think that "the universe"," said Brigid, using air quotes, "decided to literally put a new ruler in place, a new ruler of the entire fabric of space and time—I should say—so that I can stop being bored? I couldn't have taken up spelunking, or got a tattoo or gone to Thailand? The entire known universe had to be potentially fucked up so I can find some purpose. I have to say I find that pretty bloody unlikely."

Her mother shrugged. "It was just a suggestion. I don't know. No one has ever asked me to become co-ruler of the universe, so I don't have a lot of context. It does sound like quite an opportunity though, doesn't it?"

Everyone at the table made positive, supportive comments about what a great opportunity it sounded like.

"What happens if you don't do it?" asked her father.

"I haven't really had any of this laid out for me rationally to be honest. Some handsome guy tried to trick me into it, then some demons tried to abduct me, then I had a chat to some Man on a beach, then I decided to come and ask you about it, so I don't know what happens if I don't."

There was a pause.

"Can you speak to him about it then?" asked Frank.

"Who?"

"Mur-arb. Can you speak to him about it? Find out how he feels about the whole situation? I mean, you've been going through third parties and who knows what agendas they have. Talk to him and see what his perspective is on all this. You never know, he might be doing ok on his own."

"I very much doubt that," muttered Pat under her breath.

"Just talk to him? How am I supposed to just talk to him? Ring him? Call out his name three times? He's not Beetlejuice."

"Michael?" Frank craned his neck around and called over to the angel who was sitting on the sofa sifting through old copies of *Earth Garden*. "How would Brigid get in touch with Mur-arb, if she wanted? Do you have a way of tuning into him or something?"

Michael leapt up, eager to be invited into the conversation.

"What's that? How can she talk to the Great and Glorious Ruler?"

"Is that what he's calling himself? That rings some alarm bells, I must say."

"Er," Michael twisted the magazine backwards and forwards in his hands, "that's not really something I know a lot about. Sorry. I mean, I would have had some ideas with the last guy, but things have all changed now and, well, the line of authority is a bit difficult to discern."

"How about meditation?"

Everyone turned to look at Lauren.

"Meditation?"

"Isn't that the way you communicated with him back in the day? If it worked all that time ago then there's no reason why it shouldn't work now, surely."

Brigid crossed her arms. "It's not the worst idea I've heard lately. In a sea of what has mainly been bad ideas."

Lauren and Brigid weren't surprised to learn there was a fully equipped meditation room set up, seemingly just for the occasion.

Twenty-six

"Psssst."

Michael had been waiting outside for Guinnie for fifteen minutes. He hadn't seen her all day, and felt she was deliberately avoiding them, but he could feel that she was . . . somewhere. In the aether. But the aether was a no smoking zone, and he also knew that she would have had to drop down to earth level for a sneaky dart before too long. Sure enough, she appeared, and in a moment her already beatifically radiant face was lit by the flare of a match.

"Psssst."

She took a deep drag. "Jesus, Michael, are you psssst-ing me?"

"I don't want to bother you if you're busy."

"I'm always busy."

He sidestepped a puff of smoke. "We need to have a chat about Brigid."

He noticed that Guindaline was tapping her foot impatiently.

"I mean, I feel like we should probably be on the same page here."

"Yes? Why?" Her piercing eyes always made him nervous, and they looked more than usually intimidating today.

"It's about Brigid. It's about what's going on with Brigid."

"Yes?"

He didn't know why she needed to make things so difficult between them.

"We both know that she is a slightly unique charge. But—and I'm just speaking for myself here, throwing around some ideas, sending it up the flagpole to see who salutes it—it's just that I feel like this new development has taken us all unawares and I'd like us to compare notes to make sure that we are making the right decisions. Regarding her actions. And how we can best help her."

She waited for him to continue. He stared at her.

"As it were."

"Why are you so scared of me?" she snapped.

"Because you make me feel like a trainee angel again, getting in trouble for not polishing my sword properly."

She rolled her eyes. "And I, in turn, find your pathetic terror of me just . . . pathetic. I can't respect you when I know you're nervous around me. It's such a turn off."

"Maybe if you didn't look at everyone as a sex object then that wouldn't be a factor in your decision making."

She ground the cigarette out under her ballet slipper. "Go on then."

"*We* know that she's *the* Brigid, Goddess of the Flame and of the Well, Divine Mistress of Spring and New Growth, Font of all Inspiration and Creativity. We know that she's here on the planet having a sabbatical, and we're meant to keep her safe. And to speak plainly we didn't get much of a say in that. But now that she's been enmeshed in the whole Mur-arb thing again I'm very nervous. This changes everything. I feel like it changes everything, anyway. We got her away from him very effectively when she was younger."

"I feel like I was the main player there, but ok."

"Yes, you were. You, and the Deshas. There are much higher stakes now though. Back then we could ask for advice, and we got some of the higher ups to tell us if things were going ok. All of our team leaders have disappeared, there's no line of command and as far as I can tell there's no one to go to for advice at all. We're flying blind. Everyone who knows who she really is, is gone. There's no CEO any more or anything."

He peered at her for a moment, trying to gauge her reaction. "It was only the Upper Realm who knew her, wasn't it? None of the Shadow Lands people know about this, do they."

Guinnie shook her head. "No, was just us. Need to know basis."

"So now anyone else who knows about it has disappeared. Is Brigid supposed to team up with Mur-arb now? Are we supposed to let that happen? If you ask me, I think it's probably a good thing. There needs to be someone in charge, after all. I would have thought that she would be a good option to step in for the time being while we wait to see what's going to happen next. Even if it is combined with this Mur-arb character."

"If she was in her true form, maybe. Maybe she would be a good option. Theoretically. But she's not in her true form, is she? She's Brigid Humboldt, which is a whole other ridiculous issue, and she's in no way equipped for this."

"But maybe with Mur-arb she would be? That's what I don't know. Is this her destiny? Is this supposed to be what happens? This is what has me so confused. This is what's causing me stress and to be honest, it's starting to give me migraines. I'm an angel, for goodness' sake. I'm not supposed to be able to get headaches."

Guindaline sounded serious for a moment. "We have to rely on our intuition. What we think is the best for her. And I don't think this a good idea."

"Why? Is this a competitive woman thing? You don't like other women having power?".

"Get stuffed Michael. That sort of comment is the reason you give me the shits."

"What else can I assume? We know that she's having trouble in this life, that she feels lost. This would give her meaning. Step into her own power."

"That shows how much you know. She's in this incarnation for a reason. Think about how much pressure *we* feel. Well quadruple that and you wouldn't have an infinitesimal inkling of what a goddess would feel. She wants a break, for pity's sake. Do you think encouraging her to take on the role of the actual stand in CEO will give her that break? It could totally destroy her. She could end up as a shell."

"Oh." Michael looked a little forlorn. "I hadn't thought of that."

"No, you hadn't. But sure, make it about my need to be competitive with other females. That is the absolute blindingly obvious thing to make it about. There could have been no other option."

"Sorry," he said weakly. "I've been working really hard on my ingrained and conditioned misogyny."

"Not hard enough."

"It's just that, I didn't know that you cared that much about her. You're always so annoyed by her."

Guinnie crossed her arms and sighed. "Am I annoyed at the fact that someone gave up on being a goddess, which is, to be honest, my dream job. And for what? To be a human? Yes. I think that she had delusions of inferiority and she is absolutely kidding herself if she thinks that this is a 'break.' But the fact is, this is what she wanted. She chose to come down here, she chose to be a human and she chose to have her memory wiped. She *chose* it, and even though I wasn't there while she and the CEO thrashed it out, from what I've been told she had some fairly strong feelings about it. She really wanted to do this. So, do I think that being strong-armed into this, upping her stress level and taking this on is a good idea? No, I absolutely do not. Not at all. And there's also the fact that . . ."

She glanced around, not nervously, but making sure that there was no one else to hear them.

"From what I hear, Fraster is pushing for this."

"Or Mur-arb is and Fraster is advocating for him."

"No." she shook her head vigorously. "It's that Fraster putting ideas in his head. Seriously, remember Mur-arb back in the day? He had no firm ideas. None. He couldn't find his backside with both hands. And a map. And a flashlight. And a recorded tour guide. Do you honestly think that being, the one who once cried because his tofu went mouldy, could mastermind this great take over?"

"Still," said Michael, mulling over the new information. "Egragore knows what he's doing and I think that he's got her best interests at heart. And he knows all the politics and things that we're not privy to." He thought for a moment longer. "Yes, I mean I think that you've come up with some great points and it's definitely a strong argument, but when it comes right down to it, Egragore is probably the closest thing to a boss that we have right now, and if I have to choose one person to trust and look towards, then my money would have to be on him."

"Fabulous," said Guindaline tersely. "I can't say I'm surprised, but I am disappointed. I guess I'll have to do this myself."

And she flickered out of view.

Twenty-seven

The room was scattered with seagrass mats and corduroy beanbags. Candles were propped in hand thrown, unmatched pottery and interestingly chunky pieces of driftwood that Pat had collected from beaches around Australia. As she bustled around rearranging things, she insisted on lighting some sandalwood incense cones, even though Brigid protested strongly it would play havoc with her sinuses. She also found a jar of something called "flying ointment" that she swore blind was an ancient recipe used by her Witch ancestors to assist in out of body experiences. Apparently, the mix of frankincense, rue, mugwort, wormwood, and some other ingredients that her mother would rather tap her nose and wink than list, would transport her to the spiritual plane. Brigid thought it smelled like feet but consented to her mother putting it on her pressure points and some of the more accessible chakras.

Frank said that sitting cross-legged on the ground would give her the best chance of really getting into a deep state, but Brigid said there was no way that she was going to jeopardise all the hard work of getting unguent wiped on her bits by getting a cramp in her legs in the middle of whatever was going to happen. She eventually acquiesced to lying on one of the beanbags. She also requested the ancient space heater be moved out of the small room lest it set something (possibly herself) on fire.

Eventually she snapped and said that for people who were intent on her getting into a higher state of altered consciousness and relaxation they were pretty intent on pissing her off. They filtered out, her mother muttering something about "of all the people chosen to be a god's muse, I don't see how . . ." but the door closed behind her chagrin, and Brigid was left alone.

As she sat there in the dim, increasingly warming room, she realised she probably should have chosen a less sleep-inducing position than reclining on a beanbag. She shook herself and sat up, practising the breathing and "thoughts-drifting-away" methods that usually enabled her to get into a state where she felt a little less wound up than usual. The house under her was quiet. They were doing such a good job of not distracting her that she wondered if maybe they'd gone out. She could hear creaks above her as the cold wind started to twist around the house, and she gradually began to feel a familiar space open in her mind in the gap that grew between each breath. Her heartbeat seemed to slow, and thoughts melted away except for one word: Mur-arb.

Mur-arb.

Mur-arb.

"Is this really a good idea?"

Her eyes flew open, and her beautiful guardian angel stood in front of her, hands on hips, a frown on her face. She was chewing on something Brigid could only assume was gum and looked unnervingly beautiful.

"What the hell?"

Guindaline moved the gum in her mouth from one side to the other and pulled her fingers through her golden hair.

"Have you been smoking?"

Guinnie ignored her.

"I said, is this really a good idea? Trying to summon up this guy, or whoever he thinks he is. Have you thought this through?"

"He's the new CEO, if you're interested at all, and that would make him your boss, so I'd think you'd be on board with my talking to him."

"Whatever. He doesn't know what he's doing. And I don't trust him."

"So, the CEO. You're saying you don't trust the CEO. Nice."

Guindaline rolled her eyes. "Oh stop. You don't think he's the rightful CEO any more than I do."

"Actually, he's an old friend of mine, and I'm just trying to support his . . . new endeavours."

"I know he's an old friend of yours. He was seen as a not entirely healthy influence if I remember correctly. He wasn't really helping you develop into your. . . full human self. Teenage," she corrected herself. "Your full teenage self."

"You've been ignoring me and now you want to have a say in my life? Now? Just when I'm potentially doing something interesting? I think your issues have more to do with you than me."

"Why are you so stubborn? Still?"

"I think you're jealous," spat Brigid, immediately regretting her words and realising how stupid they sounded. An angel, jealous of her?

"Yes, you're absolutely right. I'm jealous. I'm very, very jealous of your amazing life. I wish I was just like you."

"Well?" Brigid threw her hands up into the air. "See? This? I'm trying to do it. I'm trying to make my life more interesting, and you're trying to stop me."

"This," said Guindaline firmly, gesturing to the incense, the balm, the candles, "is all a bad idea. What *he* wants from you is a bad idea."

"Why? What do you know?"

"Nothing." Guindaline dropped eye contact. "Nothing. I don't know anything. I just think it feels like a bad idea, and you shouldn't get mixed up with what's happening."

"But I am already mixed up with it. I'm already connected. I may as well go along with it at this stage."

"Fucking Egragore." Guindaline thrust her hands back onto her hips. "Fucking idiot. Why are the hot ones always so stupid? He should be more clued into all of this."

"Anyway, if it was a bad idea then Michael would tell me not to."

"Oh, Michael," spat Guindoline with contempt. "As if he would know anything. With this lot around you no wonder you're so clueless."

"If you think everyone around me is so clueless," said Brigid, "then why have you been so conspicuously absent? If you think you're the only one with any sense then maybe you should have been, oh, I don't know, *doing your actual job a bit better.*"

Guindoline glared at her. "This is more complicated than you realise," she said.

"I don't think it is that complicated, and I think you should go off and do whatever it is that you do, and leave me to make my own decisions, with the help of my *friends.*"

"Fine, I will then. But don't come crying to me when everything goes to shit."

And she was gone.

Brigid closed her eyes again, trying to recapture some inner peace. But the guardian angel's words kept ringing in her ears.

Stupid angel.

Mur-arb.

Mur-arb.

She recited the name over and over in her head, visualising a bright light above her flooding her body with warmth and peace. She briefly wondered if she should be going for the "reverential and worshipful" vibe and request time with him. But if he was asking for her help, he probably knew what he was letting himself in for and trying to convince him she was reverential and subservient would be starting off on the wrong foot—if in fact he would believe it for a second, which she was almost certain he would not.

The brain space in which she had this thought passed, and it drifted away.

Mur-arb.

Mur-arb.

Unknown ages passed. She looked out from a dark cliff onto an ink black sea. The blackness above her throbbed with pink mist, and waves and eddies slid beneath her, hiding whole civilisations within their depths. Her mind stretched out into the expanses before her, and she held it all within her own self—all the knowledge and responsibility of the aeons. The moment floated in time; suspended.

And floated.

Where the hell was he?

A bubble the size of the universe that could fit within her hand popping to nothingness.

This wasn't working.

Dammit.

She opened her eyes, irritated and disappointed, and stood to turn on the light.

"Oh good, you're awake," said Mur-arb, standing near the doorway twisting a grey hat in his chubby hands. "I didn't like to disturb you, but I was feeling a bit silly just standing here in the dark. That beanbag does look comfortable though, so I'm not surprised you fell asleep. There's nothing like a good, roomy beanbag. I wonder if we could just pop a lamp on rather than the light? They never turn the lights out where I'm living, and it's just nice not to have to squint for a change."

He reached out his arms to embrace her awkwardly.

"It's good to see you again. I'm so glad you called for me because I've had a bugger of a time trying to get into contact with you. I didn't think of this though. Genius!"

"I can't believe that worked," she muttered, tentatively hugging him back. He smelled of patchouli and beeswax and was unmistakably the man who had tried to shake her hand in the takeaway shop.

"Meditation is an incredibly powerful tool of manifestation. I used to tell you that, remember? Believe and you will achieve."

"Actually, that's a new one. You wouldn't have said that in the '80s because that's part of a whole new bullshit thing going on these days. I hope you're not a fan of it because we'll be having a full and frank discussion if that's the case."

He regarded her from an arm's length, grinning broadly.

"See? This is why I need you. I don't know what's going on half the time. Maybe seven eights of the time. A lot of the time, anyway. I need you to sort things out for me. Egragore tells me you don't want to, but see, Cosmic? I'm someone now. I'm the CEO or something. It's all about me. About us. We can be in charge of . . . everything. The way it's been presented to me makes perfect sense. You have to say yes."

"My name is Brigid now. And what were you doing in the souvlaki shop anyway?" she asked.

"Souvlaki shop?" He looked puzzled for a moment.

"Yes. The night that . . . well, it was the night that things really started to happen for me. It was raining. Melbourne. Australia."

"Hmmm." He frowned and tapped his chin. "Souvlaki shop you say? I don't quite know which . . ."

"How often do you come down to Earth anyway?" she asked suspiciously. "So often that you have to work out which Souvlaki shop is which?"

"Oh yes, I remember," he said hurriedly. "*That* souvlaki shop. And sorry about the rain. I thought if those weather deities came and hung out with you, they might trigger a memory or something."

"You thought continual rain might remind me that I was a deity thing?"

He shrugged.

"In Melbourne?"

"As I said, I'm still working this all out."

"I didn't even recognise you. In that shop, I mean."

"Well, no, of course not. I'd never actually physically manifested for you. Although I was slightly disappointed that you didn't get my . . . vibe. Not to worry. I didn't really know what was going on myself. I was feeling a bit lost and was wanting help and all of a sudden, there I was. Bits of me were there anyway. I think I was just projecting. And from what I've heard you'd begun to attract the attention of . . . other forces."

"They were demons, I think. I feel like I've been attracting demons. There was this tarot reading and . . ."

"Oh dear, you're not into tarot cards, are you? I must say, I expected more of you than that. So very show pony, I've always thought."

"They weren't my idea."

"Anyway, don't let stereotypes colour your view of everyone you might meet. Just because someone is demon-ish doesn't make them bad, you know."

She wrinkled her brow. "I feel that being demon-ish is kind of the literal definition of "being bad", but alright then."

They sat on the floor, she back on the beanbag bag, he on a patchwork pouffe that had been extracted from a dim corner of the room.

"So, you wanted to talk to me about something?" he asked. "Anything in particular, or just a general chat? Both are lovely, of course. I hear and honour all aspects of the conversational experience, and I commit to listening with an open and non-judgemental heart."

Brigid ran her tongue over her teeth. "Apparently, from what I've heard, you want my help, but to be honest I'm hearing a lot of different things and I just wanted to talk to you directly, I suppose. About, you know, what's going on exactly and what I'm supposed to do. I suppose some guidance would be nice."

Her voice trailed off.

"Egragore explained it to you though, didn't he?" Mur-arb looked at her hopefully. "Because he knew exactly what he was supposed to do and what he was supposed to say to you."

"Oh, yes," said Brigid, feeling strangely protective. "No, he explained everything. It was the things he was explaining that I wasn't too happy about."

"Let me know how your interactions with him go. I've been hearing worrying things about him, and I'm not so sure he's going to have a place in our Bright Future, if I'm being totally honest with you. Fraster and I have serious doubts about whether he is One of Us."

Brigid made a mental note to do absolutely nothing of the sort. Mur-arb leaned forward and took her hands in his.

"But it is so wonderful to see you again. And you're so grown up. Oh, we had fun, didn't we? We were a meeting of minds, we really were. You had such fire, such promise. Do you remember the things we were going to do together, how we were going to change the world?"

She smiled in spite of herself. "I wanted to build the world's biggest bookshop."

"Outside of the planet's typical temporal dimension if I remember correctly. And the books would perform themselves for their audience."

"And I wanted a practise archaeological dig where kids could dig up real ancient artefacts."

His grip on her hands tightened. "Your ideas were so *fun*. You had so many ideas."

"But we couldn't do any of them. They were just dreams. Neither of us knew how to make them happen."

"We could have if people had given us a chance. We just needed direction, we needed someone to point us in the right direction. That's what Fraster can do for us. Juniper should have done it back then, but he had no idea. Look what happened when things got too hard, when I became too assertive. When I started to be my true self, to come into my power. That's what I understand now; now that it's all been explained to me."

"Yes, look I'm really sorry about that, by the way. It was a pot that I made myself, a coil one from memory. I'm not sure exactly why Juniper used it and I've always felt a bit bad. But I don't think . . ."

"Yes?"

"It wasn't my understanding that it was because you were too assertive, it was always my understanding that it was . . ."

She pulled her hands away and sat back. *Because dad told me you kept trying to fix things and putting cumin and paprika in the date fudge and then accidentally blocking the waterwheel and cutting off power to the house for a week.* But she didn't say this. Let him think that he was assertive. It seemed . . . kinder.

"You will forgive me if I'm still a bit freaked out by all this. Until recently I thought this was just dreams and imagination. A fantasy world."

"A mere fantasy? That's what everyone wanted you to think. To remember. They didn't understand."

"They just knew I needed to be a child and not have all the pressure. I was feeling overburdened and had to concentrate on my future."

"What a future it could have been."

Silence.

He peered at her carefully. "So how has the promise of your life turned out? Is it amazing? Is it exciting? How has the girl who wanted to create an archaeological theme park ended up? Are you doing glorious things with exciting people?"

"I'm ok." She bit her lip, feeling tears pricking behind her eyes.

"OK?"

"I'm fine," she said, more forcefully this time. "This is how life is, alright? This is how life goes for people. No fairy tales. We do what we can do."

"But it can be. It can be for you. Why are you trying to be normal when that's not what you are supposed to be? The very fabric of reality was altered for you. And now it's happened again. Are you so desperate to be mediocre that you're just going to walk away from that?"

"Of course I don't want to be mediocre."

"Are you sure?"

They sat in an uncomfortable silence.

"You tell me what you want then," she said. "You tell me "The Vision" and I'll tell you why I can't."

He stood up, exuding nervous energy as he began to pace around the room.

"I have been given a chance. Another chance, don't you understand? After you left, I was nothing. Without your mind to connect to I had nothing. I was put into a pot, exorcised into a pot. An actual, handmade pot. No way out, no connection. Obviously once I was in there, I expanded the space so I had some room to move, but still. All our plans, all our ideas. Nothing. It was me, in a pot, with my yurt and some llamas. I invented new flavours of kombucha. Many, many flavours of kombucha."

He squatted down in front of her, eager for her to understand the full force of his words. "I can't express to you how bad that was." His eyes searched out hers. "It tastes like piss. Like fizzy piss. Do you understand?"

"You don't need to convince me," she said, holding up her hands in surrender. "That stuff is foul. You wouldn't catch me drinking it."

"Well, then." He sat back, calmer. "That was my so-called life. Are you understanding me? Without you, my life was reduced to making new and interesting flavours of urine. The endless tasting."

"Can I just ask though, why did you keep drinking it if . . ."

But he was off again.

"And you, your life? Are you satisfied? Because from what I can tell you're stuck in your own eternal loop of metaphorical kombucha tasting, and you aren't any happier than I've been. But I thought I was happy, that's the worst bit. That's the true tragedy. I thought that was what I wanted! I'd made the best of it, and I thought I was happy."

"But surely if you think you were happy then . . ."

"No, no listen. It's all been explained to me now. I see clearly. Suddenly," he sprang up again, picking up the box of matches from next to the incense cones and nervously lighting them and putting them out with his thumb. "Suddenly I'm yanked out of all that, and everything, *everything* is open to me, to us. I have the chance to be literally—and I'm not over exaggerating here, even though it sounds like it—I am literally the ruler of the universe. Everything is open to me."

"But I still don't understand how."

"No one does. That's just it, no one does. Isn't that just perfect? And so very . . . us? I'm now the ruler of the universe and no one knows why, and no one knows how, but it just . . . is. Isn't that just so deliciously random? I didn't have to win it, or debate with anyone or anything unpleasant like that. It just happened. There had to have been a reason behind it."

"I feel like there wasn't though," said Brigid objectively. "As you said, it was random."

"Whatever has happened, they love me up there. Trust me. They love me. They're jumping through hoops to do what I want. I've been getting some wonderful advice, mentorship, if you like, from one chappie especially. They're as keen to get on with things as I am, but we just need you to pop up and we'll be getting started."

"What things?"

Brigid didn't remember him being this driven back in the day, she reminded herself. Things might have been different if he was, but . . .

"I can't do it without you," he said finally.

"That's very gratifying. And very sweet, but—"

"No, I literally mean I can't do it without you. We are the yin-yang. I was talking to Fraster the other day and apparently the whole yin-yang theory was based on our energies. Ours! Together! He was very emphatic about this; very, very emphatic. It was exceedingly important to him that I, and by proxy, you, really get our heads around the fact that our energies are. . . really quite important. I can't work without you; none of my powers work, and my plans can't happen. And none of your dreams can happen either, not without me. Life is just—"

"Piss tasting kombucha," she finished despondently.

"Exactly!"

"But Fraster is really quite terrifying," she protested. "He tried to kidnap me. With a demonic horde, for goodness sakes. Do you really think that you should be listening to him? As far as I can see, I should be staying a million miles away from him."

"Oh no, no," said Mur-arb, leaning forwards, his eyes bright. "He's really taken the time to spell this out to me clearly; he knows that I sometimes get muddled, and he's been such a help. That was just a ... misunderstanding. He can get too eager, you see, and he is so eager to help me with my true destiny. And yours. Your true destiny. He cares so, so much and you must forgive him for going about it too enthusiastically. There could be so much more for you." He leaned forward, stressing each word. "You are worth more than this. Than this world. You could be everything. Change everything."

"But that's impossible."

Staring into his eyes though, she wondered, was it?

"We could be as we were supposed to be. Until people who didn't understand stopped us. He said that . . ." His words petered out. "No, *I* think this. I think this is all the truth. And I think that you know it too."

His eyes mesmerised her, and she wondered how she could have ever thought of them as merely jolly or confused. Within them, she saw eternity, the depth and breadth of everything, as he had said, laid out before her.

"This is who you really are."

What the hell had she been thinking? Why had she been waiting? Why had she been holding back? She could be part of so much more. As if a bolt of lightning had gone off in her consciousness, she realised the fact she'd been stalling was part of the stupor she'd been occupying all her life. Such a small, small life. She was worth more than this. Her life was worth more than this.

"Oh, alright then. If you really want to, I guess we could give it a try. But I'm not wearing robes, and there won't be anyone bowing at me."

"Excellent." Mur-arb clapped his chubby hands together. "Excellent. And I know just where we can begin."

In a remarkably short amount of time, Brigid's physical reality had been projected into the Heavenly Realm. She found herself sitting on a sun lounge on a beach made of diamond dust with a margarita in her hand, while surrounded by a range of rather stern looking beings who wanted to discuss the viability of installing men's and women's specific toilets instead of the politically correct unisex ones they were having to currently tolerate.

Twenty-eight

"And another thing, why didn't I get a better guardian angel?"

Brigid had burst into Egragore's office only thirty seconds earlier, and already he was not enjoying it.

"I was in *extreme danger* down there, and I was left with her." She gestured towards Guinnie, who was flirting with Amber in the foyer. "I think that being more competent than your own guardian angel is a sad state of affairs, don't you? I would have thought I was worth a bit more than that."

"Why didn't you get a better guardian angel?"

Egragore dropped his pen and looked up from his desk, his eyes weary.

"Because you were not in the least bit important until very, very recently. No one knew of your existence. They weren't going to waste one of their high-quality angels on a no-one whose main aim in life was to get through period 6 without making a twelve-year-old cry. Anyway, what's to say that your angels are so dreadful? I've got no idea what the criteria is to be honest, but they seem to have been dealing with you pretty well so far, in the face of what looks like incredibly dull odds at times. Look this has nothing to do with me. I'm just having to clean up everyone's absolute mismanagement. Half of the rubbish I'm having to deal with has nothing to do with me. I don't even hear about it until it goes belly up. And angel allocation isn't my job because until very recently I lived in the Shadow Lands, if you remember."

"But I'm the muse of the Great and Glorious Ruler," she said. "Someone competent should have been keeping an eye on me."

"Oh, for pity's sake I wish you wouldn't use that expression. It confuses the wraiths. They don't know if you're making fun of him or not when you use it. And anyway, you weren't originally, were you? You were just any other run of the mill kid involved in some hippies' religious delusions. Trust me, if we put our best and brightest on to everyone who falls into that category, we'd be so short staffed it wouldn't bear thinking about. From what I can tell the top-notch angels are allocated to people who have potential for great things, who are expected to get the attention of evil forces purely because of their sheer magnetic personality and talents. People they're scared of. And as I said, maybe your angels are top-notch. I don't know what is used as a basis for comparison. Michael is well rated, anyway. I don't know what you're complaining about."

Brigid looked around for somewhere to sit. The last few days hadn't unfolded as she'd expected. Choosing a modular curved hand-shaped chair, she slumped into it and sighed as she looked vaguely around the room.

"I'm bored," she said.

"I'm working."

A pause.

"You were more fun when we were down on Earth," she said finally.

"I had more fun down on Earth." Egragore pushed aside some of the reams of paper. "And I never thought you saw me as "fun" down there. You were always annoyed at me."

"I'm annoyed a lot of the time. You shouldn't assume it infers dislike."

He took off his black rimmed glasses and stood up from his desk, an intense look on his narrow face. Stepping quickly across the room, he glanced out of the door, looked up and down the corridor and then closed it silently. As he took a seat next to Brigid, she saw that the hunted look on his face wasn't annoyance but worry.

"Do things seem odd around here to you?" he asked, his voice barely above a whisper.

She frowned. "Odder than what?"

"Than," he gestured with his hands, "just odd, I suppose. A strange vibe. Do things feel strange to you?"

"I feel as if you're asking the wrong person. This is all strange to me."

"You've spent a lot of time with Mur-arb over the past few days. How does he seem?"

"Perhaps you should talk me through what you think is odd and we'll start from there."

Egragore leapt back up and began pacing nervously around the room. He slid his hands into the pockets of his black pants then out again. Finally, he grabbed a stress ball from the desk and rolled it around in his palms.

"I think something is going on. I think I'm being sidelined. There seem to be a lot of meetings going on behind closed doors involving agendas that are never sent to me, and I don't like it."

"While we're on that point, can I ask whether you're actually in charge here? Because you certainly gave me that impression, but I agree, no one seems to be talking to you or taking any notice of you at all."

"We have always had a kind of amorphous leadership structure."

"Sounds productive."

He briefly wondered whether it was appropriate to divulge the details of everything to Brigid, given that her position seemed largely ceremonial, but decided what the heck, no one else was talking to him anyway, and he really needed someone to bounce ideas off.

"So," she said, after he had explained to her the whole *the door was open, so we moved in* concept to her, "what you're telling me is you're a bunch of cuckoos."

"What?"

"Cuckoos. They're a bird."

"I know what a cuckoo is. I just don't understand the pointlessly distracting analogy at this particular juncture."

"They take over other birds' nests. They put their own eggs in them and then the chick hatches and throws everyone out and it gets all the attention."

"It's an inaccurate analogy to start with because we didn't throw anyone out. They were already gone."

"Are you sure?"

"Of course, I'm bloody sure. Don't you think I would have noticed if there were angels hovering around everywhere being glorious and understanding and holy at me? I would have noticed angels, alright?"

She shrugged her shoulders. "I just think that taking over when everyone was out is poor form, that's all. It wasn't your place."

A memory was niggling at the back of her mind, just poking, waiting for the right time to speak up.

"They weren't "out". We went through this. I used a white board, remember? Some of your scientists turned on some machine and the fabric of reality was rendered in half and Mur-arb was the new boss. We've been through this."

"And me."

"Yes, and you. You were the new boss too."

There was a pause.

Niggle.

"How is that going anyway?"

"Not as interesting as I'd have hoped. I've been making a library, which is fun, but now I come to think of it, Mur-arb has been in meetings with that awful Fraster for most of the time, so I haven't had that much to do. Mur-arb and I have to be in the same fractal zone or some such, but we don't actually co-create. Or something."

And the thought found its voice.

"You know, I don't think the angels mind not being here."

"How could you possibly know that?"

She told Egragore about the man on the beach. And the fact that he really hadn't been hating the fact he was having a holiday.

Egragore stared at her. "That's quite odd."

"That's what I thought."

"Huh."

"So maybe they'll be back any minute and you don't have to worry about all the meetings and Fraster being a dickhead."

"I never said Fraster is a dickhead. He's my colleague."

She raised her eyebrows at him.

"Yes, alright," he admitted. "He can be a bit of a dickhead."

Once again, Egragore glanced around furtively. "But seriously, I think they're going to stage a coup."

She leaned in, assuming an equally furtive expression. "Who?"

"Fraster. And the rest."

"But why? What are you doing to annoy them?"

"I'm not a huge fan of plunging souls into a flaming pit of repentance for an unspecified amount of time where they flail around in agony and fear regretting their earthly choices."

Brigid looked at him aghast. "Of course, you're not a fan of that. Who would be?"

"Fraster. He's awfully keen on the idea. He's recently built this big pit thing out the back. I suspect it's just a practise one, but it's grim, let me tell you."

"I thought you were all just reapers and mid-level tempters?"

"We are, for the most part. With some wraiths and the like thrown in for flavour, but yes, for the most part that's what we are."

"So why would you be intentionally causing torment to souls? It sounds demonic."

"Yes, it does rather. That's why I have a problem with it. But I seem to be a bit outvoted."

Brigid frowned. "Remember when Fraster used all those demons to try to capture me?"

"Yes," said Egragore uncertainly.

"Mur-arb told me that it was just a blip. A mistake. But doesn't that seem strange to you?"

"How strange exactly?"

"Oh, for god's sake, how can you be so naive? He is using demons. Does your lot typically work with demons?"

"Goodness no," said Egragore, aghast. "They're against everything we stand for. We believe in repentance and the possibility that all souls will reach heaven. Demonic entities, well, they hate us. You," he corrected hastily. "They hate you. Humans. Things with souls."

"Didn't it raise any warning signs when he used a fucking demonic army to try and kidnap me?"

"Fraster has always been somewhat lax with the rules. But he's my friend. Or colleague, at least. He was so helpful when I first arrived here. He just wouldn't."

"You can be really stupid for an eternal being or whatever you are," she spat at him. "He's obviously trying to bring the Great Abyss here . . . to heaven."

"Heavenly Realm," corrected Egragore automatically.

Her face was pale, and she unconsciously raised her hand to her throat, massaging herself. "If it's true, it's disgusting. It's against nature."

"For someone who didn't even believe in all of this a few weeks ago you certainly seem to be having some strong feelings now."

"And you're in denial," she snapped. "What are you even doing? Are you going to sit by while heaven is taken over by demons? I'm going to speak to Mur-arb." She jumped up. "He will absolutely not stand for this. I bet he suspected this and it's why he was so intent on bringing me here, because he knew that I could get something done about it. I know that he's quite fond of Fraster, but I can guarantee that I'm a better friend to him than that awful creature."

As she flung open the door, she turned to face him, purpose and fury blazing in her eyes. "This is what I'm here for, don't you understand. This is why I've been brought up here. This must be it. To stop this from happening. I'm here to save souls."

She stepped out into the corridor and was gone.

Egragore sat in his room long after she had left, silence falling in the building around him. The drop lights above him threw out a bright tinny shine, and he waved his hand, bringing the levels down to what he felt were more appropriate to his mood. Manipulating the air in front of him, he changed the vista outside the glass screen that covered two walls, from an immersion of billowing cumulus clouds that he liked to ironically display during the day (heaven, and all that) to an endlessly deep inky blackness, pricked with thousands of blazing pinpoints.

He stood and rested his head against the screen, feeling the cold coming from it as if he were really looking out onto the depths of space.

Not that there was day, or night, in this place, of course. But at least it was something different. Downstairs, as he had come to call it, there were no windows and no vistas to choose from, real or pretend. There was little to remind you of Earth, unless it was the officious, managerial side of the Earth; all tick boxes and flip files and mercurial management types changing procedures and routines at the drop of the hat.

But he had made it work, hadn't he? His time in the Shadow Lands had been one of unprecedented growth. He knew what was expected of him: the refinement of souls, working with them to enable them to take their place up there. And if not, if it was hopeless, then allowing them to plunge themselves into the Great Abyss, as upsetting as that was.

It had always been a matter of choice, even if they hadn't known it at the time.

And he had liked it, hadn't he? Liked his work, liked the potential, been proud of what he had been entrusted with. But now . . .

There was a gentle tap on the door and for a moment Egragore wondered if he'd heard anything at all. But then it came again. "Come in," he called out, his voice sharp in the dim quiet.

Cashion pushed the door open, blinking in the gloom. "Hello," she called nervously.

"I'm just here."

She walked over to him, her footfalls silent on the plush carpet. "Are you alright?" she asked.

"That depends," he answered. "What's going on out there?"

"I'm not really sure," she said. "There was a vote earlier, and I was the only one who objected. I don't know where everyone is now."

"Was it about me?"

She nodded. "And that woman, I think."

"Really?" He frowned. "I don't see what she has to do with this."

He felt tired. More tired than he had felt in over 600 years. "Are you going to stay up here? Or go back down to the old offices?"

"I'm not sure. I don't know if there will be a role for me if they continue on this path. I thought I might go down to Earth. Do you think there would be something for me to do down there? I'd ask Fraster but he's not around. And I know it's not really your area but do you think you could put in a good word for me?"

Egragore rubbed his eyes. He didn't feel like career counselling a wraith right now, but he could feel her disquiet, her uncertainty. "You could find a castle to wander around in, I suppose. You have that whole grey wispy thing that people love to be scared of. Would you like to try that?"

"I've never done anything like that before."

He summoned a file from the air and flicked through it, finally drawing a business card from within. "Here," he said. "Crinbourne Castle in . . ." he narrowed his eyes. "Essex, I think. Yes. Its wraith was accelerated a few years ago, and they've been doing very badly since then from all accounts. Sounds familiar. I believe I spent time there, back in the day."

She raised her eyebrows.

"When I was a human, that is. There's no use refusing to talk about it now, is there? Everyone knows I used to be human so I may as well be up front about it. So, would you like to go and rattle a few chains about?"

"Oh, yes," she smiled, her face lighting up. "I'm due for a change."

"Here you go then." He handed her the card. "Knock yourself out. Have a blast."

She took it and headed for the door, turning back momentarily to peer at him in the gloom. "Will you be alright?" she asked with genuine concern.

"I'm sure I will." He smiled, shoring up his shoulders. "Of course, I will. The CEO gave me this job, you know. Personally. I spoke to him face to face and everything. I'm sure it will take more than a few mid-level tempters to throw me off my mission." His voice faltered. His mission, was it?

"If you're sure then," she said, looking at him closely and with no further words from Egragore, she was gone too.

It seemed to be the day for women leaving his office awkwardly.

Twenty-nine

As far as Brigid could make out, Mur-arb had fashioned for himself various little micro-universes within the confines of the Heavenly Realm, and he rotated around them depending on his mood. His abilities to create change had increased dramatically since her arrival, and he'd been making the most of this. The mountainous faux-Andean world complete with llamas, yurts and *zea mays* was his current favourite, and the enormous pink balloons emblazoned with booth photos of he and Fraster that covered the tops of the mountains instead of snow were a fun if certifiably insane touch.

The Aqua world was suitably blue and relaxing, and devoid of great white sharks, as far as Brigid could tell, but, once again, the fact that the entirety of the ocean was covered by upside down beach umbrellas containing popcorn caused Brigid to wonder if this element was a deliberate inclusion. If this was the fact, then the mind that created it was of concern. If not, then the fact that he was creating what seemed to be actual worlds, but with little control over them, was also something that made her wonder exactly what was going on.

Despite all the distracting and entertaining creations that lay at his fingertips, Brigid eventually found Mur-arb sitting in the small throne room that had been his sole domain when she'd first arrived. He slumped in his chair, staring into space, and didn't seem to notice as she threw herself into the room in a manner she judged as "feistily assertive". A frown creased Mur-arb's forehead, and his eyes were deep pools of something Brigid wasn't entirely sure she liked the look of.

She hadn't had much of a chance to speak to him since she'd arrived, but she assumed this was because he was so busy making cotton-candy bio-spheres or whatever it was he'd been so excited about. She was rather pleased, in a motherly kind of way, that her presence had expanded his power, so he was able to do all of these endearingly lame things, but now she needed his full and total attention.

"I need to talk to you about something super important," she said as she approached the throne. "Are you, I mean, can you . . ." The words she wanted to say were along the lines of "Can you please mature for five minutes because I think your crony is manipulating you to try and cause the downfall of the human race or at least something along those lines" but she suspected that was way too many concepts to throw at him at once, and she would lose him to the new world he'd created, the one constructed entirely of jumping castles, before she had even started. "Do you have a minute to chat?" she said finally.

Mur-arb's eyes moved to find her, although his head stayed slumped in place. A deep sigh seemed to emanate from the very core of him. "I'm busy."

"You don't look very busy," she said. "And this is important. Look, I know that it probably hasn't been on your radar what with all your," she gestured her hands in what she felt was an umbrella/balloon kind of motion, "'creations", but I've just been talking to Egragore, and he and I are really concerned that—"

A noise rumbled from Mur-arb, a voice she hadn't heard before. "I said I'm busy. I need to think about who I can trust. I have a lot of thinking to do. On my own."

"I don't think that's the deal," she said, pushing on despite feeling the pricking of worry start to creep up her arms and edge around her neck and scalp. The very stillness of his being rang the first stirrings of warning within her. "I don't think I'm supposed to let you be." Her forced laugh echoed nervously around the sparse room. "I think we're a job lot now." She smiled widely although her cheeks began to scream in protest the longer her words hung in the air, waiting for his reply. "You know, Yin and Yang. Remember?"

"Actually," he said finally, his body relaxing somewhat as he swung himself around to face her, "since you brought it up, it's more along the lines of your being my battery. That's how I've been led to understand it."

"I'm sorry?"

"Yes." His smile matched hers, his interest in the conversation finally seeming to pick up. "Yes, apparently all we need is for you to be near me and I have the powers of creation. So technically, I could lock you in a box and go off and do my own thing. Or lock you in a coil pot, which might be more fitting." He laughed at the expression that these words brought to her face. "Oh, don't worry, I'm only joking."

She smiled nervously at him.

"I'm joking about locking you in a pot. I'd make sure it was a nice room, I promise," he continued, and his words were punctuated by a high-pitched giggle.

"Are you alright?" Her disquiet grew. "Has something happened?"

"You tell me? Has something happened?"

"I don't think so. Unless. . . I'm not sure what you mean." She glanced towards the door, wondering if this might be an opportune moment to slip out of the room.

"Apparently something is "super important", so I'm *super* keen to find out what it is." His eyes blazed with what she thought might be insanity, and she again sized up how quickly she would be able to make it out of the room. "If something is that important to you then I really do need to know what it is, don't you think? You've been having lots of lots of little discussions, from what I've been told. Hatching lots of plans. An absolute hive of schemes and ideas. You and that reaper friend of yours."

"Well," she began slowly. "I'm not sure how much you know about what's been going on around here, but things may not be quite as they seem."

She told him about the absent angels, the fact that everyone, as far as she could make out, was trespassing, the odd behaviour of Fraster, and the concerns she had about the ulterior motives of the entire middle management.

When she'd finished, he looked at her for a few moments. "So, what you're saying is that demons are trying to take over the Heavenly Realm."

"Yes." She was surprised at his ability to quickly precis the barrage of ideas she had just thrown at him. "Yes, that's pretty much it."

"And that I'm some kind of patsy whom Fraster and his minions are using as a way to gain power. That I'm being manipulated as some kind of demonic plot. That Fraster is working against my best interests."

"Yes," she said again.

"And you and that Egragore came up with these amazing deductions, did you?"

"Well, yes." She briefly wondered how she was now the one rendered idiotic by the conversation.

"Fraster," called Mur-arb, his voice rising as he continued to maintain an unsettling eye contact with Brigid. "What do you think? Am I being manipulated by some kind of demonic plot? Or maybe it's the ones coming up with the ideas that are the problem, hmmm? Don't you think that makes far more sense?"

From behind the throne stepped the tall figure of Fraster. A light smile played over his thin lips, and he held out his hands by way of welcome. "My dear. So lovely to see you again. Of course, it would have been a lot sooner if those angel friends of yours hadn't got in the way, but better late than never. And, as you may have noticed, this," he held out his arms as if to gesture to everything surrounding them, "is an angel free zone now." He breathed a deep breath through his nose, tilting his head back and half closing his eyes. "It already smells better in here, doesn't it? Without all that *goodness*. Without all that smug arrogance that goodness drags along with it. Without all that disgusting pax."

Mur-arb raised his eyebrows, not necessarily taking on Fraster's words. "Yes, yes, but what do you think? Am I being manipulated by a demonic plot?"

The two beings smiled widely at each other, and Fraster rested his long fingers on Mur-arb's arm. "Do you *feel* manipulated?" he asked with a wry grin, and they chuckled together.

"No. Not by you, anyway." He turned the full force of his dark eyes on Brigid's shocked face.

"I don't understand."

"Oh, my dear," said Fraster in the manner of a genuinely concerned and emotionally bereft elderly uncle. "I'm so sorry, but that's quite the point. Your "not understanding" has been the lynchpin of quite a lot of this, hasn't it, My Leader?"

"Yes, I'm afraid so," agreed Mur-arb. "Fraster was reasonably sure that you wouldn't have agreed to pop up and help us if you had understood everything, so we kept things on the down low, as it were. Of course, you always were so *good*, weren't you? You were always essentially good at heart, and coupled with the fact that you also, and I don't think I'm understating this, felt I was an absolute and complete fucking imbecile, I decided we couldn't really go wrong, could we? You've never respected me, you've never liked me. You mocked me even when you were a child."

Brigid gawped at Mur-arb still, her mind racing through all possible scenarios. "No! I thought you liked me. We were friends."

""Like" is a very strong word," said Mur-arb benignly. "I don't think we should just throw it around willy-nilly."

"Why? We used to be friends. I mean, pretend friends admittedly, but friends. What happened?"

"Because you let them take me," he snarled. "And you let them take you away. You could have made them keep us together. Do you have any idea what my life was like after you left? And here I was thinking that you were an innocent party, too. Thankfully the scales well and truly dropped from my eyes, and not a moment too soon. Do you have any idea what my life was reduced to?

"It wasn't much of a bloody party for me either," she protested.

"That's your own fault, your own weak pathetic fault. You could have chosen to do anything, and you wasted your life. But me, I was kept in one of your ridiculous, ugly handmade pots. A hideous handmade clay pot. Me, who could have had the world at my feet. Absolutely impotent. A shell of what I could have been, what I wanted to be, until that ridiculous Juniper had his way with me. But then, oh then, I found myself up here, a complete stroke of serendipitous luck, we thought. But maybe destiny. The angels leaving, the rightful CEO abandoning things, and then my arrival? It had to be preordained."

"No, everyone just took a holiday and . . ."

Fraster cleared his throat to interrupt but Mur-arb held up his hand "No, Fraster, I need to tell her now. There won't be another chance, and I won't find what is to come nearly as enjoyable if she never hears the truth. So, I'm brought here, but I'm clueless. No help, no power. I didn't even," and he grabbed Brigid's arm at this point, as if to ensure she really understood the emphasis of his words, "I didn't even know where the kettle was. I was nothing." He sat back, taking a deep breath and rubbing his shiny forhead. "And then these chaps all arrived, and everything started to get better."

"Egragore arrived, you mean," said Brigid. "Egragore arrived. I know that he helped you. He believed in you."

"Oh, Egragore," spat Mur-arb. "That milk sop. He just wants to make another version of heaven up here. Don't think we haven't twigged to his plans. He just wanted me to become some impotent deity that rubber stamps what the old CEO would have wanted. But really," the pressure returned on her arm, and she found herself trying to pull away from his grip, "but really, if I was supposed to do that then they wouldn't have been taken away in the first place, would they?"

"You know, from what I've been able to pick up, I think they just wanted a bit of a holiday. I tried to tell you that a minute ago . . ."

Fraster, who had been smiling calmly but seemed to have a slightly harried look in his eyes, gently removed Mur-arb's hand from her arm.

"Well done, that's right," he confirmed. "And when I, quite reasonably, explained to The Great Leader the ideas that I, that we"—he corrected quickly— "had for everything, then he saw the absolute logic of all of it straight away. He has a clearness of thought and clarity of mind that we rarely see in the Other World. He is truly a leader, and his ideas are . . ."

"What ideas?"

"That you humans have had your time," Fraster said simply. "That your ascension is over. The myth that you're the pinnacle of creation is finished and it's time for the rest of us to have a go."

"Mur-arb came up with that did he? That's his idea."

"Eventually."

"But . . . demons?"

"Yes, we demons. You were correct, of course. I am in fact a demon—a fact your Egragore has been too stupid to elucidate over the past six hundred years, despite my occasional stumblings. Demons are the only ones who don't care one whit if you humans live or die. No, I correct myself, we would, of course, like you to die, and die painfully. But we have no vested interest in your existence. We can get along perfectly well without you, although your popular culture does like to think we're obsessed with you all. Of course, bringing you and Mur-arb together was the key. Our plans would have come to naught without you." Fraster bowed deeply before her. "We couldn't have done it without you as his . . . little light, you could call it."

"I used the analogy of battery," interrupted Mur-arb.

Fraster wrinkled his nose. "I prefer light. Solar panel maybe?"

"Sun? Oh stop, she's not that powerful."

"So, you didn't need me for actual decisions? Or advice?"

"Goodness me, no. Not now. Not after he has obviously become the one that we really need. What possible advice could you have for us?" The two men laughed cheerfully. "Good lord no. You're but a conduit. A . . ."

"Receptor?"

"Oh, I quite like that one."

"Anyway, we're going to shut down everything up here, completely. Liquidate it."

"Vaporise it."

Fraster glanced at Mur-arb sharply, "Or you could just let me have the words that I choose, of course."

"I'm not going to stay quiet when my choices are better."

There was a sudden flickering and out of the corner of her eye, just out of the others' sight line, Brigid saw the figure of Egragore step back behind the curved doorway.

Buying time, she continued. "So, you're going to liquidate and or/vaporise the Heavenly Realm. Why?"

"So, they have nowhere to return to. On the off chance they do come back," said Mur-arb hurriedly. "I mean, I'm assuming they've abandoned the ridiculous human race and taken off to another reality entirely, but just on the off chance, I think we'd all feel a lot safer if we just locked things down here."

"And then what?"

Mur-arb looked questioningly towards Fraster, and Brigid understood fully that whatever was afoot was not of his doing and no longer under his control. But she could, she thought, perhaps wrestle things back in her favour. There must still be, at Mur'arb's core, the heart of the doddery man who loved creating weave patterns with afghans and bottle-feeding orphaned wallabies.

The shadow cast by Egragore could be dimly seen wavering by the doorway, and she soundlessly begged him to step back. Her best chance now was finding out as much as possible while they were both in a chatty mood.

"We don't want the risk of them coming back and reinstating humans as "special friends", do we now?" said Mur-arb. "The delusions of grandeur that those creatures have." He shuddered.

"Disgusting," agreed Fraster.

"Their time has finished. It's a natural evolution, if you like. Everything comes in cycles. That's right, isn't it?" he asked, looking to Fraster for confirmation.

"Yes, that's right."

"I take it this is all your idea?" Brigid reluctantly rested her eyes on the demon Fraster.

He smiled, his thin lips exposing oddly small teeth. "Oh, my dear, please believe me wholeheartedly when I promise you that our mutual friend needed little to no encouragement to embrace this plan. Anyway." He clapped his hands quickly, the short sharp sounds echoing in the sparse chamber. "This has been fun and has, I hope, satisfied your need for some dramatic flair, My Leader? But it's really time we got on. We're hauling out of here, you might say, but we need to put you and your friend somewhere where you won't bother us anymore."

"And everyone else has just gone along with this, have they?" asked Brigid. "All the other Shadow Land beings have just gone along with your plans? They all hate us, too?" Brigid looked accusingly towards Mur-arb. "But why do you hate humans? We were your friends. You lived with us. At least, you lived in our commune. Not all of us could see you, but we were kind, weren't we? We talked to you, meditated with you, helped you."

"And then I was banished. Because you couldn't handle my true power."

"No," she clarified. "It was because you kept causing the power to go out and one of the toddlers thought you were a poltergeist and kept having night terrors. That's why you were banished. And when it was discovered that you and I were co-dependent Mum and Dad decided I should go to an actual school. No-one hated you."

She saw Mur-arb frown, but Fraster abruptly steered back the conversation.

"You need to understand it honestly isn't about hate. It's about indifference. And I must say, my little "throwing human souls into a burning abyss as way of purification" lark has removed any reservations some of them may have had about the inherent kindness they still believed they needed to have."

"So, you've deliberately desensitised them?"

"Lovely, yes, that's a good way of putting it. I've desensitised them. Nothing like hearing humans screaming in agony "for their own good" to stop any last vestiges of empathy or pity from holding on. A few lingering wraiths and the like have scampered off though; don't think I don't know about that. Don't think I don't know about that, Egragore," he called loudly.

There was a pause, Brigid's heart caught in her throat, and the figure of Egragore appeared casually in the doorway.

"Hi, guys. Hey, Brigid. How's it going?" He waved casually to the room. His relaxed insouciance was betrayed by the way his eyes darted huntedly around, sizing up exactly what he was dealing with. He pushed his dark fringe out of his eyes, and his boots echoed off the walls as he walked over to Brigid and stood close to her. Catching her eye, he gave her a wink, and she smiled tightly. Why on earth had he just walked in here? Why had he walked into this trap?

"You've been listening then?" asked Fraster.

"Yes, yes," he confirmed. "And I'm rather smugly pleased to see I was right all the time."

"About?"

"About the fact you had, shall we say, ulterior motives in constructing that whole fiery pit of doom."

Fraster mimed applause and smiled benignly. "Yes, you did get that right, so well done to you. I'm afraid you got everything else gob smacking wrong though, didn't you?"

"You mean the whole bit where you're a demon trying to destabilise the Heavenly Realm and I didn't notice; always making excuses for your bad behaviour? Plus the fact that you've got the new ruler on your side, and it looks like you'll take some kind of revenge on me and destroy planet Earth?"

"Yes, that bit."

Egragore shrugged casually. "To be fair, you can't bat one hundred every time, can you?"

"Now of course," continued Fraster, "if I was being sportsmanlike, to keep the analogy going, I would give you the chance to repent and pledge allegiance to our new ruler."

"I wouldn't accept it," blustered Mur-arb, but Fraster held up his hand in sharp irritation.

"As I was saying, I would give you a chance to become part of the glorious new future, but—"

"Well, I wouldn't—"

Fraster's loud hissing noise of irritation cut off Egragore's words.

"*BUT*, given that you still hold the essential humanity of your birth . . ."

"You do need to fully explain this human thing to me sometime," said Brigid out of the side of her mouth. "That conversation keeps getting side-tracked."

"It's just that I was born human. It's not important. I'll tell you about it later if you want."

"I think you probably should have told me about it properly before now."

"Right, look, never mind," Fraster barked with irritation. "Just forget it. You're both going someplace where you can't interfere with our plans anymore, and that's all there is to it."

He waved his hands in the air in a counter clockwise motion, muttered some words under his breath, and Egragore and Brigid found themselves unable to move or speak.

Fraster stood so close to Brigid that she could feel the coldness emanating from him. "I'll have you know," he hissed, "that I wanted to plunge you into the Great Abyss myself, but as Mur-arb reminded me that would render him useless. So, the second-best option is to lock you away. And you." He turned to regard Egragore with a baleful glare. "You may as well keep her company. We both know you can't be destroyed, but I have no doubt you could still be an irritant to me." He threw up his hand and a hidden pressurised door sighed open. "We have prepared an area for you to stay in. It isn't too horrendous; you can thank Mur-arb for that; apparently he still has some sympathy for you." He addressed this to Brigid, whose eyes bulged wide with frustration and fear.

"Not a pot," volunteered Mur-arb almost plaintively. "See, I'm not putting you in a pot."

Brigid felt herself involuntarily moving, as if on casters, and in a moment she and Egragore were on the other side of the door.

"Don't relax too much though, my friends," she heard Fraster call through the gently closing door. "As soon as we work out a way to get rid of you entirely you can be sure we'll take advantage of it."

Given the fact that Brigid was rendered immobile and her mind was focussed on the prospect of indefinite imprisonment, she didn't notice the figure of her guardian angel, who had momentarily materialised, surveyed the scene, rolled her eyes so hard that they almost fell out of her head, and then dematerialised.

Thirty

"I fucking told her," stormed Guindaline, slamming back into the Earth's sphere of reality with all the power of a freight train, and a good deal more attitude.

"I told her this very firmly. Very firmly. But why would she listen to her guardian angel? What possible reason would there be to listen to your own fucking guardian angel? I *told* her she shouldn't have gone and you," here she pointed a perfectly manicured finger accusingly at the occupants of the room, "you lot were complicit in it. Ohhhh, just meditate and talk to him," she mimicked mincingly in a manner that was totally unlike the way any of them sounded but said volumes as to the disdain she currently had for them. "Because now she's worked out that the demons are trying to take over everything, and they've put her and Egragore in a time lock and I can't get into that to help her. I certainly don't have those kind of powers. Do you?" She swung around and assailed Michael with the full force of her accusations. "I bet you can't either, can you? Can you?"

Frank and Michael stared at her in bemusement from their place on the sofa, which was pushed companionably up by the fire. Pat and Lauren sat at the dining table, busily weaving hemp fripperies. The dinner detritus had been moved, the dishes had been cleared away, and everyone was settling down over steaming mugs of chamomile tea. Only an hour had passed since Brigid had gone upstairs, so it wasn't unreasonable that no real alarm bells or concerns had begun to creep into their consciousness.

"She's worked out that the demons are taking over, and she's been locked up?" Frank looked concerned, if somewhat doubtful. "Already? That's quick work. Are you sure?"

"Of course I'm sure. Time is different up there," the guardian angel snapped, in a manner that made it quite clear she didn't have any intention of explaining the intricacies of dimensional time differences to an idiot.

"Still," said Frank. "Even so."

"What's that, dear?" asked Pat, looking up from the ball of hemp twine that appeared to be evolving into a gemstone encrusted dream catcher.

"Apparently Brigid has been locked up. Not quite sure why. Why was it again?"

Guinnie held her hand up as if to silence him and turned her attention back to Michael. "Can you please go up there and get her?"

Michael smiled nervously. "Actually, I tried to pop up there the other day to get something out of my locker and . . ." He dropped his eyes from hers. "No go. I think my privileges have been revoked. Or something."

She shook her head, exasperated. "That's what I suspected. I think those of us who haven't just disappeared are being chilled out. I could only materialise for a few seconds before I was sucked back down here. I think this is bigger than we first thought."

"Bigger than the entirety of the Heavenly Realm disappearing for no good reason, and being invaded by the Shadow Lands, which now seems to be populated by the inhabitants of the Great Abyss? Bigger than that?"

Guinnie looked at him sharply. She sometimes couldn't tell if he was asking very perceptive questions, or being sassy, and right now she rather suspected it was the latter.

"We have a direct contravention of article R57* of the Paranormal and Extra natural Beings Covenant for a start," said Guinnie, ticking things off on her fingers, "which says that a human's free will can't be compromised. Then we have the flagrant disregard by an omnipotent deity of the basic rules of, well, decency, then we have—"

"Is this new guy actually an omnipotent deity?" questioned Michael. "Because I feel like he isn't. Otherwise, he wouldn't have needed Brigid's help in the first place."

Guinnie stared at him, aghast. "But the ruler of the universe has to be an omnipotent deity."

"Yes, you would think so, wouldn't you."

She pulled a chair out from the table and perched on the edge of it, but then leapt up again and began to pace around the room. "No, you don't understand. The ruler of the universe has to be an omnipotent deity. Not on principle or any moral or ethical bullshit, but in order to hold the very fabric of space and time together. Only an omnipotent deity can grasp the whole multitudinous complexity of the entirety of every dimension, both finite and infinite, and keep them in perfect balance."

Michael stared at her blankly.

"Did you not listen to anything at Advanced Guardianship Training?"

"I'm very good at sword fighting, if you've noticed. I paid attention to the stuff that mattered."

"This stuff matters," she hissed from between thinned lips. "This stuff truly matters. I'm genuinely terrified that the entire universe might implode at any moment, and I'm going to need more help than someone who is good at bloody sword fighting. We need to fill in all the blanks about this Mur-arb guy. Frank?"

"Hello, yes?" Frank smiled up from his mug of tea.

"What do you know about this Mur-arb guy?"

"The one who's currently in charge of the universe?"

"Allegedly, yes."

"Ah. Yes." Frank cleared his throat and sat the mug down on the green tile coffee table. "What specifically do you want to know? I mean, you were there weren't you? The first time?"

"Yes, yes, of course I was. But, you know, the odd detail may have slipped past. You wouldn't say he's omnipotent, would you? Where did he come from? Is he omnipotent?"

Frank laughed. "Oh, good grief no. I mean, I don't think so. I don't think that a conjured spirit could be omnipotent, could it? You would know more about these things than I do."

"A conjured spirit?" Guinnie felt a little like she was leading a conversation with a five-year-old, but at this stage she couldn't risk startling Frank. She needed him to be very, very on the ball right now and very, very cognisant of what she was saying. "What do you mean, "a conjured spirit"? I thought he was one of those elementals. One of those residual things that had glommed onto Brigid."

"No, I don't think so. Now, bear with me. You see, some years ago, and I'm not sure how much you know about this, so please feel free to stop me if I'm telling you something you already know, but some years ago, our friend Juniper, who was I think a warlock of some kind, but I believe that a more gender neutral term of "witch" is used these days, but he called himself a warlock back then—"

"Are you talking about Juniper?" called Pat from across the room.

"Yes, love, this young lady wants to know all about Mur-arb."

"It's a pity I can't see her. I'd be able to have a chat too. Juniper was always such a sweet man."

"Anyway," prompted Guinnie, with what she felt was saintly patience, "this Juniper bloke conjured a spirit did he?" She had, of course, been around for all this, technically, but she would be the first to admit that she didn't always pay the attention that she should.

"In a manner of speaking, yes. He wanted to conjure up his own spirit familiar you see, to give general guidance and help. There was this young lady he was quite keen on, she sang in a folk band I think, and he wanted some advice around that. Anyway, he wanted to conjure up some assistance."

"He didn't think to call on his very own guardian angel, did he then?" said Guinnie testily.

"Oh, people didn't believe in that kind of thing back then. I mean, I could see Michael of course but I was still left to 'make my own meaning on the terms of my own paradigm' or some such thing. It was much more fun to throw some herbs together, wave some smoke, and conjure a spirit, wasn't it?"

"Of course, given that it seems to have worked out so well," she continued tersely.

"Funny you should say that, because he did have his own familiar that he met during his own soul flight journeys, and the spirit seemed totally up for it, and it was all going terribly well but then—"

"He used the wrong sigil," cackled Pat, unable to contain her amusement.

"That's just it. Bless, he used the wrong sigil to summon him. So, he had his whole magic hoo-ha worked out, and he was quite good at it by this stage, if I remember correctly, so he summoned it up, it arrived on the spiritual plane, it possessed the pot he had set up—"

"For a spirit to exist within the physical plane it must have a vessel to possess, as far as we know," Pat explained to Lauren. "And the closest thing to hand was one of Brigid's little knick-knacks."

"But it turns out, he'd summoned the *wrong spirit*." Frank laughed heartily at the memory.

Guinnie's stricken face indicated it was becoming very clear that she indeed should have taken more notice of what was going on at the time.

"There was quite a fuss about it at the time," added Pat.

"Of course, there was." Frank was now well into his memories. "He had summoned this new spirit; Mur-arb was his name. Lovely guy, as I've said, but a fair bit less on-task than Juniper had expected, all things considered. And then, as it turned out, he was able to physically manifest himself occasionally too, which no one was really expecting, and there was a bit of a palaver around that. What did they call that, love?"

"A tulparata wasn't it? Conjuring a thought form but not knowing what you're doing? Yes, I think the formal term for what is created is tulparata."

"That's it. And then there was all that fuss about what Mur-arb was supposed to be doing with his so-called life. Remember that?"

"Remember it? I was there for goodness' sakes. Juniper was most upset. Ranted and raved about unleashing untold horror on the universe and all that. He always was a very theatrical man. None of us had the least idea why he was so upset."

"And as it turned out, there were no untold horrors or anything of the sort. Mur-arb just wanted to live his life peacefully on this earthly plane and who could blame him? None of us could really see what the real problem was with him, apart from being annoying a lot of the time." Frank smiled sympathetically.

"Juniper wouldn't listen though. He got quite obsessed. Mur-arb had to go, he decided. Eventually Juniper had worked out a way to get Mur-arb into a vessel, trapped I think, which seemed to quieten everything, but he never managed to actually exorcise him, but as I said, that was the last I heard. It was at that time that we moved anyway. It was time to give Brigid a proper mainstream life, we decided, and after that the whole commune was divided up. And Juniper went off somewhere."

"Yes, it was all against some official covenant or other according to Juniper. He said that he'd been in contact with a whole new pantheon of beings, and they'd cleared everything up for him. Because he wasn't an officially accredited summoner, so Mur-arb had to go. Quite sad, but probably all for the best."

"And then the place he was banished to was the coil pot made by Brigid. His choice, apparently. He wanted to stay bonded to her or some such."

"Better a pot than a person, I'd think," said Lauren somewhat breathlessly. She had been listening to the one-sided conversation with a huge amount of enjoyment, bolstered primarily by the fact that everything she had suspected about life and reality appeared to be true.

Guinnie's arms were tightly folded, and her foot tapped on the slate floor.

"And now you tell me he's taken over as ruler or some such thing, which I must admit is a bit of a surprise. I wouldn't have thought he'd be much good at it." Frank shrugged.

"Brigid helping him would have given him some guidance at least," called Pat.

"Yes, that's true. She did have a good head on her shoulders when it came to giving him advice. But this young lass tells us now that he's locked her up, so I don't know what's going on."

There was a pause.

"What's she saying now?" asked Pat.

Frank peered at Guinnie carefully. "Nothing right now. She doesn't look very happy."

"Doesn't look very happy? Didn't she like your story? I could try to remember some more bits of it if you think it would help. Like how Juniper devised his own magic system that—"

Frank held up his hand. "Hang on, love, I think she's going to say something."

Guinnie continued to stare off into space.

"She's thinking," whispered Michael.

She thought for a while. Finally, she sighed heavily.

"Right, so what we have is a common or garden spirit type thing, who seems admittedly quite powerful. He got a taste for being in charge back in the '80s after being summoned by a basic incompetent. Now, as a result of what can only be described as a random freakish quirk of scientific chicanery and malpractice"—here she glared at the humans as if they had been personally responsible for the actions carried out at CERN, the home of the Large Hadron Collider— "he has been thrust into the position of having more power than he could possibly ever have dreamed of, and he may well not even want. Plus, he doesn't have a prescribed moral framework to work within, and seems to have gone with the plans of whatever afterlife faction blew enough smoke up his arse and/ or scared him the most. Is that what we have?"

Michael and Frank were unsure if this was rhetorical or if she genuinely wanted their input. They both, wisely, decided it was probably the latter and nodded.

"So, there's a really obvious solution to it then, isn't there?"

The rhetorical questions were quite scaring Michael and Frank at this stage.

"Do you think it might be a wise idea to try and get hold of Juniper about now?" called Pat.

Guinnie threw her hands up. "Finally, someone with a brain," she said.

Thirty-one

From A Concise History of The Shadow Lands, Volume 59, page 893.

How the mortal warlock Juniper became intricately involved in the greater workings of the Other World, and his round-about involvement in the fate of the Shadow Lands more specifically, has been well documented in other tomes, but how it has bearing on the topic at hand bears clarification.

In the words of a particular human who became famous primarily because he didn't die of the plague, (which cut down a significant amount of his more talented rivals), 'Some are born great, some achieve greatness, and some have greatness thrust upon them.' This is how Juniper liked to think of his life trajectory to this point. He fell upon this mainly because no one had thought up a great quote that included the idea of 'some have greatness because they had an almost pathological need to dick around with magic way out of their league'.

This dicking around with magic way out of his league had caused him no end of guilt and regret, because of the arse backwards way he went about things. Then there was his fervent desire to forget he had discovered the discombobulating and hefty truth that the girl he thought was the perfect subject of positive and life affirming forces…the child of his best friends…was in fact a goddess, and he was causing some significant grief to some of the framework of the known universe by connecting her up to Mur-arb.

He hadn't intended to connect her up to Mur-arb, and this point was the single aspect that ensured he did not receive any disciplinary action, although whether Other World beings can bring disciplinary action to bear on still-alive morals is still being hotly contested. He had originally meant to summon his own spirit guide. Juniper had wanted some life advice; direction and clarification about whether he should put all his energy into learning the banjo or the mandolin (he simply didn't have the finger strength for both), so his motives were innocent enough.

Tangentially, and bear with us for a moment as its relevance will become apparent, Brigid, Goddess of the Flame and of the Well, Divine Mistress of Spring and New Growth, Font of all Inspiration and Creativity, was tired and needed a rest. She was done. She had done all the creation and tweaking and organising the general business of helping people for many, many years and she was, basically, burnt out.

So, after a full and frank exchange of views in the Upper Realm, with some tears and some hugs, it was decided that she would spend time on earth essentially being a nobody. The CEO had misgivings, but Brigid was very firm in her opinions and beliefs and quite honestly the CEO had had enough run ins with stroppy European deities in the past to know when he was beaten.

So, a place, and a time, where she could rest and recuperate, and just generally not be worried about everything going on in the upper echelons was selected. A suitable family was chosen for her, she had a going away party, her memory was fully wiped and Bob's your uncle.

The aforementioned 'rest' was somewhat hindered by the fact that Juniper came on the scene, started up his conjuring and matched her up, accidentally, with Mur-arb, and this is where free-will can prove, to put it plainly, a bit of a bugger. Mur-arb was harmless. He was doddery, definitely, however he was an other world being, and this was not what had been planned for her. Mind melding with a summoned spirit was not what had been planned for her at all, and it should have been heartily discouraged if anyone had been given a heads up about it. But Juniper seemed quite set on it all. He saw a chance for great enlightenment, for astral clarity and for a great push forward for humankind.

Sure, it was a bit of a stretch, and it probably wasn't going to happen, but the fact is that within Brigid he saw something great, the potential, the glimmer, the possibility for amazing spiritual things.

He did have a bit of a gift, after all.

It was decided, at the very highest levels, that someone would have to have a bit of a talk with him. He couldn't just be stopped; his memory couldn't be wiped (article R57 of the Paranormal and Extra Natural Beings Covenant for Earth Based relations re: free will), and while there were covert attempts to redirected him, he proved quite fixated and didn't take readily to subtle advice. So, there was another meeting, and it was decided that, given his dogged determination and his belief that he really was working on world peace or the like, that he should probably be told the truth. To end the matter once and for all.*

So, they told him.

They took him aside, and they told him.

The CEO, that is. The CEO took him aside and told him about Brigid. About the sabbatical. And about the fact that he was really, (and they decided that they needed to speak plainly here), fucking things up for her.

And to Juniper's credit he felt extremely bad about the whole thing. There were apologies all round and yes, again some tears, but at the end of the day it was made quite clear to him that he needed to restrict any magical and or/ paranormal dealings from her entirely. She needed her peace.

Which he agreed to readily, and because the Upper Realm were a really lovely bunch, they gave a slight bump to Juniper's powers, but in a way that couldn't really harm anyone. He thought he'd come by them of his own volition, but it never hurts to have someone's ego plumped does it?

He made sure that Brigid and Mur-arb were removed from each other, he promised that he would make sure she wasn't bothered anymore, and he decided to remove himself entirely from the equation lest he screw things up for her even more.

He didn't promise not to dabble in the magical again, but he did promise not to dabble in the business of goddesses.

Which was all well and good.

Thirty-two

It was a testament to Brigid's dogged determination to get to the bottom of things, and her inability to focus on anything else while so preoccupied, that even though she and Egragore had been locked in a series of fairly well-appointed rooms, with no discernible escape plan, all she really wanted to do was find out more details about the fact that Egragore had once been human.

"There's nothing else we can do," she said reasonably. "And you can't get away from me because of all this . . ."

He looked at her with weary eyes. "It's so long ago. It's in the past."

The look on her face indicated that he wasn't having it. So, with a sigh, he told her.

Egragore had lived a fair to middling life. Not too good, not appallingly bad, but in all honesty, it was very difficult to live a really good life in England in the 1350s, what with all the filth and the dying and the rampant underlying class warfare and the persecution.

Not dying of the plague and not being flogged by an angry mob or being poisoned by a rancid potato was pretty much a good day, as far as Egragore could remember. And while he never did any of the killing or the persecuting or the selling of the rancid potatoes himself, it was hard to avoid the general zeitgeist.

He was more concerned with keeping his head down and not dying than he was with making the world a better place, so when he eventually did die (after being hit by a falling church spire, of all things) he was pleased but slightly embarrassed to find himself not only in the Heavenly Realm, but also being lauded as one of the Great Ones. He was fitted for a pair of angel wings, because, as he was told by a great shining being atop a glowing cloud, his heroism and selfless love was such as the world had never seen. For his great sacrifice to mankind, his selfless disregard for his own safety plus the fact he had saved countless children from certain death, he was being given Angel status, an honour that had never been bestowed upon a human in the vast and expansive history of space and time.

Ever. At all.

The fact he was being addressed as "Maud" with she/her pronouns was a little mystifying to him, but he reasoned that he'd never been dead before, had never been made an angel and maybe this was just how things went down around here. Who was he to judge?

Meanwhile he was happily going to accept any accolades coming his way and was hardly going to say no to an angelic feast in his honour. He really didn't think it was his place to question the decision of an omnipotent and omniscient being, even if he hadn't ever done anything to rescue a child from certain death…unless it had been by accident without him knowing about it. But, the love, the glory and the sheer magnificent awesomeness of the place in which he had found himself had already started to work on his heart and change him. He wondered that maybe if he had his time again then perhaps he could have been just a little more giving, a little more loving, and a little less obsessed with his physical safety over all other priorities.

So he was a little disappointed when it came to light that there had, of course, been a massive cock up, and the elderly woman who had been crushed to death next to him was actually the great shining being the likes of which had never been beheld in the history of all humankind. He was just some guy who was not only not a great shining being but didn't even have a place reserved in the Heavenly Realm at all. In a monumentally awkward case of gate crashing, he had inadvertently become the honoured guest at a party he hadn't even been invited to.

So, there were hearty apologies all round, some vigorous hand shaking, pats on the back and some string pulling. When he found himself in the Shadow Lands, it wasn't as a soul trying to refine itself through suffering into something better, but as a rapidly promoted reaper who got to make some of the decisions, had bodily autonomy and at least had a clue about what was going on.

It had never happened before. No matter how amazing and wonderful, or horrific and demonic the afterlife proved to be, human souls had no place in the running of it.

That was well understood.

Except this once, in an uncustomary and unorthodox and yes, possibly foolhardy manner, a once-was-human did take his place in the pantheon of otherworldly beings that divinely ruled the realms of the afterlife.

Well, he'd been in the Heavenly Realm. He couldn't exactly forget all of that, could he? He couldn't bloody well just forget everything that had been opened up before him. Not really.

Over the years he came to the conclusion that it had been the worst consolation prize in the history of forever, because if he had just been sent to purgatory as a struggling soul, then at least he would have had a chance at heaven. As it was, he was doing a job he couldn't stop doing because he was expected to be grateful it had been given to him at all, and there was no chance of getting out of the situation. To make matters worse, he had Fraster being an arsehole to him for all eternity because Egragore was now his superior and humans were seen as little more than vermin by a surprisingly large number of the afterlife community.

"So that's it," he finished despondently. "That's my story. I hope you will now understand why I don't usually open with it when I meet new people."

"It's bloody embarrassing," agreed Brigid.

"Yes, I've been treated with a delicious mixture of contempt, dislike and second-hand embarrassment for hundreds of years, so it's been an absolute pleasure, let me assure you."

"It does make the Heavenly Realm management look a bit slack. Or outrageously incompetent and unbelievably negligent."

"That's one of the reasons why I do what I do," said Egragore. "I don't want any more stuff ups. A clerical error has essentially ruined my afterlife, and I'd prefer it if that didn't happen to any other poor souls."

Brigid smiled at him. "I would have liked to know you when you were a human."

He laughed. "I was a bit of an arsehole. And I smelled. The hygiene in the afterlife is much better, that's one advantage."

She reclined on a navy-blue lounge that seemed to have been placed so as to jarringly clash with the rest of the décor. Across from the lounge was a large blackwood credenza, jammed full of miscellaneous games and jigsaws that were missing precisely 3 pieces each.

"Here we are then."

"Yes, here we are."

"Any plans?"

"Not a one."

"Excellent. I trust something will come to us."

Egragore looked doubtful. "From what I have seen of your mate Mur-arb, and Fraster, I think our best chance of getting out of here is one of them forgetting we exist and leaving a gate open."

"Let's be on the lookout for open gates then."

"I suppose so."

They sat in silence for a while.

"How human are you still? Do you know how to do human kinds of things?" she asked him suddenly.

"What do you mean "how human am I"? I look human. What else is there?"

Her eyes twinkled.

"You don't mean . . ."

She leaned forwards, her eyes searching his face for the answer she was looking for.

"What do you know about backgammon?" she asked.

Thirty-three

The cafe was decidedly retro: spacious, garishly carpeted, orange laminated tables set with plenty of space between them. The kind of place that had been found in department stores all over Australia until the 1990s. Back when profit margins became more important than whether nannas were able to buy their grandchildren a bowl of chips and a frog in the pond on their day out, or a harried retail worker was able to grab a quick and cheap cup of Styrofoam tea during their fifteen-minute break.

Now the luncheon world was all gourmet sandwiches and chunky cut potato wedges with sweet chili sour cream for the kids, which cost more that the movie ticket once had, or standing in line for ten minutes to buy an overpriced coffee that could double as a hot milkshake, and there was your break gone and there was no time left for a ciggie, was there?

But this cafe steadfastly remained a last dinosaur among eating establishments. A place where you could grab your tray and slide it with a satisfyingly smooth hiss along the metal shelf, surveying the food that sat, quietly and deliciously in its own juices, under the Perspex shields.

Bowls of chips for $1, and of course sauce was always free, and from the squeeze bottle; there were no ridiculously tiny plastic packets here, where you had as much chance of shooting sauce into your eye when you pressed it as you did of directing it onto your chips. Plates of rissoles and instant mashed potato, crab sticks, ham sandwiches on white bread, and horrifyingly yellow yet pleasantly gelatinous custard slices with the perfect plastic tooth achingly sweet white icing, little cups of jelly with a choccie frog on top, and of course, milkshakes in huge metal cups, made with full cream milk, syrup, and with a dollop of ice cream plopped in the top. A much-maligned plastic straw topped it off. Turtles? Who cared about turtles? It was more important that some poor kiddie's straw didn't collapse after ten minutes and fall into the drink, which indubitably happened with those ridiculous paper ones, and of course International Roast coffee and tea in the bag. Costs had to be cut somewhere, after all.

Although it was primarily fuelled by white flour and sugar, and while nary a food allergy or diet choice was catered to (unless meat and three veg is a recognised diet choice, in which case the cafe was utterly inclusive) both locals and kitsch connoisseurs flocked to it. It was cheap, it was tasty, you got your food quickly, and you could sit at the orange laminate tables and chat for as long as you wanted without fear of being moved on. Also, it provided, hands down, the best tomato sauce any one had ever tasted.

Or had tasted in recent memory, anyway.

The rumour flew around, with reliable regularity, that Juniper's *Tasty Licks*, as it was called, was going to close. Some of the most prevalent reasons were: that the owner couldn't afford to pay the overheads; that the building was being bought by a Chinese conglomerate; that it was only a matter of time until it went the way of all old fashioned cafes and was razed to the ground. However, it stubbornly continued to stay open, and no one could work out why.

The answer was, of course, magic. It had taken Juniper a long time to hone his magic skills into a true craft; mistakes had been made, there had been casualties along the way that he sorely regretted, but now, finally, in the golden years of his life, he was making damn sure that he was using his powers wisely. Wisely and sensibly, making sure that the children of the 21st century were able to eat their chips and milkshakes without any interference from macrobiotic, gluten free, or vegan naysayers.

It seems to be a strange hill to die on, that if one was going to stake their entire life's learnings on a just one issue, supplying citizens with sugar and carbs would certainly be a road less travelled, if not a road absolutely never used and with a large "keep out" sign leaning drunkenly on the rusted gate. But no one was privy to this information, and Juniper worked doggedly away at keeping the Shield of Ignorance activated, ensuring a steady stream of food be provided to his cafe, and that no child should suffer the dietary life that Brigid had been subjected to decades earlier.

If he had to do penance, then he was going to enjoy himself while doing it, and he was going to bring happiness to the world.

And because of this, he wasn't hugely surprised when Frank and Pat, along with two angels, arrived in his cafe one Friday just at closing time.

He had aged, of course. They had all aged. But his particular kind of aging had resulted in a kind of exhaustion around the eyes, a greyness of long plaited hair and goatee beard that one often didn't see outside a man who had been in prison for the better part of the last fifty years. He looked haggard; he looked tired beyond measure; he looked worried. The constant wild darting of his eyes spoke of a man who had seen too much of this world (and indeed, a variety of other worlds), and he was quite frankly over it.

But the way his eyes lit up when he saw Frank and Pat, the way the years dropped away from his face so you could see the young, hopeful, slightly delusional young man, would bring a smile to the hardest of hearts, the way he wrapped his arms around both of them in turn and told them that it was really, really amazing and wonderful to see them after all these years was genuine. It would lead the casual observer to realise that perhaps his life hadn't been quite as gruelling and unforgiving as the geography of his face implied.

After he had put them to work tidying up for the day, and wiping down tables and rearranging the laminated menus, he made them all a cuppa and offered them a seat in the main body of the café, where they all politely made small talk and completely avoided mentioning the reason that Pat and Frank had made the five-hour drive to see him.

They noticed he was glancing over their shoulder repeatedly, with all the intensity of a first-time flyer waiting for their bags at baggage collection.

"Look, I don't want to be weird or anything," he said finally, "but can you see the angels who are standing over there?"

"I can," confirmed Frank. "But she can't. It's ok, they're with us. They're . . . the good guys," he finished weakly.

"Oh, thank god." A look of relief washed over Juniper's face. "I was worried that they might be . . ." He shook his head as if to rid himself of unpleasant memories. "I don't see things that aren't there very often anymore, and I just wanted to make sure they hadn't come for me. That it's not my time."

Frank glanced over his cup of tea at Michael and Guinnie, who were lounging in the olive-green bench seats that ran along the far wall and tearing open packets of sugar. "You wouldn't have thought there was anything to worry about with those two surely? Not with the wings and the halos and the golden glow of otherworldly goodness? I mean, they don't look like trouble, do they?"

Juniper frowned and shook his head, flinching at some long-ago memory. "I just don't know. I just don't know anymore. You just never know."

Pat reached across the table and laid her hand on his. "I thought you would have moved on from all of this," she said gently. "You know we don't blame you for what happened."

He laughed a hollow, mirthless laugh. "Except it was all entirely my doing, and I'm the one who brought him to this plane, through my own incompetence and hubris."

"Yes, that's true," said Frank, ignoring the glare from his wife. "It *is* your fault, what happened, but we don't *blame* you, if you know what I mean. I mean, we were all young, we were trying out different things, you just made a mistake, that's all. And I mean, nothing dreadful happened at all. We just realised that we shouldn't, you know, mess around with sprits, I guess."

"But it could have though. That's what's always stayed with me. I summoned a random, powerful spirit that took a shine to your daughter. He must have recognised her residual power."

Here he stopped, seeing the puzzled looks on Pat and Frank's faces. Across the room, Guinnie looked up, frowning at this comment, but Juniper moved on quickly, seemingly keen to keep things moving.

"But Brigid was all right and no harm was done. How is she these days, anyway?"

Pat cleared her throat, responding to an imperceptible nod from her husband. "Actually, that's what we've come here to speak to you about. Now, I don't want you to get upset, but . . ."

And she told him.

He responded fairly well, considering.

Considering the fact he'd just been told a spirit he had brought to this earthly plane had somehow been appointed as leader of the universe, had gone rogue, and had imprisoned Brigid, and that now they needed him to come up with a way to vanquish him. Again.

He responded fairly well, considering all of that.

The way he dealt with it, as far as they could see, was to ask if they'd like another cup of tea, and then disappear behind the swinging doors of the kitchen for half an hour.

"What's going on?" called Guinnie eventually, after they had moulded all the sugar on all the tables into a kind of medieval castle arrangement and then reminisced about old times and previous charges. "Have you sorted it? Can we go now?"

"Soon," replied Frank, who wasn't at all sure whether it would be, but didn't need impatient angels on his hands at this stage. "Should I go in there and see what's keeping him?" he asked Pat, who had started knitting.

She shrugged. "Maybe he's done a runner out the back door. I feel like he still frightens easily."

Frank looked at her aghast. "Surely, he wouldn't have run off? Surely, he understands how important this all is?"

"It's precisely the fact that he understands how important this all is that he may have run off," she said, pulling herself to her feet and placing her handbag, the one made of recycled seat belts, on the table. "But come on, let's go and see, at least."

Winding her way through the maze of tables, and around the back of the bain-marie, Pat pushed through the swinging doors and stepped into the kitchen.

It looked, to all intents and purposes, like a perfectly normal commercial kitchen: stainless steel benches, ovens, racks of utensils and a large fridge/freezer at the back. What was slightly unexpected was what appeared to be a medium sized time vortex throbbing away right next to the warming ovens.

Not that they knew it was specifically a time vortex. But a vortex is a vortex is a vortex, and it didn't take a genius to know one when they saw it.

"No wonder he didn't want us to come back here," said Frank. "That's got to be against health and safety regulations."

Pat edged around the back of the warp in space, which twisted and gleamed casually to itself. A faint hum emanated from it, and it seemed to possess the vague smell of cinnamon.

"It's just floating here," she said. "Just casually floating here. I bloody well bet this is where Juniper escaped into."

"I must say," said Frank, "that creating a vortex in your own commercial kitchen isn't really the way to make up for past magical mistakes, is it? I mean, if he's really interested in protecting other people and not, you know, interfering with reality, then I would have thought that installing a vortex right where people could walk into it willy-nilly is a pretty poor showing. He certainly hasn't become any more sensible over the past few decades."

At these words, a few streamlets of energy zapped out towards Frank, who jumped back with a small yelp.

"He did tell us not to come back here, didn't he?" said Pat. "I suppose that was his way of keeping everything in its place." She leaned forwards and peered into its depths. "Juniper?" she called, her voice disappearing as if whisked away down an airplane toilet. "Juniper? Are you in there? We're still waiting, you know, dear."

The colours and kaleidoscope shapes within the tunnel took on a new hue, and with a faint popping noise, Juniper stepped out, holding several metal trays in one hand, and a cumbersome plastic container in the other.

"Hello, yes, sorry about that," he apologised. "Didn't mean to take so long so sorry about that. How long was I gone exactly?"

Frank looked at his watch. "Forty-five minutes."

"Oh, that's alright then. I thought for a moment it could have been days. It's happened before. I was just grabbing some new vanilla slices and sauce.

And I needed to have a quick chat with someone. And now what's done is done."

He displayed both hands and, sure enough, they contained a tray of vanilla slices and a large container of sauce.

"Is that . . ." started Pat uncertainly, ". . . is that your cupboard then?"

"In a manner of speaking." Juniper smiled. "It is my cupboard, I suppose, yes."

He laid his cargo down on a bench and turned to face them, clapping his hands, and grinning widely. "So, let me make dinner and then we can talk. Properly talk. Do you think the angels are hungry?"

"No, they don't eat. At least, I don't think they eat. I just assumed that . . . hang on." Frank disappeared into the body of the restaurant for a moment before returning with a slightly crestfallen look on his face. "They say they're starving and would each love a bowl of chips if it's not too much bother.

"Wonderful." Juniper grabbed an apron and set to work turning on the large fryer.

"And some vanilla slice."

Juniper gestured to the tray he had moments ago lain on the bench. "Heaps there. Just grabbed a fresh lot."

Pat glared at Frank, trying to gesture "you ask him" with her eyes, but her husband just shrugged his shoulders and made that "I have no idea what you're talking about" face that all couples married for decades have evolved their own unique version of. Finally, Pat couldn't hold it in anymore. "So, where does it actually . . ."

"I suppose I should explain myself," said Juniper, cutting over her words. "I know you need an answer about the whole Mur-arb situation, but I needed to compose my thoughts for a moment. I have to confess your revelation was quite a shock."

"Yes, yes," dismissed Pat, "and we do need to get back to that because it's awfully important, but right now I think I'm more interested in that great vortex thingy, to be honest."

Juniper glanced up from the bag of chips he was opening. "Oh, that? Yes, I'm pretty proud of that, all things considered."

"Juniper, what *is* it?" Pat didn't intend to sound accusatory, but, after all, he had made an absolute mess of things in the past, and she couldn't put her hand on her heart and swear she thought he'd been able to get much better with time. She gestured to the vortex still swirling away in the corner, its myriad of colours twisting away into the infinite distance.

"This," said Juniper, his eyes lightening a little, "is my pièce de résistance, my love, the true source of all my success." He choked up at the very thought of it. He stepped back and stretched out both arms in a kind of supplication. "This is the culmination of all the years of work and study, soul searching and deep, deep reflection. This is my time vortex."

Thirty-four

Fraster had taken to pacing over the last few days, and he wasn't entirely happy with this development. A steely glare, a steady hand and a deliberately unnerving tapping on his desk had been the tools of his trade until now. The pacing was new, and he didn't like it. It did not at all project the image he had worked so hard to refine during the previous eons, one of quiet but determined control and methodical superiority.

No, the pacing made him look nervous and unsure what to do next, although this was appropriate because it was exactly how he had been feeling since he'd secured the woman and Egragore in the time lock, then attempted to direct the actions of Mur-arb, who was proving to be as stubborn, wilful, and cluelessly obstinate as a toddler.

He had, for some naïve and ridiculous reason, thought this would be easy.

He should have known better.

So, he paced. This was accompanied by an anxious pulling on and rubbing of his right ear, plus frequent full body sighs. It was not the demeanour he was used to projecting, and he didn't like it one bit.

"FRASTER!" came a yell from a room somewhere off to his left. He flinched involuntarily and waited to see if running footsteps would attend to the call. Surely someone, anyone, else would be there? He stretched his already preternaturally agile hearing, striving to hear movement from somewhere in the realm, but there was nothing. Nothing? That was impossible. He had allocated various subcommittees into roles just yesterday, and they should be on to at least their third meeting. Now he thought of it, where were the progress reports that—

"FRASTER!"

The bellow came again, the sound reverberating around what Fraster now realised were empty corridors, and he jolted to his senses, realising that if he didn't pay attention to Mur-arb quickly then there was no knowing what would happen. Making his way to the small airlock that Mur-arb had decided to occupy, he entered nervously, his eyes darting about. He literally didn't know what to expect. Mur-arb was becoming increasingly erratic in his creations and whims, and Fraster wasn't completely confident he wouldn't be coming face to face with a T-Rex or a wendigo. But there was simply Mur-arb, sitting in a straight-backed chair, a cup of tea in his hand and a book on his lap, a pleasant smile resting lightly on his lips.

"There you are. I was wondering if I'd accidentally banished you too." He laughed, raising his cup companionably.

Fraster laughed back, nervously smiling, until his slightly lagging brain registered what had just been said. "I'm sorry? What do you mean banished "as well"?"

Mur-arb replaced the cup onto the saucer and somewhat fussily placed both on the side table that had appeared beside him, concentrating deeply on arranging it in the middle of the table, just so. He took a crisp white cloth serviette, folded it meticulously into the shape of a swan, and placed it perpendicular to the cup, staring at it intently for a moment, before carefully unfolding the swan and draping it over the cup. He frowned at his handiwork intently for a few seconds before turning back to Fraster.

"Yes, I've been meaning to speak to you about that. I've decided we really don't need anyone else here, so I've banished all of them. Well, I say "banished", but that sounds far more aggressive than it is. I mean, I'm not aggressive. I haven't aggressively banished them, I mean."

Fraster stared at him in horror. "You mean you've. . . I mean, there's no-one . . ."

Mur-arb smiled widely and waved his hands in the air. "That's right. There's no one else up here now. Just us. And I must say, that's easier, don't you think? So much easier than having all that noise around all the time. All those voices."

His smile disappeared and he jumped to his feet, walking rapidly over to the long feature of one-way glass that stretched down the length of the curved room. Pressing his forehead against it, he cupped his hands around his eyes and peered through, his breath making clouds of condensation on the dark glass.

"Did you hear that?" he said sharply. "Did you hear her? I think I heard her voice." He listened intently for a moment before turning away. "Maybe not. It's hard to say. Since I created a new world for them yesterday, they've been moving further and further away, so it's getting harder to hear what she's doing. But I didn't want her cooped up in those small rooms, you understand. It's very important to keep things in captivity comfortable and stimulating. They're doing it in all the zoos. On Earth, that is." He looked perplexed. "Must we destroy the zoos? I don't think we need to destroy them. Or the sanctuaries. They don't have to be all destroyed in your plan, do they? Or was it my plan? I'm becoming so forgetful lately."

Fraster realised he needed to tread very carefully now, in a way that he may not have ever had to be careful in the past. The shock of Mur-arb's words seemed to have jolted him back to some kind of control

He would be damned if this being was going to break him now; he hadn't come all this way to see some addled Woodstock refugee get the better of him. Maybe the whole problem was that he'd been assuming rational behaviour out of a being that had never claimed to be rational and for that matter laid no claim to any kind of coherent thought.

He had found that assuming other creatures were not idiots never ended well.

"You think it's best for just you and I to take care of everything, do you? Excellent idea."

He followed Mur-arb's eyes to look out through the window. It seemed to be night through the glass, and the light of the room they stood in meant it was impossible to make out anything clearly, but he thought he could see trees clustered close to the window, and then extending off some way into the distance.

"Yes, of course. All we have to do is keep track of Egragore and Brigid now, and there doesn't need to be an entire legion for that, does there? The biome is self-sustaining, so we don't even need to care for them, as such, everything is provided. We're essentially just, as I said, zookeepers. Do you remember…" he shook his head, as if searching for an answer in a magic eight ball. "Do you remember why I'm angry at her? I know she's done something dreadfully bad, and she needs to be locked away from everything for the good of the universe, but I can't for the life of me remember why. Because if it isn't that dreadfully terrible then maybe she could —"

"Right." Fraster spoke slowly, measuredly. "That's our only job, as you see it, yes?"

"Of course." Mur-arb glanced up, a look of concern flitting across his face. "Or is there something I've forgotten? I feel like there may be something I've forgotten. Apart from destroying Earth, and I'm really beginning to have second thoughts about that."

It was at that moment that Fraster realised the Great and Glorious Ruler had utterly untethered himself from reality, and that the fate of everything might, in a very real sense, be in his own hands. For someone who had dreamt of complete control, it wasn't sitting as well with him as he had hoped it would, and quite honestly none of this was going to be much fun if he didn't have at least a basic staff.

Dammit.

"If you could just get back to the banishing of all the Shadow Lands staff that you mentioned a moment ago."

"I was quite nice about it, you know. I don't think they minded."

Fraster swore under his breath. No, he was willing to bet they hadn't minded, given they now didn't need to deal with this shit show.

"But of course, you don't have to be nice. Remember? Remember how we talked about the fact that you don't have to be nice? You're the boss, after all. You don't have to be nice to anyone. At all."

"Even you?"

"Obviously, I'd prefer it if we could have a cordial working relationship but after all, remember, I'm here to serve and help you."

Mur-arb sighed. "Yes, you keep saying that, but I don't really think I'm cut out for all of this." He jerked suddenly, grabbing the nape of Fraster's shirt, pulling the man towards him. "I didn't ask for all this, you know. I didn't ask to be here. I don't think I asked for any of this".

His voice petered out and his eyes took on a vacant expression again. Fraster prised his fingers away from his frightfully expensive shirt and smoothed it down. He added the act to the list of things that the great buffoon would inevitably be made to pay for.

"So, you got rid of everyone?"

Mur-arb nodded vaguely.

Fraster tapped his fingers against the cool dark glass. "And this? You said you've made a new world. What do you mean?"

"I just gave them some more space. And some trees. She always liked trees."

Fraster took a deep breath through his nose and contemplated that for a moment. It couldn't hurt, surely. They were still in a time lock; just because it was bigger now and had some foliage in it didn't alter that crucial fact.

"Alright, fine." He cleared his throat and attempted to sound kind, empathetic, grandfatherly even. "I can tell you're finding everything quite challenging."

"Oh, I am, I really am. I wish that—"

"And I can tell," he continued rapidly, fully intending that this be a very one-sided conversation. "But remember, you don't have to worry about a thing. I'm happy to act as your humble servant and assist you in any way that you need."

"I feel like I was too hard on her. Do you think I was too hard on her? I think I yelled. Did I tell her I hated her?" He rubbed his head. "How could I have done that? What came over me? I don't even know my own mind anymore. I think there's something wrong with me."

"Look, just between you and I, the last CEO was emotionally unstable, too. He regularly seesawed between callous genocide and all-encompassing love, and to be honest, from what I can tell, the humans never knew what they were going to get. Have you ever read their Holy Books? Nasty. Mood swings are just to be expected given the huge weight you're carrying on your shoulders, and I think that the sooner you come to terms with that, and find something to keep yourself busy, then the better for all concerned. I think what you're going through is just a perfectly normal part of the job."

"Maybe I do need something to do." He glanced towards the window again. "Perhaps I should just pop in and—"

"If you could just cast your mind back a few days—I know it's hard but do your best—remember when we talked about turning all of the planet Earth into a lovely big pit? About how all humans are vermin and need to suffer? And while messing with their psyches is all well and good, and we've been doing a fabulous job of that with rising rates of depression and anxiety, it just isn't enough. My invention of the internet has been a fabulous tool to really dull their senses and make most of them hate each other. But if you could recall, some of them are still slipping through the net and being just a bit hopeful. Being, as I am, a demon, I'm not really a huge fan of that."

Mur-arb tried to interject, but Fraster ploughed on.

"And yes, I know you're not a demon, or even very demonic or hate filled, unless . . ." he raised an enquiring eyebrow, but Mur-arb shook his head, ". . . alright, not filled with hate as such, but you were terribly hard done by when it comes to the humans, weren't you?"

Mur-arb looked uncertain.

"Remember," said Fraster, pushing the point. "Remember you got summoned, very incompetently, really only half formed, if I can say that without you taking offence, and then essentially exploited for their own gains."

"From what I've heard, they didn't really exploit—"

Fraster held up his hand. "Exploited to the point that you didn't even realise you were being exploited. Can you imagine that? That's humankind for you. Fetid arrogant vermin. And then this person," he gestured to the land outside the window, "this person doesn't even have the decency to stick by your side and support you. Imagine that. You could work so very well together, but without even a nod at your past history, she goes straight over your head and tells everyone you're incompetent."

There was silence as Mur-arb thought about this, the expression on his face one of despondence rather than, as Fraster had hoped, maniacal anger.

"You can't trust anyone." Fraster's voice dropped to a whisper. He reached out his clawed hand and laid it on the ruler's arm. "Everyone has left you. Except me."

"No, I banished them. They would still be here—"

"Untrustworthy," he hissed. "Deceitful, all of them."

"But I thought you had committees?"

"We don't need them." Fraster made a snap decision. "We don't need them. We can do it on our own. We can turn the entire planet Earth into a vast eternal purgatory, and you can finally be vindicated. We throw them into fiery pits, they die, obviously, then their souls get stuck right where they died and they're in torment eternally. And I literally mean eternally because there's nowhere else for them to go anymore. It's quite empty up here and . . . well, as far as I can tell there's not much happening in the absolute lower reaches either. They're basically on standby waiting for my reports, too."

"Look, old chap, I appreciate it, I really do. I appreciate that you're trying to cheer me up and all, but my heart just doesn't seem to be in it."

Fraster regarded him grimly. "I didn't want to have to do this," he said slowly, his hand reaching into the pocket of his coat. "I really didn't want to have to do this. But you must understand that things are unworkable with your flip flopping all over the place."

Slowly, he drew something out from the fold of his jacket, a misshaped coil pot that looked as if it were made by a ten-year-old. It only just fitted into his cupped hand. Mur-arb's eyes widened in shock as he saw it.

"Where did you get that," he asked, visibly shaken.

"Do you recognise it?" This was purely for theatre. Of course, he recognised it. Fraster had personally spent time on Earth searching for it, and it had been a singularly unpleasant experience. But he'd needed a contingency plan in case his Plan A had become less than eager to fit in with his machinations, and it looked like his efforts had been worthwhile.

"I don't want to banish you back into this. It's never pleasant to bear the brunt of a failed exorcism, is it? But I need you to take your responsibilities more seriously now. You can't keep wandering off and making mini universes filled with sentient hash browns. You need to focus, and what you need to focus on is reducing planet Earth to a flaming purgatory. Do you understand?"

Mur-arb nodded.

"And then you can make mini universes filled with sentient hash browns, if you really want, but I suspect we can find you something more interesting to do, don't you?"

Mur-arb stared at him; his eyes indecipherable.

"I know that threatening you is very ugly and a much less stylish move than I usually like, but here we are. I feel as if I have your attention now?"

Mur-arb pressed his lips together. Sweat beaded on his forehead and his face was motionless. He stared, like a rabbit deciding whether it wanted to make friends with oncoming headlights. Fraster moved the pot slightly, and Mur-arb jumped, jerkily. "I suppose I don't care about the Earth that much," he whispered.

Fraster smiled with relief. "That's the spirit."

"And I certainly don't care enough about the humans to end up back in that void."

"That's where you go when you're exorcised, is it?"

Mur-arb shuddered involuntarily. "A void. It's terrible. Just all that . . . nothing. I know about it. I'm aware of the nothingness but can't do anything about it. I can't move; I can't speak."

Fraster tapped his cheek thoughtfully. "That sounds quite interesting. Do you think there's any way you could make that happen down on Earth?"

"Oh no, I couldn't possibly. I can't bear to even think about it."

"Not even just a few pockets? For the really annoying ones?" He could tell he'd pushed the deity about as far as he could and decided to settle with what he'd achieved so far.

He stood. "I do wish you'd left me with some help. It was very silly of you to get rid of everyone. It's difficult to get things done without a staff, you know. I was going to implement a staggered roll out of the fiery pits to really get a good amount of terror and abject despair going on down there." He took a deep breath. "That amount of fear is really very good for the lungs, you know. It's a heady brew. But I suppose you don't get much of a buzz from that kind of thing, do you? Anyway, I can't do a roll out on that kind of scale without committees." He paused. "Would there be any point in me threatening you to get them back?"

Mur-arb looked alarmed. "Oh, please don't. I don't even know where I put them. I dematerialised them and projected them somewhere . . . somewhere nice I think, but I really couldn't say where."

Fraster decided this wasn't a hill he needed to die on.

"I could create some new staff if you like?" said Mur-arb.

Fraster shuddered. "That would be worse than none at all. I'd have to do all the training, and I have little to no interest in that. No, we'll just have to make do. And no hard feelings about the pot, I trust?"

Mur-arb looked at him. "Does it matter?"

"No, I suppose not, now you come to mention it." He turned back to the dark window. "Are you just going to sit here?"

"I don't really have anything else to do."

"No messing around trying to get Brigid out and begging her forgiveness, all right?" He waved the pot in Mur-arbs general direction. "Don't want to have to pull out the big guns, do we?" But the deity was already staring off into space, seemingly lost again.

Fraster didn't dare contemplate what would happen if the little man lost what was left of his mind. The sooner his plan came to fruition the better.

Thirty-five

The waiting seemed endless.

It felt like it had been weeks, but there was nothing to really record the passing of time.

Egragore paced fitfully around the room, his mind too preoccupied to settle on one task. Not that there was anything to do here, he thought ruefully. He couldn't even cast his mind out into the universe anymore and touch on what was going on around him. For the first few days he'd been able to identify lone, isolated messages travelling through the aether, but as the ExactoLock technology solidified it meant that everything in its boundaries stayed within its boundaries.

He had no idea how Brigid had been able to create the worlds within the world, but she had spent so much time in silent thought, so much time still, so much time in what he assumed was mediation that, really, anything could have been going on in her mind without him knowing about it.

On his second trip past the steel rimmed windows, he glanced out and frowned as his eyes lighted on the distant figure sitting alone on the moss-covered trunk of a massive fallen tree. This particular window, he knew, looked out upon an area of temperate rainforest, one that Brigid seemed increasingly drawn to.

This sense of awareness, of knowing where she was at all times. This hint of knowledge that glimmered around the edges of his brain had been gradually becoming more of a part of him, until he had discovered yesterday that he was able to seek her out in the entire realm, just by turning his attention to her.

He wondered if it was something that she had done. Whether it was a connection that she had made with her own mind, or whether it was a feature of the world that they now seemed to live in.

The pressure sealed door opened at his touch, and he stepped out into the vast, frigid wilderness. He summoned a fleece jacket into his hands, knowing that she wouldn't have thought to take one herself.

As his feet sank into the waterlogged ground, he thought of their first meeting and the way their friendship had developed. When had he stopped seeing her as merely a means to an end, something that was useful for getting him further towards what he wanted? When had she taken on a life of her own in his mind? It had been such a long, long, long time, but there were still human feelings there.

Apparently.

He wryly considered the fact that Fraster had been right about that all along.

She heard him as he approached and she glanced up, her expectant face causing his stomach to sink even more.

"Anything?"

"Not yet."

He handed her the jacket and sat down next to her on the damp tree, grimacing. "This is going to go right through my trousers."

She put on the coat without comment, and he marvelled at how their actions had become so automatic, that looking out for each other had become just a matter of course. It was as if he was becoming more human again, the more time he spent here.

She was so still, looking out over the far-off mountains frosted with snow. The wind blew straight off the Antarctic, and you could feel the aged expansiveness of the frozen continent from here. He tentatively reached out for her hand, and she let him take it, her fingers tightening around his slightly as their palms touched.

"So, does anyone know where they are?" she asked after a few minutes of silence. "Michael and Guinnie and the rest?"

This stillness was new to him. Looking back on the woman he had first met, a woman whose mind was constantly flitting around from idea to idea, whose nervous energy was a force within itself, he could feel a dramatic change.

Something was happening, he thought.

"I'm not sure. I've lost communications. From what I can tell, they've gone entirely. They're not appearing on any data, all of the Earth-based workers have gone, and no one has any idea where. It's like they've just vanished." His voice trailed off.

"Disappeared from this universe."

She turned her head to look at him for the first time, her eyes deep set and dark in her face. "They're my angels," she said simply. "They're supposed to be here to help me. It's not fair that just when I really need them, they're gone. I don't have anything else. I can't do this on my own."

"It's not their fault," he said. "You know they would be here if they could."

"It's the bubbles," she said.

Caught off guard, he didn't understand her meaning, and he frowned at her, perplexed.

"Like the wrinkly man said when I met him. Each universe is a bubble. Sometimes they link up, and then we can cross over, and sometimes they just . . . stand completely alone."

Her fingers tightened around his, more as a source of comfort to her than anything else, he suspected. "We're in separate bubbles now. And I feel like we're supposed to do something, but I'm not sure what it is.

"Let's go for a walk," she said.

"Not too far though. The ExactoLock won't register us if we go too far; that's how they work. We'll simply wink out of existence."

She stopped and held her head still, as if listening. "I need to spend more time in meditation," she confirmed. "I think I'm getting close."

Thirty-six

"Mate," Frank said slowly. "Let me get this straight. You've created a time machine, time vortex—whatever it is, it's bloody impressive—and you're using it for transporting tomato sauce?"

"And vanilla slice," he clarified.

"You couldn't grab some wagon wheels while you're there next time, could you? Some of the good ones. They're tiny these days. It's bullshit. Don't look at me like that, Pat, it annoys you as much as it does me."

"If we could just move away from food for a moment." Pat sounded more irritated than usual. "I think this vortex might be the answer."

Juniper looked at her blankly.

"It's a time machine," she said, stating what she felt was bleedingly obvious. "Do I need to spell this out? You could go back and, for example, not summon Mur-arb in the first place. You could undo the whole problem. If you'd never summoned him in the first place then he couldn't have become the ruler of the universe and, well, Brigid wouldn't have become involved either and none of this would be a problem."

Juniper chewed on his lip thoughtfully for a moment. Finally, he sighed heavily. "I know that sounds like the solution to the problem, but I strongly suspect a move like that would only add to our predicament. If what you say is true, and Mur-arb and Brigid have been drawn into what sounds like events undulating with pivotal importance to the entire fabric of space and time, then trying to undo it would create a paradox. If I even could undo it. There are deep waters running here, undercurrents in which darker forces than I understand are swimming. I've been warned off once before and I'm loathe to step in again. And anyway, the whole stuff up with Mur-arb was a very important learning experience for me. It made me the practitioner I am today. I don't think I'd even want to undo that."

Pat stared at him stonily. "Don't you think that's a little, how can I put it, selfish?" Her seemingly endless wells of patience had now thoroughly dried up.

"Er, well, it's the paradox that's the real issue. The paradox and the possible implosion of the universe that we need to be careful of. I think that's the key issue here, now I come to think of it. And I just can't do anything else that will affect Brigid, alright? She needs to be left alone. I know that she needs to be left alone. That's my one, absolute definite."

"But she hasn't been left alone," snapped Pat. "That's the problem, she's involved and we're trying to extricate her."

He grabbed his head, a truly pained expression on his face. "You don't understand," he nearly sobbed. "There is more to this than you understand. More than I can tell you and I don't want any of this to be happening."

"Well, it is happening," she said. "And if you know more than you are letting on then you have a duty to help us. Or to fix it. Or to do *something* for god's sake."

Pat looked over at the slowly vibrating vortex. There was no sound but the hum of the fridge in the corner. No road noises could be heard from outside, and the cafe lay expansive and silent. There may as well have been nothing at all in existence but three fairly ordinary humans and an utterly improbable machine.

"Do you know if anyone else has one of these?" she asked, a thought growing in her consciousness.

Juniper shrugged. "I don't think so. Not that anyone else has told me, anyway. It's not as if there's a spell we can just whip up to create a time machine. Otherwise, everyone would have one."

"So, you just tinkered around?" asked Frank.

"It was deduced and thoroughly educated tinkering," said Juniper somewhat pompously. "Years and years of study and experimentation."

"So, you studied and experimented and came up with . . . this."

"Yes."

"A better experiment than the last one, mind you," said Pat. "I'm surprised you had the hide to do it after the last stuff up."

"As I said, years of study and education and meditation and communing with spirits, I—"

"Came up with the only time machine in existence."

"Yes."

"Doesn't that sound a little improbable to you?"

"Improbable? How so?"

"I'm sure smarter people than you have tried to do it but with no avail. Don't you find it a little odd?"

"Odd. Maybe. I suppose now you mention it, it's a little—"

"Staggeringly against all the odds?" Frank had now joined in.

"Makes you think that maybe there was something else in play, doesn't it?" said Pat?

"Does it?" Juniper was now looking back and forth between the two.

"It does," agreed Frank.

They lapsed into a thoughtful silence.

"Almost like something knew we would need a time machine," he continued.

"Or someone," mused Pat.

"Someone, indeed."

"But as I said, I can't go back and undo what's been done."

"No, quite right, you can't go back and completely undo what's been done. You can't go back and stop yourself inadvisably summoning a paranormal being."

"You'll never let that go, will you?" said Jupiter.

"You said before that there was more but you couldn't tell me." Pat was now looking at him closely.

"I misspoke."

"I bet you did. But you meant it, didn't you?" she pushed.

"I can't tell you. I swore that I wouldn't."

Pat looked thoughtful.

"You promised someone that you wouldn't tell, is that it?" said Frank.

"Someone, something. Yes."

"When was that?"

He scrunched up his face. "Mid '80s."

"Ok, hear me out. Do you think that you could, hypothetically, tell me . . . before it happened?" Pat seemed to be choosing her words carefully.

"What do you mean?"

"Well, if we go back to before you swore yourself to secrecy, and told me, then strictly you're not doing anything wrong are you?"

"We?"

"No, sorry. If people. Hypothetical people," clarified Pat. "If hypothetical people went back in time, separately, and happened to meet up. Hypothetically. And then just happened to have a conversation."

"A hypothetical one," added Frank, helpfully.

Juniper looked puzzled. "I don't know if that would work."

"Which bit?"

"I don't know if I would remember the things that I know now if I went back in time to before I knew it."

Frank grabbed a coke from the fridge. "I don't think that's how time travel works," he called out.

"Which bit in particular?" asked Juniper.

"I don't think that you forget things that you don't know yet."

Pat looked slightly defeated. "I'm really not following this now."

"Trust me then," said Frank. "I've read The Brief History of Time."

"So, in that case we could go back and . . . tweak things," suggested Pat.

"Tweak things?"

"That's right . . . tweak things."

"Lay some seeds. Have a chat. Shoot the breeze." Frank felt, somewhat disloyally, that Pat was just saying anything that came into her head now.

Juniper lifted the drained chips out of the fryer and dumped them into a tray. Salting them thoroughly he drew down sauce and vinegar from high shelves and laid it all out. He carried a tray to the angels table, and they enthusiastically dug in.

"So, are these two your guardian angels then?" Juniper asked Pat and Frank.

"No, they're not ours," said Pat. "They're Brigid's."

"Why aren't they with her then."

"It's got something to do with her being…what is it exactly?" Frank called to Michael. "Why can't you be with Brigid? Inter dimensional thingy, wasn't it?"

"Something like that," said Michael through a mouthful of chips.

"Why are you here then?" asked Juniper directly to the angels. "Why are you hanging out with her parents? Haven't you got anything better to do?"

"What are they saying?" asked Pat after a moment.

"Apparently they knew that there was going to be food, and they had heard about my menu." He raised a can of coke at them in salute.

"About this vortex situation," said Pat, endeavouring to get Juniper back on track.

"Look, I'm happy for you to use the vortex if you think there would be a use for it, but I'm sorry, at the moment I really don't know if that would work,"

Pat gestured towards the portal. "May I?"

"You want to go through my time portal?"

"If it's alright with you."

"I mean, it's not something to be entered into lightly. I've been very highly trained, and I've got a vast amount of experience in treading between the two tenuous worlds in the dimensional—"

"Get your hand off it, mate," interrupted Frank. "You go back thirty years and nip into Coles to buy sauce. You're hardly negotiating peace treaties with the Habsburg Empire, are you? And trained? You told us yourself that you got lucky with your tinkering."

Juniper eventually agreed, providing Pat with a rundown of what she would experience on the short but potentially discombobulating trip. And a shopping list. And then, she, in turn gave him a very specific note about where to be, at a very specific date, in a very specific year.

As it turned out, she enjoyed revisiting her old haunts so much that she didn't come back for three weeks, and even then, she forgot the groceries.

It was a cafe not unlike the one that Juniper ran in the year 2019. Not unlike it, for the very good reason that this was the one that his was based on.

Juniper had always been sentimental.

They walked towards each other slowly as if testing the waters, smiled widely with a certain joyful knowing, embraced, and sat down. A man and a woman in their 60s, dressed in clothing that didn't look too out of place, although the outfits in question wouldn't be bought (from a Vinnies op-shop no less) for another few decades.

And as evidence that Juniper's concerns about creating a paradox and possibly plunging the universe into a black abyss of doom were misplaced, the high waisted corduroy pants that the woman was wearing were, at the same time, being worn by a young man who walked past the café some 20 minutes after the woman and the man sat down for a cup of tea. These pants found themselves donated to a charity bin 5 years later, spent some time in a box in the back of a combi travelling across the Nullarbor, had a litter of kittens born in their cosy nestled crotch, were donated again and eventually wound their way to a tip shop, where the woman gleefully found them in 2017.

Not the main point, however. The point was that the man and the woman sat and talked. They laughed, they cried, they held hands companionly and, after Juniper had taken a deep breath and explained the amazing reality of the true nature of her only daughter, Pat drew herself up and made plans. She found a cheap motel to spend the night in, passed a few productive hours in Melbourne's reference library and the next day, bought a bus ticket along a road that she knew well, given she had/ was currently living there at the time.

She didn't know if this was allowed, she didn't know if potentially meeting a younger version of herself was going to present a problem, and she didn't know if it was even going to work, but she had been given a vital piece of information that she thought maybe, just maybe, would be what they all needed to get themselves out of this mess.

Thirty-seven

As they walked through the dense, damp forest that was springing up around them, Egragore tried to ask Brigid what had been going on.

"You badgered me relentlessly until I told you about being a human," he complained. "Now there's something I really want to know, and you won't talk to me. I could feel something in my mind poking around. Like . . . fingertips. Exploring. Poking around. It felt a bit invasive to be honest."

"Yeah, sorry about that," she said somewhat guiltily. "I was looking for someone else, but I wasn't very good at it to start with. I don't think I left anything out of place, did I? And I tried not to look at anything that I wasn't supposed to. Still . . ."

"What?" he frowned at her reddening cheeks.

"Seriously, you're into ankles?"

"I thought you said that you didn't look at embarrassing bits?"

"It was right there. In lights. It's clearly a thing."

"How did you. . . how did you learn that you could do that?"

"I'm not sure, I just knew. Or I knew that I should try, anyway. I felt like a little light went off in my head. Or an alarm. An alert. I felt like there was a signal, anyway, telling me I should try."

"That meditation seems pretty powerful."

She shrugged. "Or something."

"And did you find the person that you were looking for?"

She nodded. "Yes, eventually. I got better at it quickly."

"So, who were you . . ."

"Ssshhhh." They walked around a huge boulder, pushed aside dripping branches, and stood in front of a white wall, completely incongruous in the alpine environment. It glowed slightly, and as Brigid pressed her ear against it, Egragore could hear a low thrum deep within it.

"Here," she said, standing back and resting her hand lightly against it. "This is where we wait."

The fact that everything was damp, and mossy, and generally sodden made the wait unpleasant, but at least the boredom inspired Brigid to tell him who she had been looking for, and why.

"He's very confused," explained Brigid. "And scared. He knows that he's made some bad decisions, but he's very easily influenced, always has been. Once I managed to get in there, into his mind that is, and calm him down, he realised that he's been completely manipulated. And he's so, so sorry poor love. He wants to make things right now."

Egragore hugged her to his chest and rubbed his hands against her back; the cold was biting now night was falling, and their breath hung in the misty air around them. Suddenly, the low thrum became a metallic buzz, and an invisible door slid open on a stark white interior, revealing the person they had been waiting for, wearing his favourite fisherman's cap again, and a crocheted shawl.

In this doorway stood Mur-arb.

"I'm sorry it took so long", he muttered nervously. "I had to wait until I was on my own. And it was hard to hear you through all of this". He gestured to the built environment around them.

"It's alright." Smiling, Brigid stepped towards him and wrapped her arms around him. "It's alright now."

"Is it?" The worried look stayed on his face, and the furrows in his brow seemed permanent now. "Because he will be frightfully angry with me when he finds out what we've done. Do you think we could maybe not tell him? Could we maybe hide somewhere? Or go on a nice holiday? Yes, a nice holiday! That would be the ticket. And he has the pot!" His words were rushed in the eagerness to tell her this news. "The pot, the one Juniper put me in. I don't know how Fraster got it, but he did, and he's threatened to put me in it if I don't do his bidding. Before, when I thought that he was on my side, that he was talking sense, he was so nice to me, so reasonable. But now he seems to have turned. And if I don't do what he wants . . . ."

"Which is?" asked Egragore

"Turn the earth and everyone on it into an eternal purgatory."

Egragore glanced at Brigid, whose face had paled.

"So, the fiery pit that he made was just a practice. A dress rehearsal. He wants to transform the planet."

"Shit." She spat out the words and began to pace. "I'm not ready," he heard her mutter. "I'm not ready. I can't do this yet. I'm nowhere near ready. It's not clear."

She grabbed Egragore's arm and pulled him away, out of ear shot of Mur-arb who was wringing his hands nervously and beginning to tell a wall sconce about his plight.

"We need more time," she said. "If that's what he wants to do, then I'm sure he needs more time, but I'm not ready yet. I'm nowhere near ready. I'm still "me.""

"What do you mean? You're babbling."

'I can't do this," she snapped, her voice rising. "I'm not ready yet, I told you. This is big, really big. This is more than I can do with . . ." she threw her arms open, "this. It's more than I can do with this."

"I don't understand you," he said.

She shook her head. "I don't understand it fully yet. At least, I don't know enough yet. But I don't think I have any choice. It's alright," Brigid said, stepping back towards Mur-arb and gaining his attention. "We're in this together. Stronger together, right?"

Mur-arb nodded.

"We need to get rid of him and then we can make our own plans. Make the Earth more secure again. Try to stabilise it and get things in order."

Brigid squeezed Egragore's hand. "You will help, won't you?"

They stepped inside the room and the door slid shut behind them again, sealing up the ExactoLock forever. Egragore looked at the seamless wall. "I don't understand how you two communicated through that," he said. "It's meant to be utterly impenetrable."

"I don't really care at this stage," she said, moving quickly through the room and glancing out into the corridor, beckoning the two men to follow her. "I'm pretty focussed on working out what we should do next, and avoiding Fraster."

"We do need to find him, you understand," said Egragore, "if you're going to vanquish him or do whatever it is, you're going to do."

"I haven't quite worked that out. Any ideas are gratefully accepted."

"We could put him in his own pot?" suggested Mur-arb with a giggle. "Find something ugly and exorcise him into it."

"Do you know how to do that?"

"I don't," said Brigid. "But I'm not discounting any idea out of hand at this stage."

As they turned another winding, anonymous corner, there was a dark blur in front of them, and the demon Fraster stood, his glowering form appearing gradually, bit by bit, until an inky blackness filled the entire corridor, and a sense of evil pervaded their senses.

"Shit," exclaimed Brigid. "Quick, go down to Earth," and linking hands, they dropped their levels down so they were standing on a grassy hill, in a grove surrounded by oak trees.

Brigid frowned as she looked around. "Where are we? Did one of you direct our coordinates? I've never seen this place before."

"Never mind that," said Egragore. "How did Fraster partially manifest? He's not supposed to be able to do that. That's another level of being entirely."

Mur-arb made an uncomfortable nervous sound in the back of his throat and kicked at a loose tussock of grass. "That may have had something to do with me."

Brigid and Egragore turned to glare pointedly at him. "What exactly do you mean by that?"

"I felt a bit overburdened by the amount of responsibility I was dealing with, so I gave him a bit of it."

"A bit of what?"

"Responsibility. And power. Extra power. I'm sorry," he said, his words a rush, "I'm sorry but he made so much sense and I really thought that he was the only one on my side."

"How much?"

Mur-arb had visibly paled by now, and his eyes glistened. "Quite a bit."

"How much?" Brigid and Egragore spoke in unison, their voices steely.

Before Mur-arb could answer, the air around them dropped in temperature and a rushing sound filled their heads. With a noise like a person being sucked into an airplane engine, Fraster appeared in front of them.

"One could start taking this personally," he said as his fully formed self brushed some non-existent dust off his sleeves with a sneer. "I just wanted a little chat, and you all ran off to . . ." He glanced around himself. "Ireland, by the look of it. May as well see the world before I set it all on fire."

"I don't think so," snapped Brigid, looking around for some kind of vessel. Egragore frowned quizzically at her, and she hissed under her breath, "We need to find something to send him into. Find a container of some kind."

There was a flicker of movement from Fraster as he pulled the old, roughly made coil pot out from under his black jacket. "Something like this?" He smiled that skin crawling smile that made Brigid shudder despite herself.

Mur-arb took a step backwards, his hands jolting out in shock. "No, please put that away," he gasped. "I did what you wanted. I gave you the power to create and destroy. You promised you'd get rid of that."

"Ah, that I did, that I did," lilted Fraster pleasantly. "But, you see, I'm a demon. Why do people forget that? I mention it quite often these days if anyone would bother to LISTEN TO ME."

The roar of these last words shocked the small group in front of him into silence, and they barely dared to breathe as he began to circle around them.

"I will no longer be treated like your lackey," he hissed at Egragore. "Or an idiot." This, he directed to Brigid. He sneered.

"Or a lapdog."

With this he stopped in front of Mur-arb. "A tame little lapdog. A supportive, all enabling little lapdog." Each of these words he punctuated with a vigorous shake of the pot, and with each shake Mur-arb shrunk back, seemingly reducing in stature in front of their eyes.

"I have made myself quite clear to you. Quite clear. Even your addled potato brain should have been able to understand what I have spelled out. If you don't see our plans through, then here you will go."

Mur-arb's white face trembled.

"It's alright though. I can understand your fear. I wouldn't like to be plunged into a void filled pot for the rest of eternity either. I get it, I really do."

He reached out and rested a friendly, skeletal hand on the deity's shoulder. "And it's quite easy, I promise. It's quite easy to avoid this fate worse than death."

He stood back and lifted his hands in the air, gesturing to the lush green countryside around them.

"You know what you have to do."

Brigid drew in her breath sharply.

Mur-arb's eyes were filled with tears.

"Can't you do anything?" whispered Egragore.

"I'm trying," she hissed. "But they seem to be just as powerful as each other at the moment. It's like trying to move a brick wall. I told you, I'm not ready yet."

"I'm waiting." Fraster continued to glare at Mur-arb.

"What is it to be? The pot or the planet? Ooh, this is quite fun; it's like a really high stakes game show, isn't it?"

Brigid tried to move over to Mur-arb, tried to take his arm to let him know she was there, that he wasn't in it alone, but she seemed unable to move.

"Stay there, you poisonous viper," snapped Fraster. "You've done quite enough, wouldn't you say? I will give you one last chance, Mur-arb. Plunge the human race into eternal purgatory or spend your own eternity in here. Which is it to be?"

As he raised his voice in command, a cloud that had been covering a distant hill began to change in form, almost as if smoke was drawing into it, helping it increase in size. Not just in size though, as a darkness behind him began to form. A thick, almost viscous darkness that seemed to be gathering together and sucking from its surroundings all glimmers of light or brightness that dared to exist.

This darkness grew and moved toward them, and within moments Brigid could see shapes within it. At first just a teeming mass, but gradually, as they began to move closer, a demonic army became visible. Thousands of screeching, clawing, undulating, deathly hordes stretching out behind Fraster as far as the eye could see, covering not only the lone distant hill, but now the entire horizon.

In this mass, Brigid recognised many of the kinds of beasts she had seen in the battle near the park, but also new, larger, and more horrendous looking creatures. She looked around vainly for Michael, or Guindaline, or any other angels at all, but there was no one to help this time.

To Brigid's horror, she saw Mur-arb turn towards her, saw him mouth the words, "I'm sorry," through tear-stained cheeks, and then the ground she was standing on began to tremble.

At first, she assumed it was the unspeakable army that forged towards them that was causing the earth to shake, but within moments she realised it came from the ground itself. Could it be that an earthquake, or some such geological event was, however improbably, striking rural Ireland just at the exact same time as a demonic horde was forging towards them? As Mur-arb and Fraster joined their hands together, raised them, and turned towards the demonic mass, she fell to the ground and pressed her hands to her head to try to protect herself from the rending, grinding, splitting horror that was unfolding around her. She felt Egragore take her hand and they wrapped their arms around each other as all sense of time disappeared from their consciousness. The earth they crouched on buckled and groaned with death agonies such as the world had never seen before. The sounds, smells and movements blurred into one reality as the heat of infernos burned the very air they struggled to breathe.

Brigid was vaguely aware of the death screams of thousands of beings, but she didn't know if she could hear these with her ears, or if they were being projected into her very being. A deep visceral revulsion filled her, a deep certainty that this went against everything that she stood for, everything that she was created to bring to fruition. Two forces were pulling against her, one a very human, very instinctive desire to protect herself, to curl up as small as she possibly could and just try to withstand the horrors around her. The other force, more hidden but still definitely there, told her to leap up, to grab the fabric of reality and meld it all back together again, to not only put a stop to what was happening but to bring it back to wholeness with her bare hands.

But Brigid, very scared and very human, could only cower next to Egragore, and pray for it to be over.

And after an endless time, it was.

They stood up. A dry, rocky desolate hell-scape stretched infinitely around them, punctuated with deep holes filled with fire and on it the demonic army swarmed, as if ensuring that any last signs of life were well and truly gone. In the face of so much destruction, so much unspeakable despoilment, Brigid felt utterly and impossibly small and helpless. The demon Fraster towered above them, seemingly grown in stature with the apocalyptic happenings, and Mur-arb lay on the ground; foetal, keening softly to himself.

Before she could move, even if she'd had the presence of mind to do anything, Fraster held out the clay pot towards the Great and Glorious Ruler, muttered a few archaic words, and with a drawn-out sucking noise, Mur-arb was dragged into its narrow neck.

"No!" Mur-arb's cry was snatched away, made smaller as it was whisked into the little clay vessel.

Brigid leapt forward, and in so doing she made a grab for the pot in Fraster's hand.

"He did what you wanted!" she yelled, anger blazing in her eyes. "He did everything you wanted. He just didn't understand. He didn't understand."

As she looked, blazing, into Fraster's cavernous face, she had the complete and overwhelming realisation that this, all of this, the destruction, Fraster, the evil that had engulfed possibly the entire planet was a step too far.

And it wasn't going to happen.

Any of it.

Not on her watch.

There was a small 'click' in her mind, as the final piece slipped into place, and the words that had been said to her all those years ago, came back to her.

"When the worlds tremble, stand strong. Creation is in your heart."

It suddenly dawned on her this hadn't been just a feel-good motto to help her out at job interviews and to give her ideas when she was trying make her first souffle. She realised who it was that had given her these words, and that this was it.

"This is not your place," she said, her voice seeming to come from somewhere beyond her, but also from a place within her that was ancient and long dormant. "This was never your place. How dare you. How dare you assume to think you ever could have dominion here. You have swum in waters that were not meant for you, little demon. You have chosen the wrong path."

Egragore heard the change in her voice, and was blinded as a hugely bright, yet warm and lifegiving, light filled the air. He flinched, throwing his hands up to cover his eyes, and for a brief moment he thought it must have been a trick of the light when he saw her transforming before his eyes.

She seemed to be growing taller, her hair growing a deeper red, falling down her back in waves so different from her usual ginger shoulder length frizz. Her nose straightened, her chin lifted, a circlet of leaves seemed to be growing at her brow, and he imagined he could see rays of light surrounding her body. An aura of green gold surrounded her, lifting her up so that her feet were no longer touching the ground.

"I will not let a ridiculous insignificant mortal female call the shots here," snarled Fraster, waving the chipped and damaged pot in Brigid's direction. "This isn't about you; it was never about you. You were just a succubus, a hanger on, everything about you is an accident, and its pure folly that you have been allowed to be involved in this as long as you have. A ridiculous quirk of fate that it is high time I put a stop to."

She wavered. Had she been wrong? Maybe he knew more than she did? Was she a succubus? Was this a quirk of fate? Was she wrong?

She flickered, the aura dimming and withdrawing back into her body. There was another pulse, another voice that echoed inside her head, not imagination, not a memory but an actual voice, yelling the truth into her very soul.

"When the worlds tremble, stand strong. Creation is in your heart."

Fraster raised his hand in a gesture that could have been anything, really, but as he did so, Egragore saw Brigid's eyes turn golden, and a light shoot from them which illuminated the demon in a spotlight of deep clarity. Suddenly Fraster seemed to be falling, the land sliding away beneath his feet. He stumbled, the pot falling from his outstretched hand into the sea of mud underneath them that was beginning to pulse and move like a gelatinous sea. The pot sat for a moment balancing, almost floating on what was now a viscous muck. Egragore made a move to grab it, but a bubble of unspeakable gas burbled up from below and engulfed it, sucking it down toward the living core of the planet and taking with it the sad, lost deity.

The land around them seemed to have begun to fall away again, terraforming and undulating in a manner similar to, yet completely different, from what had previously existed. A deep hum filled Egragore's ears, a hum so deep that, had there been any Tibetan singing bowls left on the planet, they would all have rung out a symphony in reply. But they were all gone, and as it was, all Egragore could do was throw his arms around a nearby boulder and hold on.

Later, he would feel slightly embarrassed that during this universally historic event, he spent most of his time hugging a rock, but the fact was, it was all he was capable of doing. The entire sky had begun to glow with the greens and golds of an aurora and his eyes were drawn up to where a now silhouetted figure stood on the cliff above them, a cliff that was rising out of the very earth as he stared at it in awe. The cliff rose, the woman grew, and the broken earth hummed with anticipation.

He glanced around to reassure himself that Mur-arb wasn't standing nearby, creating a new world as a mood swing struck him, but this, on reflection, seemed entirely different to the toy box bubbles that seemed to be his stock in trade: more real, more majestic, more . . . everything.

Brigid stood there, filling the sky, a golden glaze of light filling every facet of the world around him now, a singing noise, impossibly sweet ringing in his ears, filling his head. His voice seemed high pitched now as he tried to call out to her, but he felt unworthy even to speak her name and the words fell back into his mouth.

As Egragore watched, Fraster and the swarming hordes behind him seemed to grow smaller and smaller, and for a moment he thought that they were retreating, running away in abject terror at the recognition of the glory that had grown before them. But then he saw that they *were* shrinking; shrinking in the face of the penetrating light and angelic singing. As they dwindled in size, their tiny running bodies scattering around in chaotic panic, until they sank into the spongy ground.

Everything else grew brighter and brighter. So bright that even Egragore's otherworldly sight was dimmed and he flinched, throwing his arms up in front of his eyes.

Bridget spoke, and her voice seemed to be part of everything: part of the sky, part of the trees, part of the very fabric of the earth. She plunged herself into the very heart of the planet, creating a hum that drew up around them, resonating with deep, visceral sounds, like the heartbeat of the universe, as the very fabric of everything seemed to self-heal and repair itself. As the humming continued, Egragore realised it was coming from the very molecules of the planet itself, and everything around them began to fall back into an essential "rightness".

Bridget stood, impossibly tall and bright, her arms raised above her; her fiery hair cascaded down to the ground. Her head was thrown back, her eyes closed, and the humming sound came completely from her yet was totally separate from her. A green line, like the first wisp of flame along the side of a piece of paper when touched with a match, crept over the surrounding hills. It ran along the edges of the barren hills, like a child colouring the outline of a picture with the fluorescent marker, and once all the edges of the hills were lit with a bright green, once all the browns and greys were highlighted, the filling in began.

Life-giving green swept across the land, transforming the rocks and desolation into a verdant, life filled expanse once again.

This was happening as far as Egragore could see, and although it was beyond the limits of his sight, he knew that this was happening everywhere; green was repopulating the planet, seas were filling, poles were icing and plant life was rising from forest floors. Trees reached into the sky, their growth accelerated beyond belief, as the branches filled with first buds, then blossoms, then the rich green of deep summers growth. Within minutes, he heard the first tentative whistles of birds, and he saw smaller animals rising up out of the ground, fully formed and seemingly born of the dirt.

The humming reached a crescendo that even he could barely tolerate, creating a crushing pressure that roared in his ears. As he grabbed his head, certain he would not be able to bear it for one more second, it was over. The noise stopped as abruptly as if someone had flipped a switch and there, around him, was Earth as it had always been, as he had known it, as it was meant to be. Recalibrated, fresh, and new.

Thirty-eight

A small, crumpled figure slumped on the ground in the distance, lying below the now much smaller cliff as if she had tumbled from it at the height of her creations. Egragore leapt up and ran towards her. No longer the goddess figure that had called this world back into creation, but his Brigid. Reaching her, he rolled her over, his breath catching in his throat at what he might find. He pushed the rusty red hair he was familiar with out of her eyes and cupped her face in his hands. Seemingly unmarked, but too still. He felt her neck for a pulse, or some sign of life.

"Jesus, be careful," she snapped at him, pushing her body up into a seated position. "Your hands are freezing. And clammy. Fuck me, I've got a headache." She rubbed her forehead and grimaced. "That was way harder than I remembered. Getting back into a human body after that palaver is a really *really* bad idea. *Bad* idea. Not a fan."

He grinned despite himself, and she pushed his hands away, then realised what she had said. "What do you mean, remembered?"

"I've done it before," she said, pushing her now matted hair out of her face. "Haven't I told you that? I could swear I've told you that. You never bloody listen."

"You say a lot of stuff," he said. "I'm bound to miss something."

Brigid caught sight of one of the strands of hair that she was attempting to tie back and let out an irritated groan. "Couldn't I have kept that ultra red goddess-y colour? It hardly seems fair that I end up with a headache and drab hair again. I must see if Gloria can colour match that tone next time I'm in the salon."

Egragore caught sight of someone waving at them, just in front of the closest hill. "Wait." He shielded his eyes and looked into the distance. "Who are they? Is that your parents?"

She waved at the couple holding hands in the distance, "Yeah, they just came through Juniper's time vortex. Mum needed to give me a bit of a kick start in the end, bless her. No one can ever tell me that 40 somethings don't still need their mums."

"Wait, what? Time vortex?"

"Never mind." She laughed. "Add it to the list of things we need to talk about."

Pat gave her a questioning hand wave to which Brigid replied with a double thumbs up, and a huge grin. She blew her dad a kiss, then Pat and Frank looked around, seemingly satisfied at what their daughter had managed to pull off, and they wandered off to examine what appeared to be an ancient well in a grove of trees.

"Apparently," she said, unsteadily getting to her feet with the aid of Egragore's firm arm, "this is what I do. I call things into life or some such. Healing and shit. It used to be my job, I think. Like, way, way back. A thousand years or so. Which explains a lot, to be honest. I'm surprised that you didn't know about it, but I guess that ancient Celtic goddesses might be a bit beyond your job specifications."

Egragore stared at her. "Look, this is throwing me a bit. I mean, I thought we were, well, you know, making some progress in our relationship, if you will, but now you throw this at me, and I feel a bit stupid that you didn't mention it earlier. I feel like there might be a bit of a power imbalance now."

"A power imbalance," she said, raising her eyebrows. "Are you asking me to apologise for being a Goddess?"

"Are you a Goddess?"

"If you think I'm going to saddle myself with someone, reaper or whatever, who isn't able to handle being with a strong woman then I'd be better off going and asking Juniper if he wants to shack up with me."

Egragore was momentarily at a loss for words.

She giggled, her mood seemingly not yet stabilised. "I'm joking. But this bit is serious. I am a Goddess, in my own right, nothing to do with Mur-arb. It turns out that was just another one of those odd quirks of life, like the Hadron Collider thingy. Just a synchronicity, if you like, that doesn't actually mean anything. I am a Goddess, and I was chosen to be Mur-arbs co-deity, but the two things were mutually exclusive."

"Synchronicities usually do mean things though," said Egragore sceptically. "I find it very odd that you're randomly swept up in two very improbable things like this."

Brigid shrugged. "Maybe. Who knows? Even we don't know everything. Maybe it's the call of, you know." She gestured upwards. "Someone higher up. Part of their grand plan or some such."

Egragore frowned. "Higher up than the Heavenly Realm? There is no higher up than that. The CEO, that's it. That's the final arbiter."

"Oh really? So, because you haven't experienced something it doesn't exist?"

He shook his head as if to jolt loose some of the many things he was finding difficult to understand.

"You have guardian angels. Why would you need any of those things if you were a goddess? What the hell does a deity need with a bunch of piddling guardian angels? Can I assume then that you're the actual Goddess Brigid?"

She nodded.

"The actual Goddess Brigid. That's incredible."

"The actual full name is Brigid, Goddess of the Flame and the Well, Divine Mistress of Spring and New Growth, Font of all Inspiration and Creativity, but it's ok, you don't have to use it all the time."

Looking around he rubbed his hands across his eyes and took a deep breath. "Then why did you get into so much trouble and need me to help you out of it?"

"You need to understand I didn't know any of this for most of the time that we've known each other," she explained. "You're speaking as if I've been keeping this big secret from you, but I've literally been keeping it from myself. My memories were wiped until. . . wait, I'll get mum to explain it."

She called out to Pat, and she and Frank gradually wended their way over to where Brigid and Egragore were standing.

"Thanks for helping me out with all of this," Brigid said, gesturing about to express that by "this" she meant everything. "Would you like to fill us in on some of the details? I'm still not sure exactly what happened."

Pat flashed a beatific smile and hugged her daughter. "I'm so glad we all ended up here. I've always wanted to visit Ireland. It's like a dream come true."

"Mum," warned Brigid.

"It was a bit of a gamble," Pat admitted. "But once Juniper told me that you were a goddess, having a lovely little life on earth, I decided that there must be a way to trigger that memory if, you know, push came to shove. So, I looked back through some mythology and folk lore, found something that would mean something to you, in your original incarnation, then spent some time explaining it to 10-year-old you. It was a bit tricky, I had to time my visit for when I was out. 1986 me, I mean. I didn't want to run into myself. Very awkward. I would have had words to say about the perm, for a start. All those chemicals, I can't believe I got sucked into society's idea of beauty. But yes, I gave you the words of power and knew that, when it was time, then they would . . . activate you, I suppose. As I said, slight gamble but it paid off. You see, I couldn't change anything as such, but I could just implant that little memory, so if everything got extra terribly awful, then the memories of who you really were would come back and you would," here Pat clicked her fingers together, "do what you do."

"Fix the very fabric of reality you mean."

"Yes, dear. And you did a lovely job. Now if you'll excuse me, I believe that's New Grange over there, and there seems to be not a single tourist about, so I'm going to make the most of it. I wish I had my camera with me- I need some photos."

Egragore just stared. He was literally lost for words.

"And as for why I needed Michael and Guinnie, I am a real human you know. Despite all this."

She gazed off into the distance, the light from the sun making it very clear that it was, in fact, morning. "Anyway, we don't need to understand all of this do we? As far as I can tell, everything is back to normal, or at least as normal as . . . hang on." She frowned and narrowed her eyes for a moment, scrunching her face and gazing into the middle distance. "Oh bugger, I can't step up anymore. Can you?"

Egragore too glanced around himself. That was odd. He felt entirely human. He couldn't explain exactly what was different, but he felt . . . himself again. It had been a long six hundred years, but he realised that the feeling of humanness that filled him was completely natural and 'right'.

Brigid looked around her, scanning the ground and tilting as if she had just heard something. "Oh my god, Mur-arb. He's down there somewhere," she said. She paced the ground for a moment, bouncing lightly on her toes as if testing the ground. "Yes, he's here. I can hear him. He's crying." Her own eyes filled with tears. "This is just awful. Damn Fraster for all of this."

"Can you retrieve him? Maybe release him or something?" asked Egragore. "Poor Mur-arb. None of this is really his fault. He didn't really stand a chance, did he?"

Brigid closed her eyes and became very still. After a few moments, a faint glow appeared above the ground about twenty metres from where they stood. "There," she said. "I've released him. Not in his corporeal form, I've released him into the aether, his true, spirit form. He's happier that way. And he never asked to be created, did he? Poor bugger. And I think that was the absolute last bit of my juice. I strongly suspect that I've got nothing even vaguely other worldly left in me."

A shimmer appeared in front of them, a shimmer that resolved itself into a tall man wearing a sharp, expensive looking grey suit. His black curly hair was clipped efficiently, and his chiselled jaw and dark features spoke of a man who was used to being in control. Brigid regarded him with a frown for a moment before laughing.

"Oh, hello there. I'm not used to seeing you in a shirt and without the tan, and with some fat on you. Did you decide to get off that beach and do some actual work then, you slacker?" She stepped forwards and threw her arms around him, hugging him tightly. The man smiled expansively, returned the hug with just as much warmth, and with a last noiseless click, reality slipped back into its regularly scheduled programming. Keeping his arm around Brigid he reached out and shook Egragore's hand with a warm firmness that cannot be taught, no matter how many leadership seminars you go to, which filled Egragore with a deep, soul enriching joy. The field they were standing in was warming up now, and a heady scent of damp grass and clover filled their nostrils.

"Thank you both for taking care of things while we were gone on our", he cleared his throat, "enforced vacation. That Hadron collider situation threw us for six. I should never have given humans such an interest in science. I was told it would end badly for me. Never mind, I knew you'd sort things out, you know. You didn't have to worry about her."

This he addressed to Egragore.

"Things got a bit hairy for a while there though," protested Egragore.

The man smiled again, and his smile had the amazing quality of convincing you that, things were alright.

"Who knows," he said, his rich deep voice making Brigid blush a little. "I don't have to be in charge all the time, you know. And Her Upstairs is particularly happy with you this time. She's going to put you up for a commendation from what I've heard."

Brigid clapped her hands together. "I do appreciate some external validation," she grinned. "I'd love a certificate or a medal or something if there's one going."

Egragore's eyes darted to Brigid's. "Sorry, but you lost me again. Who is "Her Upstairs"?"

Brigid patted his hands. "I think that's classified, sorry." She looked to the man for clarification. "Yes?"

He nodded. "Yes, need to know basis only, that one." He taped the side of his nose and winked.

"But what's going on," interrupted Egragore, "with us I mean. I feel different. Unusual. Or, normal again I suppose. I'd appreciate some intel on what's going on."

The man regarded him for a moment. "That would be because you're mortal again. You've been granted another chance. How do you feel about that? I did feel bad about the whole demotion business you know; I really did. Things were a bit tricky there for a while; we were trying out a new management structure and we had got some new advisers in which, you know, can go very well or very badly. Once again, valuable lessons were learned on all counts, but I think we've really got a handle now on what works and what doesn't. You're happy to stay as a human, are you? I've moved ahead with that assumption."

"That depends." Egragore seemed to slip back into reaper mode momentarily. "Do you know if all the Realms are back in order? I mean, are they back how they used to be. How they're supposed to be? With, you know, the upper areas and the lower orders and everything . . . calibrated?"

"I think you will find", said the man, "that things are just how you would expect them to be. Maybe even better. This one here did some tweaking when she was recalibrating, didn't you?"

Brigid blushed a little. "That purgatory thing was shit, honestly, wasn't it," she said. "I've always been a bit of a universalist. Everyone should get to the Heavenly Realm and all that."

The man gave her a grin and she smiled back in a way that made Egragore feel once again that he had little idea what was going on.

"Anyway, as long as it's all settled for now, we don't need to worry about those kinds of things for ages and ages, do we?" Brigid said. "Where we're going to end up and all that? We have our lives to live, don't we? Properly this time. As whole people. What do you think of giving Ireland a whirl?" she whispered to Egragore.

The man in the suit nodded as confirmation. "Ages and ages if you like. And when you're done here this time, well, there will be jobs. If you want them. Nice ones."

"That can wait," she said, holding out her hand to Egragore who took it, thinking that feeling vaguely bemused seemed to now be his default position and he realised, for the first time ever, that he was absolutely fine with it.

"Are we going to have a lovely life?" Brigid called, half joking, to the man as he walked away. The man gave a little wave that could have meant anything really, and as he disappeared into the fresh new green of the rolling hills, Brigid took a deep breath, smelling the lush newness of the sun touching her world, and, with a happy little smile, knew that she could probably now be anything that she wanted to be.

The End

Eva Leppard has been writing since she was very young and has often wanted to apologise to her primary school teachers for the voluminous pages that she used to write about kittens and bunnies doing not very much.

She now lives in the Tasmanian bush with an elegantly sufficient amount of children, and a disturbingly large number of rescue animals, many of which she raised by hand whether they liked it or not.

In a piece of karmic rebalancing, she has made up for the boredom that she put her teachers through by becoming a primary teacher herself, and spending much of her time reading 20-page stories about kittens and bunnies doing not very much.

www.ingramcontent.com/pod-product-compliance
Lightning Source LLC
Chambersburg PA
CBHW010345220726
48290CB00016B/2643